"I'm not what you think I am,"

he said. "You think I'm some kind of gentleman, you think all you have to do is tell me 'no' and 'don't,' even though you damn well want it as much as I do. You think because I'm some kind of hero, I'll keep both of us from going too far. You think you can put me upstairs in some guest room, while you sleep one flight away, with your bedroom door unlocked and open, as if I'm strong enough to keep us apart. But guess what? You leave that door open and unlocked tonight, and I'm going to take it as the invitation that it is—because I don't want to be strong enough anymore. I'm not a hero, Lucy, and I'm tired of playing one."

She was trembling. "Blue, you're right. Part of me wants to be with you that way, but I can't—"

"Maybe you can't, but I sure as hell can."

Dear Reader,

There's a nip in the air, now that fall is here, so why not curl up with a good book to keep warm? We've got six of them this month, right here in Silhouette Intimate Moments. Take Modean Moon's *From This Day Forward*, for example. This Intimate Moments Extra title is a deeply emotional look at the break-up—and makeup—of a marriage. Your heart will ache along with heroine Ginnie Kendrick's when she thinks she's lost Neil forever, and your heart will soar along with hers, too, when at last she gets him back again.

The rest of the month is terrific, too. Jo Leigh is back with *Everyday Hero*. Who can resist a bad boy like T. J. Russo? Not Kate Dugan, that's for sure! Then there's Linda Randall Wisdom's *No More Mister Nice Guy*. Jed Hawkins is definitely tough, but even a tough guy has a heart—as Shelby Carlisle can testify by the end of this compelling novel. Suzanne Brockmann's TALL, DARK AND DANGEROUS miniseries continues with *Forever Blue*, about Lucy Tait and Blue McCoy, a hero as true blue as his name. Welcome Audra Adams to the line with *Mommy's Hero*, and watch as the world's cutest twin girls win over the recluse next door. Okay, their mom has something to do with his change of heart, too. Finally, greet our newest author, Roberta Tobeck. She's part of our WOMEN TO WATCH new author promotion, and once you've read *Under Cover of the Night*, you'll know why we're so keen on her.

Enjoy—and come back next month for six more top-notch novels of romance the Intimate Moments way.

Leslie Wainger,
Senior Editor and Editorial Coordinator

Please address questions and book requests to:
Silhouette Reader Service
U.S.: 3010 Walden Ave., P.O. Box 1325, Buffalo, NY 14269
Canadian: P.O. Box 609, Fort Erie, Ont. L2A 5X3

FOREVER BLUE

SUZANNE BROCKMANN

Published by Silhouette Books
America's Publisher of Contemporary Romance

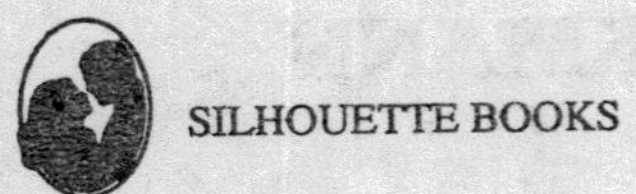

ISBN 0-373-07742-4

FOREVER BLUE

This edition published by arrangement with Harlequin Books S.A.

Printed in U.S.A.

Books by Suzanne Brockmann

Silhouette Intimate Moments

Hero Under Cover #575
Not Without Risk #647
A Man To Die For #681
**Prince Joe* #720
**Forever Blue* #742

*Tall, Dark and Dangerous

SUZANNE BROCKMANN

lives just west of Boston in a house always filled with her friends—actors and musicians and storytellers and artists and teachers of all kinds and shapes and sizes. She sings in an a cappella group, manages the professional acting careers of her two children and handles publicity for her church's Appalachian Benefit Coffeehouse.

For Jodie Kuhlman and Patricia McMahon,
for their amazing brainstorming power
and naming skill,
and for Sarah Telford,
for lending Lucy her little black dress.

Prologue

Lieutenant Blue McCoy was the point man, leading the six other men of SEAL Team Ten's Alpha Squad across the marshlike ground. He moved painstakingly slowly, inch by inch through the darkness, touching, feeling the soft, loamy earth; searching for booby traps and land mines before actually putting his weight down on any one spot.

He watched the shadows, scanning the brush in front of him, memorizing the placement of each faintly silhouetted leaf and branch, alert to even the most minute movement.

The sounds of the night surrounded him. Insects buzzed and clicked; a dog barked maybe a mile away. An owl called through the darkness, its eerie cry proclaiming itself lord of this nocturnal domain, king of this night world.

It was a world in which Blue McCoy belonged, a world where he could lead a group of men so silently and invisibly through the darkness that the crickets at their feet didn't sense their presence.

It had taken them more than an hour to cross the open field. Five more yards and they'd be in the cover of the brush. They'd be able to move faster then. Faster, but no less cautiously.

Blue listened, so in tune with the land around him that he *was* the night. His heart beat slowly in time with the silent, age-old rhythm of the earth and he thought of nothing—nothing but survival. All the noises and sounds of the air force base where Alpha Squad had been just ten hours earlier had long since evaporated, leaving only the night. There were six other men behind him, but Blue heard not a sound from any of them. He knew they were there only from faith, but it was a faith in which he had no doubts. The other SEALs were guarding his back as he led them forward. He knew they would die to protect him, as certainly as he would give his life for them.

Blue sniffed the air and froze, catching a faint, musky odor. But a second sniff convinced him that it was only an animal, some kind of rodent that moved as silently through the night as he did. It wasn't a human smell, and human animals were the prey he was hunting tonight.

Directly through the woods, dead ahead at twelve o'clock, forty yards distant, was a cabin. According to the spooks from FInCOM—the agents from the Federal Intelligence Commission—inside the cabin was United States Senator Mike Branford's fifteen-year-old daughter, Karen. The latest infrared satellite photos of the cabin revealed that at least four members of the terrorist group that had kidnapped her were inside the cabin with her. Another ten people were sleeping in a second structure, twenty yards to the northeast. And two five-man units of terrorists patrolled the surrounding woods. Only minutes ago, one of the units had come within four feet of Blue and the Alpha Squad. The unit commander had lit a cigarette, tossing the smoking match inches from Blue's hand before ordering his men to move on.

With their faces painted green and black, and with their intensive SEAL training, experience and discipline, Alpha Squad *was* invisible, embraced by the darkness, enshrouded by the cloak of night.

As the SEALs positioned themselves in the brush that surrounded the cabin, Blue turned to look at his commanding officer and best friend, Lieutenant Joe Catalanotto. Blue could barely see Joe Cat's face in the darkness, but he saw the man's nod.

Time to go.

Out of the corner of his eye, Blue caught the stealthy movement of Cowboy, Lucky, Bobby and Wes as they faded toward the northeast and the second structure. They were going to secure that building and neutralize the terrorists inside.

That left Joe Cat and Harvard cooling their heels outside the main cabin while Blue crept inside to snatch back the girl.

H. stood guard while Joe and Blue scanned the exterior of the cabin, in particular the window that was to be Blue's insertion point, his way in.

There were no booby traps, no alarms, no extra security. That was because the quarter mile surrounding the cabin was loaded with booby traps, alarms and armed security patrols. It was also because Aldo Fricker, the terrorists' leader, had forgotten the number-one rule: Never assume. The terrorists had left their vulnerable underbelly unprotected because they'd assumed that no one would be able to penetrate the fiercely guarded outer perimeters of their compound.

They were wrong.

Al Fricker, meet SEAL Team Ten's Alpha Squad.

As Blue watched, Joe Cat quickly and quietly cut the pane of glass from the cabin's window. Harvard gave Blue a boost up, and he was inside.

Blue did a quick scan of the interior with his night-vision glasses, quickly locating the senator's young daughter. She was curled up in an old brass bed in the southeast corner of the room. From what he could see she was still alive. The four guards were in sleeping bags or stretched out on the bare floor near the door. Blue took off his NVs and waited several seconds for his eyes to grow accustomed to the dark again, listening to the quiet breathing of the sleeping guards. It wouldn't do any good to wake the girl up while wearing the NVs, looking like some kind of alien from outer space. She was going to be frightened enough as it was.

He took four syringes from his battle vest and moved silently through the room, giving each of the guards a carefully dosed guaranteed good night's sleep. He sealed the needles back up and packaged the now-empty syringes in a bag marked Biohazardous Waste. A quick search of the cabin convinced him that no other guards were lurking, so he moved toward the senator's daughter.

He flicked on his penlight, shielding the light in the palm of one hand as he looked down at the sleeping girl. She was curled in a fetal position, knees tucked into her chest, one arm up, wrist attached by handcuffs to the brass headboard of the bed. Her hair was tangled and knotted, and dirt and blood from abrasions streaked her face and bare arms and legs. She was wearing a pair of blue shorts and a sleeveless top. Both were badly torn.

The bastards had hurt her. Karen. Her name was Karen Branford. They'd beaten her. Probably raped her. Christ, she was *fifteen* years old.

Rage filled him. Hot, molten and deadly, Blue felt it seep through his body, under his skin, spreading out all the way to his fingers and toes. It was a familiar sensation in his line of business. Normally he welcomed it. But tonight his job wasn't to fight back. Tonight his job was to take this battered little girl out of here and get her to safety.

When he adjusted his headset, pulling the lip microphone closer to his mouth, his voice was steady. "Cat," he said almost silently to his commanding officer. "They hurt her."

Joe Catalanotto cursed. "Bad?"

"Yeah."

"Can she walk?"

"I don't know," Blue said.

He turned toward the girl again, sensing from the change in the sound of her breathing that she was awake. Awake and terrified.

Quickly he knelt down next to her, holding the penlight so that it lit his camouflaged face.

"I'm Lieutenant Blue McCoy, miss," he said in a low voice. "I'm a U.S. Navy SEAL, and I'm here to bring you home."

She stared at him, eyes wide, taking in his uniform, his gun, and he knew she didn't understand.

"I'm an American sailor, Karen," he said. "I'm a friend of your daddy's, and I'm gonna get you outta here."

At the mention of her father, understanding and hope flared simultaneously in her brown eyes. She had been clutching at her torn shirt in a futile attempt at modesty, but now she removed her hand to cover his light.

"Shh," she whispered. "You'll wake the guards."

"No, I won't," Blue said. "They're not going to wake up for a while. And when they do, they're going to be in jail." He extracted his lock pick from the waterproof case in his vest and set to work on her cuffs. Three seconds was all it took, and the lock snapped open.

As she rubbed her wrist, Blue slipped off his pack and battle vest and quickly unbuttoned the camouflage shirt he wore underneath it. It was damp with perspiration and probably didn't smell too good, but it was the best he could offer her under the circumstances.

She accepted it silently, slipping it on and buttoning it clear up to her neck.

Blue had to give her credit. After her initial surprise and fear, she now gazed back at him unflinchingly. Her eyes were clear and brave. He'd seen brown eyes like hers somewhere before, a lifetime ago. The owner of those eyes had been fifteen years old, too....

Lucy. Little Lucy Tait. Hell, he hadn't thought about *her* in years.

Blue glanced at his watch, double-checking to make sure his pack was secure. According to the plan, diversionary tactics should be just about ready to start. Blue took a deep breath, looked down at Karen and quietly asked, "Can you walk?"

The young girl stood up. The tail of Blue's shirt came all the way down to her knees. "Better than that," she said stoutly, "I can run."

Blue smiled for the first time in what seemed like hours. "Well, all right. Let's go."

They were halfway through the brush, when Blue heard the first shots ring out. Joe Cat and H. were right behind him, and he sensed them both turning toward the sounds of the skirmish, wondering which men of Alpha Squad were involved, wishing they could go toward the fighting and provide backup.

"This is the wrong way," Blue heard Karen gasp. She pulled free from his grasp, looking wildly around.

He took her arm again. "No, it's not—"

"Yes, it is," she insisted. "I tried running this way before. There are nothing but cliffs. There's no path down to the ocean. We'll be trapped!"

The kid had tried to escape. Blue marveled at her guts. She *was* tough. Again he couldn't help but think about Lucy Tait. He'd been a senior and Lucy had been a little freshman, and the first time they met, she had been getting the stuff kicked out of her by a gang of kids. She was bloody and clearly the odds were against her, but she had a defiant lift to her chin and a "you can't beat me" glint in her brown eyes.

Cowboy's voice came in over Blue's headset. "Cat! About four tangos broke free. They're heading in your direction!"

"Copy that," Cat replied. He turned to Blue. "Go."

"We're going to parasail down to the water," Blue told Karen. "There's a boat waiting for us."

She didn't understand. "Parasail? *How?*"

"Trust me," he said.

Karen hesitated only a fraction of a second, then nodded.

Then they were running again, this time without Cat and Harvard on their heels.

The forest opened up into a field, and Blue felt vulnerable and exposed. If one of the terrorists broke through Cat and Harvard's ambush . . . But they wouldn't.

"Knock the hell out of them for me," he said into his lip microphone, and he heard Joe Catalanotto chuckle.

"You bet, buddy."

Blue stopped at the edge of the cliff and made adjustments to his pack so that Karen could be latched against him and they could parasail down to the water together.

She didn't complain, didn't say a word, although he knew that the proximity of his body to hers had to remind her of the brutalities she'd endured over the past four days.

But he couldn't think about that; couldn't wonder, couldn't focus on her pain. He had to think about that ship bobbing in the darkness, made invisible by the night.

He flipped on the homing device in his vest, reassured by the series of blips and beeps that told him the ship was indeed out there.

"Hold on," he said to the girl, and then he jumped.

Blue was on the deck of the USS *Franklin* when the chopper carrying the rest of Alpha Squad touched down.

He looked closer, trying for a quick head count. It was a reflex from the time all those years ago when Frisco had gone down. He hadn't been KIA—killed in action—but he may as well have been. He still hadn't recovered from his injuries. His leg had damn near been blown off and he was still in a wheelchair—and still mad as hell about it.

Frisco had been Alpha Squad's unofficial goodwill ambassador. He had been friendly and lighthearted, quick to talk and to make friends with everyone around him. He had a sharp sense of humor and a fast wit—he soon had strangers laughing and smiling wherever he went. And his friendliness was sincere. He was a walking party. He always had a good time, whatever the situation.

In fact, Alan "Frisco" Francisco was the only SEAL Blue knew who actually enjoyed basic training's endurance test called Hell Week.

But when Frisco was told that he could never walk again, he'd stopped smiling. To Frisco, losing the use of his leg was the worst thing that ever could have happened to him. Even worse, maybe, than dying.

Blue watched the men jump down from the big bay doors of the helicopter. Joe Cat—his dark hair worn longer and tied back in a ponytail, his stern face relaxed in a smile nearly all the time now that he was married. Harvard—his shaved head gleaming like a coffee-colored bowling ball, looking big and mean and scary as hell. Bobby and Wes—unidentical twins, one big and tall, the other wiry and short, yet they moved in unison, finished each other's sentences. Lucky O'Donlon—Frisco's swim buddy. And the new guy—Cowboy. Harlan "Cowboy" Jones—temporary replacement first for Lucky on the same rescue mission that had injured Frisco, then temporary replacement for Frisco. Except it had been years and years, and it sure as hell looked as though temporary had turned pretty damned permanent.

They were all there, and they were all walking and breathing.

Joe Cat spotted Blue and moved in his direction.

"Everything okay?" he asked.

Blue nodded, heading with Joe toward the stairs leading below deck. "The doctor checked out the girl," he drawled. "She's with the shrink and the support staff right now." He shook his head. "Four *days,* Cat. Why the hell did it take them so long to let us go in after her?"

"Because the average politician and top-brass pencil pusher doesn't have a clue what a SEAL team can do." Joe Cat unfastened his battle vest, heading directly toward the mess hall.

"So a fifteen-year-old girl is *brutalized* for four *days* while we sit around with our thumbs up our—"

Cat stopped walking, turning to face Blue. "Yeah, it bugs me too," he said. "But it's over now. Let it go."

"You think Karen Branford is gonna just let it go?"

Blue could see from Cat's dark eyes that the CO didn't like the answer to that question. "She's alive," he said quietly. "That's much better than the alternative."

Blue took a deep breath. He was right. Cat was right. He exhaled loudly. "Sorry." They started walking again. "It's just... The girl reminded me of someone I used to know back in Hatboro Creek. A girl named Lucy. Lucy Tait."

Joe Cat eyed him with feigned astonishment as they turned the corner into the mess hall. "Yo," he said. "Am I hearing you correctly? You actually knew other girls besides Jenny Lee Beaumont in Hatboro Creek? I thought the sun rose and set with Jenny Lee, and all other girls were rendered invisible by her magnificent shine."

Blue staunchly ignored Cat's teasing tone. "Lucy wasn't a girl," he said, pouring black, steaming coffee into a paper cup. "She was just . . . a kid."

"Maybe you should look her up while you're back in South Carolina for the wedding."

Blue shook his head. "I don't think so."

Cat took a mug from the rack, regarding Blue speculatively. "You sure you want to *go* to this wedding?" he asked. "You know, I can arrange for Alpha Squad to be part of some vital training mission if you need an excuse not to be there."

"It's my brother's wedding."

"Gerry's your *step*brother," Cat noted, "and he happens to be marrying Jenny Lee, your high-school sweetheart and the only woman I've ever heard you talk about—with the exception now of this Lucy Tait."

Blue took a swallow of the coffee. It was strong and hot and it burned all the way down. "I told him I'd be his best man."

Joe Cat's teeth were clenched as he gazed at Blue. The muscle worked in his jaw. "He shouldn't have asked you for that," he said. "He wants you there, giving him your stamp of approval, so he can stop feeling guilty about stealing Jenny Lee from you."

Blue crumpled up his empty paper cup, then tossed it into the garbage. "He didn't steal her," he said. "She was in love with him right from the start."

Chapter 1

It was going to be the wedding of the year—shoot, it was going to be the wedding of the decade. And Lucy Tait was going to be there.

Oh, not that she'd be invited. No, Lucy wasn't going to get one of those fancy, gold-lettered invitations printed on heavy, cream-colored stock, no way. She was going to this wedding as a hired hand—first to keep the traffic moving outside Hatboro Creek's posh country club and then to stand inside the ballroom, guarding the pile of expensive wedding gifts.

Lucy adjusted the collar of her police uniform as she cruised Main Street in her patrol car, searching for a parking spot near Bobby Joe's Grill.

Not that she'd expected to be invited to Jenny Lee Beaumont's nuptials. She'd never run with that crowd, not even back in high school. But man, back then, back when Lucy was a scrawny freshman and blond, beautiful homecoming queen Jenny Lee had been a senior, Lucy had desperately wanted to join Jenny's exclusive club.

She would never have admitted it. The same way she would never have admitted the reason she wanted so desperately to be close to Jenny Lee—namely, Blue McCoy.

Blue McCoy.

Rumor had it he was coming back to town for his stepbrother's wedding.

Blue McCoy.

With dark blond hair and dark blue eyes that burned with an intensity that made her heart stand still, Blue McCoy had haunted all of Lucy's adolescent dreams. He was the hero of her teenaged years—a loner, quiet, dark and dangerous, capable of just about anything.

Including winning beautiful Jenny Lee Beaumont's heart.

Except Jenny Lee wasn't going to marry Blue McCoy on Saturday afternoon. She was marrying his stepbrother, Gerry. He was two years older than Blue, with a quicksilver smile, movie-star good looks and a happy-go-lucky attitude. Some people might have found Gerry the more attractive of the McCoy boys.

Apparently Jenny Lee had.

Lucy found a parking place a block down from the Grill and turned off the patrol car's powerful engine. On second thought, she turned the key again and pushed the buttons to raise the power windows. The summer sky looked threatening. Lucy was willing to bet it was going to pour before she finished her lunch.

She checked to make sure her sidearm was secured in her belt holster as she hurried down the sidewalk. She was already ten minutes late, and her friend Sarah's self-imposed work schedule didn't allow her to take more than a hour for lunch.

The Grill was crowded, as usual, but Sarah was saving a table. Lucy slid into the booth, across from her friend.

"I'm sorry I'm late."

Sarah just smiled. "I would have ordered lunch," she said. "But Iris hasn't worked her way around to this part of the room."

Lucy leaned back against the plastic cushion of the bench seat. She let out a burst of air that lifted her bangs up off her forehead. "I haven't stopped running since 7 a.m." She eyed her friend. Sarah looked tired and hot, her dark hair pulled back from her face in a ponytail, dark circles under her hazel eyes. "How are *you?*"

"I'm nine months pregnant with a child that has obviously decided not to be born until he's old enough to vote," Sarah said dryly. "It's ninety-seven degrees in the shade, my back hurts when I lie down, my sciatic nerve acts up when I sit, I have a review deadline that I can't possibly make because I've spent the past three days cooking instead of writing, my husband has been home from his shift at the hospital four hours in the past forty-eight, my mother-in-law calls every five minutes to see if my water has broken, I miss living in Boston and this is the first chance I've had in nearly a week to complain."

Lucy grinned. "Then don't stop now."

"No, no, I'm done," Sarah said, fanning herself with her napkin.

"Afternoon, ladies." Iris took her pen from behind her ear and held it poised over her ordering pad. "What can I get you today?"

"I'd like some marzipan," Sarah said.

Iris sighed good-naturedly, pushing a stray red curl back up into her bun. "Honey, I told you before, if it's not on the menu..."

"I *need* some marzipan," Sarah said almost desperately. "Almond paste. Or maybe a piece of my mother's fruitcake. I haven't been able to think about anything else for days...."

"We'll both take a turkey club," Lucy said smoothly, "on whole wheat, mustard, no mayo, extra pickles."

"Sorry, hon," Iris murmured to Sarah as she moved on to the next table.

"My life," Sarah intoned dramatically, "is an endless string of disappointments."

Lucy had to laugh. "You're married to the nicest guy in town, you're about to have a baby, you just won a prize for your music and you're *disappointed?*"

Sarah leaned forward. "I'm insanely jealous of you," she said. "You still have a waistline. You can see your feet without craning your neck. You—" She broke off, staring across the room toward the door. "Don't look now, but I think we're being invaded."

Lucy turned around as the glass door to the grill swung open and a man in green army fatigues, carrying a heavy-looking green duffel bag casually over one shoulder, came inside.

He was clearly a soldier, except on second glance his uniform wasn't quite inspection ready. The first thing Lucy noticed was his arms. The sleeves had been torn from his green shirt at the shoulders and his arms were muscular and strong. He looked as if he could easily bench-press three times his body weight. He wore his shirt open at the collar and unbuttoned halfway down his broad chest. His fatigue pants fit him comfortably, but instead of clunky black army boots, he wore only sandals on his feet.

He had sunglasses on, but his gaze swept quickly around the room and Lucy imagined that he didn't miss much.

His hair was thick and a dark, sandy blond.

And his face was one she recognized.

Lucy would have known Blue McCoy anywhere. That strong chin, his firm, unsmiling mouth, those rugged cheekbones and straight nose. Twelve years of living had added power and strength to his already strong face. The lines around his eyes and mouth had deepened, adding a sense of compassion or wisdom to his unforgivingly stern features.

He had been good-looking as a teenaged boy. As a man, he was impossibly handsome.

Lucy was staring. She couldn't help herself. Blue McCoy was back in town, larger than life.

He finished his quick inspection of the room and his eyes returned to her. As Lucy watched, Blue took off his sunglasses. His eyes were still the brightest shade of blue she'd ever seen in her life, and as he met her gaze she felt frozen in place, hypnotized.

He nodded at her, just once, still unsmiling, and then Iris breezed past him.

"Sit anywhere, hon!" she called out to him.

The spell was broken. Blue looked away from Lucy and she turned back to the table and Sarah.

"Do you know him?" Sarah asked, her sharp eyes missing nothing—particularly not the blush that was heating Lucy's cheeks. "You do, don't you?"

"Not really, no," Lucy said, then admitted, "I mean, I know who he is, but..." She shook her head.

"Who is he?"

Lucy glanced up again, but Blue was busy stashing his duffel bag underneath a table on the far side of the room. "Blue McCoy." Lucy spoke softly, as if he might overhear even from across the noisy restaurant.

"*That's* Gerry McCoy's brother? He looks nothing like him."

"They're stepbrothers," Lucy explained. "Blue's mother married Gerry's father, only she died about five months after the wedding. Mr. McCoy adopted Blue shortly after that. The way I hear it, neither Mr. McCoy nor Blue was happy with that arrangement. Apparently they didn't get along too well, but Blue had nowhere else to go."

"I guess not, since he didn't make it back into town when Mr. McCoy died a few years ago," Sarah commented.

"Gerry told me Blue was part of Desert Storm," Lucy said. "He couldn't get leave, not then, and Gerry didn't want to hold up the funeral, not indefinitely like that."

"Gerry's brother is in the army?"

"Navy," Lucy corrected her. "He's in the Special Forces—a Navy SEAL."

"A *what?*"

"SEAL," Lucy said. "It stands for Sea, Air and Land. SEALs are like supercommandos. They're experts in everything from...I don't know...underwater demolition to parachute assaults to...piloting state-of-the-art jets. They have these insane training sessions where they learn to work as a team under incredible stress. There's this one week—Hell Week—where they're allowed only four hours of sleep *all week.* They have to sleep in fifteen-minute segments, while air-raid sirens are wailing. If they quit during Hell week, they're out of the program. It's pretty scary stuff. Only the toughest and most determined men make the grade and become SEALs. It's a real status symbol—for obvious reasons."

Sarah was gazing across the room, a speculative light in her eyes. "You seem to have acquired an awful lot of information about a man you claim you don't know."

"I've read about SEALs and the training they go through. That's all."

"Hmm." Sarah lifted one delicate eyebrow. "Before or after Gerry's brother joined the navy?"

Lucy shrugged, trying hard to look casual. "So I had a crush on the guy in high school. Big deal."

Sarah rested her chin in her hand. "Out of all the people in this place, he nods at *you,*" she remarked. "Did you date him?"

Lucy couldn't help laughing. "Not a chance. I was three years younger, and he was..."

"What?"

Iris approached the table, carrying two enormous sandwiches and a basket of French fries. Lucy smiled her thanks at the waitress, but waited for her to leave before answering Sarah's question.

"He was going out with Jenny Lee."

"Beaumont...?" Sarah's eyes lit up. "You mean the same Jenny Lee who's marrying his brother on Saturday?" At Lucy's nod, she chuckled. "This is getting too good."

"You didn't know?" Lucy asked. "I thought everyone in town knew. It seems it's all anyone's talking about—whether or not Blue McCoy will show up to the wedding of his stepbrother and his high-school sweetheart."

"Apparently the answer to *that* question is yes," Sarah said, glancing across the room at the man in uniform.

Lucy took a bite of her turkey sandwich, carefully *not* turning around to look at this man she found so fascinating. Sarah was right. The question about whether or not Blue would attend Gerry's wedding had been answered.

Now the town would be abuzz in speculation, wondering if Blue was going to create a disturbance or rise to his feet when the preacher said "speak now or forever hold your peace."

The temptation proved too intense, and Lucy glanced over her shoulder. Blue was eating his lunch and reading the past week's edition of the *Hatboro Creek Gazette.* His blond hair fell across his forehead, almost into his eyes, and he pushed it back with a smooth motion that caused the muscles in his right arm to ripple. As if he could feel her watching him, he looked up and directly into her eyes.

Lucy's stomach did circus tricks as she quickly, guiltily, looked away. God, you would think she was fifteen again and sneaking around the marina where Blue worked, hoping for a peek at him. But he hadn't noticed her then and he certainly wouldn't notice her now. She was still decidedly not the Jenny Lee Beaumont type.

"What was his mother thinking when she named him Blue?" Sarah wondered aloud.

"His real name is Carter," Lucy said. "Blue is a nickname—it's short for 'Blue Streak.'"

"Don't tell me," Sarah said. "He talks all the time."

Lucy had to laugh at that. Blue McCoy was not known for running on at the mouth. "I don't know when he first got the nickname," she said, "but he's a runner. He broke all kinds of speed records for sprinting and long-distance races back in junior high and high school."

Sarah nodded, peering around Lucy to get another peek at Blue.

Lucy's police walkie-talkie went off at nearly the exact instant the skies opened up with a crash of thunder.

"Report of a 415 in progress at the corner of Main and Willow," Annabella's voice squawked over the radio's tinny speaker. "Possible 10-91A. Lucy, what's your location?"

Main and Willow was less than a block and a half from the Grill, in the opposite direction of her patrol car. It would take her less time to jog over there than it would to get to her car and drive. Lucy quickly swallowed a half-chewed bite of her sandwich and thumbed the talk switch to her radio.

"The Grill," she said, already halfway out of the booth. "I'm on it. But unless you want me to stop at my car to check my code book, you better tell me what a 10-91A is."

The police dispatcher, Annabella Sawyer, was overly fond of the California police ten code. Never mind that they were in South Carolina. Never mind the fact that Hatboro Creek was so small that they didn't need half the codes most of the time. Never mind that the police officers weren't required to memorize any kind of code. Annabella liked using them. She clearly had watched too many episodes of "Top Cops."

Lucy knew what a 415 was, though. A disturbance. She'd heard that number enough times. Even a town as tiny as Hatboro Creek had plenty of those.

"A 10-91A is a report of a vicious animal," Annabella's voice squawked back.

Lucy swore under her breath. Leroy Hurley's brute of a dog had no doubt gotten loose again.

"Be careful," Sarah said.

"I'll wrap your sandwich," Iris called as Lucy pushed open the door and stepped out onto the sidewalk.

The rain soaked her instantly, as if someone had turned a fire hose on her from above. Her hat was back in her car, and Lucy wished for both of them—hat and car—as she headed toward Willow Street at a quick trot.

With any luck, this sudden skyburst had sent that 10-91A scurrying for shelter. With any luck, the 415 had ceased to exist. With any luck...

No such luck. Leroy Hurley's snarling Doberman had treed Merle Groggin on Andy Hayes's front lawn. Andy was shouting for Merle to get the hell out of his expensive Japanese maple. Merle was brandishing his hunting knife and shouting for Leroy to get his damned dog locked up or put down, and Leroy was laughing his size forty-six–waist pants off.

It was decidedly a bonafide 415.

As Lucy approached Leroy Hurley, his huge dog caught sight of her and turned. Her stomach tightened at the animal's threatening growl. She liked dogs. Most dogs. But this one had one mean streak. Just like his master.

"Leroy," Lucy said, nodding a greeting to the big man, as if they weren't both standing in a torrential downpour. "What did I tell you last week about keeping your dog chained in your yard?"

The Doberman shifted its weight, glancing from Lucy to Merle Groggin, as if deciding who would make a tastier lunch.

Leroy shrugged and grinned. "Can't help it if he breaks free."

She could smell the unmistakable scent of whiskey on his breath. Damn, he got meaner than ever when he'd been drinking.

"Yes, you can," Lucy said, taking her ticket pad from her pocket. It was instantly soaked. "He's your dog. You're responsible for him. And in fact, to help you remember that, I'm going to slap you with a fifty-dollar fine."

The big man's smile faded. "I'm the only thing standing between you walking away from here in one piece and you getting chewed," he said, "and you're gonna *fine* me?"

Lucy stared at Leroy. "Are you threatening me, Hurley?" she asked, her voice low and tight but carrying clearly over the sound of the rain. "Because if you're threatening me, I'll run both you *and* your dog in so fast your head will spin."

Something in Leroy's eyes shifted, and Lucy felt a surge of triumph. He believed her. She'd called his bluff, he believed her and was going to back down, despite the whiskey that was screwing up the very small amount of good judgment he had to begin with.

"Call your dog off," Lucy said calmly.

But before Leroy could comply, all hell broke loose.

Andy Hayes fired a booming shot from his double-barrel shotgun, sending Merle plunging down from the tree. The Doberman leaped toward the fallen man, who struck at the dog with his big knife, drawing blood. With a howl, the animal dashed away down the street.

"Stay the *hell* away from my tree!" Andy shouted.

"You stabbed my dog!" Leroy Hurley roared at Merle.

"You coulda killed me," Merle shouted at Andy as he hurried out of the man's yard. "Why the hell didn't you just shoot the damned dog?"

Leroy moved threateningly toward Merle. "If that dog dies, I'm gonna string you up by your—"

"Hold it right there!" Lucy planted herself firmly between Merle and Leroy. She raised her voice so it would carry to the house. "Andy, you know I'm going to have to bring you in—reckless endangerment and unlawful discharge of a firearm. And as for you two—"

"I hope that stupid animal does kick." Merle spoke to Leroy Hurley right through Lucy, as if she wasn't even there. "Because if it doesn't, I'm gonna come after it one of these nights and finish it off."

"I ain't going nowhere," Andy proclaimed. "I got rights! I was protecting my property!"

"Maybe I'll just finish *you* off first!" Leroy's fleshy face was florid with anger as he shouted at Merle.

Lucy keyed the thumb switch on her radio. "Dispatcher, this is Officer Tait. I need backup, corner of Willow and—"

Leroy Hurley pushed her aside with the sweep of one beefy arm, and Lucy went down, hard, on her rear in the street, dropping the radio and her ticket pad in the mud. Leroy moved up the walkway to Andy's house with a speed surprising for such a large man, and as Lucy scrambled to her feet, he grabbed Andy's shotgun and pointed it at Merle.

Merle ducked for cover behind Lucy, and Leroy swung the gun toward her.

"Leroy, put that down," Lucy ordered, pushing her rain-soaked hair back from her face with her left hand as she unsnapped the safety buttons that held her sidearm in her belt holster with her right hand.

"Freeze! Keep your hands where I can see 'em," Leroy ordered her.

Lucy lifted her hands. *Shoot.* How could this have gotten so utterly out of control? And where the hell was that backup?

Leroy was edging toward them; Merle was cowering behind her, using her as a shield; and for once Andy Hayes was silent.

"Step away from Merle," Leroy growled at her.

"Leroy, put the gun down before this goes too far," Lucy said again, trying to sound calm, to not let the desperation she was feeling show in her voice.

"If you don't step away from him," Leroy vowed, his eyes wild, "I'll just blast a hole right through you."

Dear God, he was serious. He raised the shotgun higher, closing one eye as he took aim directly at Lucy's chest. Her life flashed briefly and oh, so meaninglessly through her eyes as she stared into the barrel of that gun. She could very well die at this man's hands. Right here in the rain. And what would she have to show for her life? A six-month-old police badge. A liberal-arts degree from the state university. A computer business she no longer had any interest in. An empty house at the edge of town. No family, only a few friends . . .

"Don't do this, Leroy," Lucy said, inching her hand back down toward her own gun. She didn't want to die. She hadn't even begun to live. Dammit, if Leroy Hurley was going to shoot her, she was going to die trying for her gun.

"Freeze!" Leroy told her. "I said to freeze!"

"Leroy, I'm holding an Uzi nine-millimeter submachine gun," a soft voice drawled from over Lucy's shoulder. "It looks small and unassuming, but if I move my trigger finger a fraction of an inch, with a firing rate of sixteen bullets per second, I can cut even a man as big as you in two."

It was Blue McCoy. Lucy would have recognized his velvet Southern drawl anywhere.

"You have exactly two seconds to drop that shotgun," Blue continued, "or I start firing."

Leroy dropped the gun.

Lucy sprang forward before the barrel had finished clattering on the cement walkway and scooped up the gun. She cradled it in her arms as she turned to look at Blue.

His blond hair was drenched and plastered to his head. His clothes were as soaked as her own, and they clung to his body, outlining and emphasizing his muscular build. He squinted slightly through the downpour, but otherwise stood there holding a very deadly looking little submachine gun as if the sky were clear and the sun were shining.

He was still watching Leroy, but his brilliant blue eyes flickered briefly in Lucy's direction. "You okay?"

She nodded, unable to find her voice.

There was a crowd of people down the block, she realized suddenly. No doubt they had all been drawn out into the wet by the sound of Andy's first gunshot. Great. She looked like a fool, unable to handle a few troublemakers, requiring a Navy SEAL to come to her rescue. Terrific.

"Leroy, Andy, Merle," Lucy said. "You're *all* gonna take a ride to the station."

"Aw, I didn't do a damned thing," Merle complained as the long-awaited police backup arrived, along with the police van for transporting the three men. "You got nothing on *me*."

"Carrying a concealed weapon ought to do the trick," Lucy said, deftly taking his hunting knife from him and handing it and the shotgun to Frank Redfield, one of the police officers who had finally made the scene.

"Talk about carrying a concealed weapon," Merle snorted, gesturing with his head toward Blue McCoy as Frank led him toward the van. "What are you going to charge *him* with?"

Lucy pushed her wet hair back from her face again, stopping to pick up her sodden ticket pad and the fallen walkie-talkie from the mud before she approached Blue.

"Merle is right, you know, Lieutenant McCoy," she said to him, hoping he would mistake the shakiness in her voice as a reaction to the excitement rather than as a result of his proximity. "I'm not sure I can let you walk around town with one of those things."

He handed the gun to her, butt first. "You let Tommy Parker walk around town with it," he said.

Tommy Parker? Tommy Parker was nine years old.... Lucy looked down at the gun she was holding. It was lightweight and... "My God," she said. "It's plastic. It's a *toy.*" She looked back up into Blue's eyes. "You were bluffing."

"Of course I was bluffing," he said. "I wouldn't be caught dead with an Uzi. If I wanted an assault weapon, I'd only use a Heckler and Koch MP5-K."

Lucy stared at him and he gazed back at her. And then he smiled. His teeth were white and even and contrasted nicely with his tanned face.

"I'm kidding," he explained gently. "If I had to, I'd use an Uzi. It's not my weapon of choice, though."

Great, he must think she was some kind of imbecile, the way she was staring at him. Lucy closed her eyes briefly, but when she opened them he was still watching her.

"I'm sorry," she said, "I really owe you one. You saved my neck back there, and . . . well, thanks."

He nodded, gracefully acknowledging her clumsy thanks. "You're welcome," he said. "But haven't we already had this conversation? I'm getting a real sense of déjà vu here." His smile flashed again—pure sunshine in the pouring rain. "It seems every time I'm in Hatboro Creek, I end up saving little Lucy Tait's . . . neck."

Lucy was shocked. "You remember me?" As soon as the words were out of her mouth she was embarrassed. Of course he remembered her. Standing here soaking wet, resembling a drowned rat, she no doubt looked not too different from the skinny fifteen-year-old girl Blue had saved from a serious thrashing out on the far side of the town baseball field all those years ago.

"I'm a little surprised to see you," Blue drawled. "I'd have thought you would've packed up and left South Carolina years ago, Yankee."

Yankee. It had been her nickname all throughout high school. Lucy Tait, the Yankee girl. Moved to town with her widowed mom from someplace way up north. She was still referred to all the time as "Yankee girl." It had been twelve years. Twelve *years*. Her mother was no longer alive. And Lucy wasn't a girl anymore. But some things never changed.

"No," Lucy said evenly. "I'm still here in Hatboro Creek."

"I can see that."

Blue gazed at Lucy, taking in her long, brown—wet—hair, tied back in a utilitarian ponytail; her unforgettable dark brown eyes; the lovely, almost delicate shape of her face; and her tall, slender body. Little Lucy Tait wasn't so little anymore. The rain had softened the stiff fabric of her police uniform, molding it against her female curves. Yes, Lucy Tait had definitely grown up. Blue felt an unmistakable surge of physical attraction and he had to smile. At age eighteen, he *never* would have believed that the sight of scrawny little Lucy Tait standing in the rain could possibly turn him on.

But if there was one thing he learned in his stint as a Navy SEAL, it was that times—and people—were always changing. Nothing ever stayed the same.

"How long have you been an officer of the law?" he asked. The crowd was gone and the police van was pulling away. The rain was relentless but warm. Blue liked the way it felt on his face, and Lucy didn't seem to be in any hurry to get to shelter.

Lucy crossed her arms. "Six months."

Blue nodded.

She lifted her chin. "I'm the first woman on the Hatboro Creek police force."

Blue tried to hide his smile, but it slipped through. "First *Yankee* on the force, too, no doubt."

Lucy must have realized how defensive she looked, because she slowly smiled, too—at first almost sheepishly, then wider. "Yeah," she said. "I suppose I've been setting all kinds of new Hatboro Creek records lately."

Her face wasn't exactly what you'd call pretty. At least, not at first glance. Her mouth was too wide, too generous, too big for her face—except when she smiled. Her smile transformed her totally, making her eyes dance and sparkle and charming dimples appear in the perfect, smooth, slightly olive-tinted complexion of her cheeks. Her nose was straight and large, but not too big for her face, revealing a faintly Mediterranean ancestry. Her eyes were warm and the deepest shade of brown, framed by thick, dark eyelashes.

Her ears were small and amazingly delicate looking. Blue found himself watching, fascinated, as a drop of rain clung to her unpierced earlobe before dripping onto her shoulder.

"I'm surprised Chief Bradley lets you patrol alone," Blue said.

Lucy's smile vanished. "Why? Because I'm a woman or because I'm a Yankee?"

"Because you're a rookie."

"I had Leroy Hurley handled," Lucy remarked, her dark eyes flashing. "Until Andy got his gun."

Blue nodded, forcing his gaze out and into the distance, down Main Street, toward the marina. How long had it been since he'd been with a woman? Two months? Three? Longer? He honestly couldn't remember. He usually didn't pay his sexual appetite much mind—until it sat up and demanded priority attention.

Like right now.

In a flash he could picture Lucy standing in the warm rain, sans uniform, water washing down her lean, shapely female body—full, soft breasts; flat stomach; slim hips; dangerously long, well-muscled thighs.... The image sent an intense rush of heat through him, heat he knew she'd be able to see in his eyes.

It was strange. In the past, Blue had always been attracted to the overly feminine type—the helpless type of woman who wore lots of frills and lace and needed to be rescued. It was true that he had in fact come to Lucy's rescue more than once, but both times she'd certainly been doing her best to save herself. She was independent and strong. Even though she was soaking wet and only a rookie, she wore her police uniform and the gun at her side with an air of authority and competence. That should have pushed him back a step or two. Instead, he found himself inching forward, trying to get closer.

"I assumed Andy was harmless," Lucy was saying with a frown. "I focused on Leroy and didn't pay Andy any attention. That was my big mistake."

"Never assume anything," Blue said. He could tell from the way she met his gaze, then suddenly looked away, that she had gotten a glimpse of the fire in his eyes. She blushed, a tinge of pink darkening her cheeks as she looked down at the mud-encrusted radio and ticket pad she still held in her hands. She slipped the pad into her belt and tried to wipe the radio clean. She appeared to be intent on fixing her equipment, but she couldn't keep from glancing at him out of the corner of her eyes.

Suddenly, Blue remembered the rumor he'd heard his senior year in high school that the little Yankee freshman girl had a crush on him. He'd been flattered and amused, and as kind to the girl as he could be without leading her on.

Was it possible that Lucy's high-school crush had survived all these years?

Blue had noticed right from the first moment he'd spotted her sitting in the Grill that she wasn't wearing a wedding band. Was it possible that Lucy was still single, still unattached?

Blue had come to Hatboro Creek today out of obligation. He'd come with every intention of enduring his visit—he hadn't planned to enjoy any of it. But he was on leave, and his leave time was infrequent and irregular. Why not take hold of an opportunity and have a little pleasure, especially since that pleasure seemed to be handing itself to him on a silver platter? Why not? Especially since the attraction he was feeling right now was stronger than anything he'd felt in a long, *long* time.

"I, um, I better go," Lucy said. "I'll need to fill out a report and..." She turned toward him, using the back of one hand to push her wet hair from her face, but succeeding in leaving a streak of mud on her cheek. "Can I give you a ride somewhere? Are you staying at your brother's?"

As Lucy watched, Blue glanced up at the cloudy sky as if noticing the rain for the first time. It was finally starting to let up. He pushed his hair back from his face but didn't meet Lucy's eyes again. "No," he said. "Jenny Lee has already moved into Gerry's place. I thought it would be better if I stayed at the motel. And it's not far. I can walk there probably faster than you could drive."

Lucy nodded, wishing almost inanely that he would smile at her again, or that he would look at her and let her get a second glance at that slow-burning heat she'd imagined she'd seen in his eyes. But it had to be just that—imagined. Blue McCoy would never be interested in her.

Would he?

"I wish I could think of a way to thank you properly for what you did," she said, backing away.

He stepped toward her, following. "*I* can think of a way," he said in his soft drawl. "There's a party tonight at the country club, a sort of rehearsal dinner for Saturday's wedding. Come as my date."

Lucy stopped short. Her first reaction was to laugh. This had to be some sort of joke. Go to Hatboro Creek's exclusive country club—on a *date* with Blue McCoy, her childhood hero? But Blue wasn't laughing. He was . . . serious?

Why? Lucy searched his eyes, looking for the reason he'd asked her out. Why? There had to be a reason.

She found the answer in the heat in his eyes, as clear as day.

Sex.

He was a man and she was a woman, and although his invitation had been to attend a fancy, high-society party, what he *really* wanted to do with her wouldn't require any kind of party dress at all. She could see all that in his eyes—and more.

Lucy was floored.

Blue McCoy wanted her. He wanted *her.* He was actually physically attracted to and interested in the tall, skinny, gawky, awkward Yankee tomboy, Lucy Tait.

Oh, she had no misconceptions about the extent of his desire. It was purely sexual. There were no emotions involved. At least not from his end. But it was clear from the look in his eyes that if she went on this date with him, he was going to do his damnedest to see that she didn't get home tonight until well after dawn.

A clear and extremely erotic image of Blue pulling her down with him onto his bed at the Lighthouse Motel flashed through Lucy's mind. Tangled arms and legs, seeking mouths, straining bodies, skin slick with sweat and desire... Strobelike pictures bombarded Lucy's senses, along with a thousand other thoughts.

She had been plenty reckless and wild before—but never in her personal life. As crazy as she'd been with her career, Lucy had always been extremely careful when it came to relationships. But ever since she'd first laid eyes on Blue McCoy at age fifteen, she'd desperately wanted to run her fingers through his thick, dark blond hair.

Lucy knew she meant nothing to Blue and would no doubt continue to mean nothing to him, even if he slept with her. She'd never made love to a man before without knowing that their relationship was going to grow, without *hoping* for some kind of permanence. Yet Blue was in town for only a few days—a week at the most. Chances were that he wouldn't be back. Maybe not for another twelve years.

As she gazed up at Blue, he reached out and touched the side of her face, gently wiping what was no doubt a smudge of dirt from her cheek with his thumb. His hand was warm, warmer even than the rain, and his touch sent a wave of fire spiraling through her, down to the depths of her very soul.

She couldn't help herself. She reached up and touched his hair. It was wet, but still soft and thick. It was remarkable. One small movement and she was living one of her wildest dreams.

Blue's eyelids grew heavy at her touch, heavy with pleasure—and satisfaction. He'd won, and he knew it.

"I'll pick you up at 1900...seven o'clock," Blue said, his voice barely louder than a whisper. "Or would you rather meet me over there, at the club?"

Lucy found herself nodding. Yes. "I'll meet you there," she breathed. Dear God, yes, she was going to do this. She was going to go to this party with Blue McCoy, and later... Later, she was going to live out one of her most powerful, most decadent fantasies.

It wasn't until after he walked her back to her patrol car, until after he went inside the Grill for the rest of his lunch and his duffel bag and with a nod headed toward the motel, and until after Sarah drove by in her little black Honda

Accord, giving Lucy a toot of her horn and a big thumbs-up, that reality crashed in.

What the hell did Lucy think she was doing? Was a one-night stand with Blue McCoy—no matter that he was the man of her hottest dreams—worth the talk and gossip and speculative looks she'd have to endure weeks and even months after he'd gone? Was one night—or even two or three nights—worth the silence that was sure to follow? Because Lucy had no false expectations. Blue would not write. He would not call. He could be killed on a training mission, and she'd be the very last to know.

Could she really love a man she knew would be loving someone else, some other woman, this time next month—or hell, maybe even next *week?*

She wished she could call Edgar, wished she could tell him about Blue's invitation, wished they could talk it over, hash it out. But even though Edgar wasn't around, Lucy knew exactly what he would have said.

Go for it.

Edgar was the only person Lucy had ever told about her high-school crush on Blue. He was the only one who had known that she still carried a torch for a guy she never even really knew.

Yeah, go for it was what Edgar would have said.

And then he would have reminded her to have safe sex.

Safe sex. Now there was an oxymoron if Lucy had ever heard one. A condom would help with some of the physical dangers. But what about her emotional safety? What kind of protection could she use to ensure herself that?

Down at the police station, Lucy went through the motions, taking a shower; putting on a clean, dry uniform; filling out the forms and reports. But all afternoon, she asked herself the same questions over and over again. Could she really go out with Blue tonight, knowing damn well where it was going to lead?

The answer wavered between Edgar's possible *go for it* and *no.* No, it wasn't worth it. No, she couldn't do this. Could she? How could she pass up her wildest, hottest sexual fantasy?

But every time she told herself no and started to pick up the phone to dial the Lighthouse Motel, where Blue was staying, Lucy remembered the liquid desire in his eyes and the hot touch of his hand on her face.

She remembered the answering pull of her own longing and need, the promise of a wild, reckless passion the likes of which she'd never known.

And she knew exactly why she'd said yes.

Chapter 2

Lucy pulled her truck into the Hatboro Country Club's elegant driveway, feeling out of place. She parked in the back lot, unwilling to leave the keys to her trusty but beat-up old Ford four-by-four with the valets. She couldn't stand the thought of them snickering as they pulled it alongside the Town Cars and Cadillacs. She also wasn't sure she could handle walking in the front entrance of the posh country club wearing this little black dress she'd borrowed from Sarah. *Little* was the key word. It was sleeveless, with a sweetheart neckline and a keyhole back, and it hugged Lucy's body, ending many, *many* inches above her knees. On Sarah, the tight skirt had been short, but Lucy was at least four inches taller than her friend. Aided further by high heels, the dress made Lucy's long legs appear as if they went on forever—an effect, Sarah had pointed out, that would *not* be lost on Blue McCoy.

Lucy glanced in one of the mirrors that lined the hall as she went in the country club's back door.

Sarah had fixed her hair, too, piling it on top of her head. It seemed as if Lucy had casually swept it up off her neck, but in reality the carefree look had taken the solid part of a half hour to achieve.

She was also wearing more than her usual dab of lip gloss. Mascara, liner and shadow adorned her brown eyes, and blush accentuated her wide cheekbones.

Lucy looked like...somebody else. Instead of skinny, she looked slender, her legs long and graceful. Instead of girl-next-door average, she looked exotic, glamorous and mysteriously sexy.

Blue probably wasn't going to recognize her. She could barely recognize herself.

Which made sense, because Lucy certainly didn't recognize this odd sensation she felt, knowing that she was here to meet a man who was practically a stranger—a stranger who could very well be her lover before the night was through.

Blue McCoy.

But he *wasn't* a stranger. Not really. After all, he'd been her hero for years. He was pure masculine perfection—if you went for the big, brooding, enigmatic type. And Lucy definitely did.

Music was playing in the country club's big ballroom, and it filtered down toward Lucy. She started up the stairs, heart pounding; she knew that Blue was somewhere up there near that pulsating music.

The country club had undergone changes in its interior decor since the last time she had been there. She couldn't remember what color the thick wall-to-wall carpeting had been, but she was positive that it hadn't been this deep, almost smoky shade of pink. The wallpaper was different, too, a muted collection of flowers and squiggles, in tasteful off-whites and beiges and various shades of that same dark pink.

Her high heels made no noise at all on the plush carpeting as she moved down the corridor toward the ballroom.

The lights in the ballroom had been dimmed, and hundreds of candles had been placed around the room—on the dining tables, on the serving tables, even in candlesticks mounted on the walls. The effect was lovely, giving the entire room a flickering, golden, fairy-tale like glow.

The dining tables covered half the room, leaving the other half of the hardwood floor open for dancing. A small band—drums, keyboard and guitar—was set up in the corner opposite the bar.

Lucy recognized many of the people scattered about the big room. It was a who's who of the county's wealthiest and most powerful citizens. The police chief and his wife were there, as was the president of the bank. The mayor and his wife were chatting with the owner of Carolina Island, the seaside resort located several miles north of the Hatboro Creek town line.

The women wore glittering gowns and the men were dressed in black tuxedos—all except for one. One man—Blue McCoy—was dressed in the resplendent, almost shimmering white of a naval dress uniform. As he turned, the candlelight gleamed on the rows and rows and *rows* of ribbons and medals he wore on his chest.

His shoulders appeared impossibly broad, with his well-tailored uniform jacket tapering down to his lean hips. He wore officer's insignia, and Lucy was reminded that Blue was a full lieutenant—unless he'd been even further promoted since the last time she'd asked Gerry about his stepbrother's naval career.

He was carrying a white hat in his hands. His hair, a dark, shining golden blond, reflected the dim light. He was talking to Mitch Casey, the chairman of Hatboro Creek's chamber of commerce. Blue's tanned face looked so serious, so stern, as he nodded at something Casey was saying. He was listening intently, but his blue eyes kept straying toward the front entrance, as if he were waiting for someone. Her? Lucy felt a flash of pleasure. He was. Blue McCoy was watching and waiting for *her*.

He held himself slightly stiffly, as if he wasn't quite comfortable in his surroundings. But why should he be? Gerry and his father were the ones who had had the memberships to the country club. Throughout high school, Blue had chosen to hang out and work down by the docks where he kept his little powerboat.

Even when Blue was dating Jenny Lee Beaumont he had stayed away from the country-club set. He'd been a loner back in high school, with only one or two friends, who were also outcasts or misfits. He wore a leather jacket and rode a motorcycle that he'd rebuilt from parts, yet unlike the other tough kids, his grades were exceptionally above average. Still, he had a reputation for being a troublemaker simply because he looked the part.

Even back in high school Blue had been slow to smile. He'd been serious and quietly watchful, missing nothing but rarely stepping in. Unless, of course, the cruel teenaged teasing and rudeness went beyond the limits—like the time five members of the boy's junior-varsity baseball team decided to demonstrate just how unhappy they were that a girl, a Yankee girl, had made the cut and gotten onto the team.

Lucy could hold her own in a fair fight, but five to one were tough odds.

Until Blue fearlessly stepped in, ending the violence with his mere presence. The other kids had learned to keep their distance from him, wary of his quietly seething temper and his ability—and willingness—to fight. And to fight dirty, if he had to.

Apparently he'd had to more than a few times.

According to the story Lucy had heard, Blue had been five when Gerry's father had adopted the little boy out of obligation. Apparently neither Blue nor Mr. McCoy had been overly happy about that, but Blue had had nowhere else to go. Blue had grown up in his elder stepbrother's shadow, clearly a burden to his stepfather. Was it any wonder that the little boy should have quickly become self-sufficient and self-reliant? And quietly grim?

Was it any wonder that both the boy and the man he'd become were watchful, intensely serious and slow to smile?

Lucy remembered the way Blue had smiled at her that afternoon. Had Blue smiled at Jenny Lee that way back in high school? It was hard to believe that he had. If he had, with a smile like that, surely Jenny would be marrying Blue this coming Saturday rather than his elder stepbrother.

As Lucy watched, Blue's attention was pulled away from both the main entrance and Mitch Casey when Gerry McCoy and Jenny Lee Beaumont swept onto the dance floor.

Jenny was wearing a long, pink dress that set off her soft, blond curls and her peaches-and-cream complexion. It had been fifteen years since she'd been in high school, but her skin was still smooth and clear. She still looked like the captain of the cheerleading squad, with her sweet smile and perfect, beautiful features—a fact that no doubt had helped her land her job as entertainment news reporter for the local TV station.

Gerry, however, looked tense, his smile forced as he led his bride-to-be in a slow dance. Was he feeling threatened, perhaps, by his stepbrother's larger-than-life presence?

Physically, the two men couldn't have been less alike. Gerry was taller than Blue but slighter, almost willowy, if that word could be used to describe a man. Although they both had blond hair, Gerry's was a lighter, paler shade, and his hair was fine and slightly thinning on top, not thick and wavy like Blue's. And though Blue's smiles were scarce, Gerry's were almost constant. In fact, Gerry's carefree, fun-time, no-worries attitude contrasted so sharply with Blue's serious intensity that Lucy found it hard to believe the two men had lived under the same roof as young boys. It seemed almost impossible that they'd shared a home and not driven each other crazy with their different approaches to life.

But the talk around town was that despite their differences, Gerry and Blue had been closer than many blood brothers, that their strengths and weaknesses had complemented one another. Lucy didn't know for sure that that was true. By the time she and her mother had moved to Hatboro Creek, Gerry was off at college, and by the time Gerry returned after college, Blue had already left to join the navy.

Lucy gazed across the ballroom, studying Blue's face, watching him as he watched Gerry dance with Jenny Lee.

His gaze swept around the room, passing directly over Lucy with no glint of recognition, as if she wasn't even there—or as if he'd forgotten that she even existed, as if she paled so absolutely compared with Jenny Lee.

Lucy's stomach clenched in disappointment. But really now, she scolded herself. What did she expect? Did she honestly think she'd be anything to Blue but a poor substitute for the woman he truly wanted? She had to keep her imagination in line here. If she wasn't careful, she'd start believing that Blue had unconsciously reached out to her because deep down he was searching desperately for a good woman to love. Or she might start believing that she could make Blue fall in love with her, that just one glorious night of lovemaking with Lucy would soften his damaged heart.

No, the sad truth was, Lucy had come here tonight with her eyes wide open. She knew exactly what Blue wanted from her. He wanted sex. No strings, no desperate search, no falling in love, no softening hearts.

She knew that, and she'd come anyway.

Except now the way Blue's eyes seemed to look right through her signified a decided lack of interest on his part.

Lucy was a fool for thinking she could ever compete with Jenny Lee. Even though Jenny was engaged to marry another man, she was so pretty and sweet it was crazy to think that Blue wouldn't be carrying a torch for her. No doubt he'd asked Lucy here tonight hoping for a distraction—a distraction that she'd failed to provide.

Lucy knew she should turn away, walk out of the room and down the long corridor to the stairs that led out to the back parking lot. But she couldn't move. She could only gaze at Blue and wish that things were different.

His rugged features were impassive, his eyes revealing nothing—no emotion, nothing. And that, of course, convinced Lucy that there *was* something Blue was working so hard to hide.

On the other hand, she had to admit it was a no-win situation for Blue. She knew that she was not the only person in the room watching him for his reaction to his stepbrother and his former sweetheart's dance. If he smiled, it would be with "bittersweet longing." If he frowned, it would be with "barely concealed jealousy."

No, Blue's were not easy shoes to be in right now, and Lucy had to give the man credit for showing up in the first place.

Shoes. Blue wasn't wearing shoes, Lucy realized suddenly. He was wearing sandals. He was wearing his gleaming white navy dress uniform with rows and rows of ribbons and medals on his chest, and a pair of leather sandals on his feet.

As more and more people moved out onto the dance floor, Blue turned away and headed for the French doors that led out onto the patio. The doors were closed tonight. It was too hot to keep them open. The air-conditioning would escape and the muggy night air would be let in.

With his hand on the doorknob, Blue turned back and looked across the room—directly at Lucy. This time he didn't look through her. This time he met her eyes. He moved his head almost imperceptibly, but his message was clear. Follow him outside.

Lucy's heart was pounding as she moved along the ballroom wall toward the patio doors. Perhaps she'd been wrong. Blue did recognize her. He did know she was here. It took her several minutes to work her way around the room, but finally she reached the French doors and slipped out onto the patio.

The sounds of the music and laughter from the party became muffled and distant as she shut the door behind her. The heat brushed against her face and arms like something solid. The moon was nearly full and it glowed through a haze of high clouds.

The patio was wide and made of carefully evened-off flagstones, with a decorative cast-iron railing surrounding it. Several chairs and tables with flickering citronella candles were set up around the edges. Japanese lanterns were strung overhead, but the pale light they cast couldn't compete with the moonlight.

As Lucy stood and let her eyes grow accustomed to the dimness, she saw Blue in the shadows, leaning against the railing, just watching her.

Blue couldn't believe his eyes. That was strange, because he'd been a lot of places, seen both the best and the worst that humanity could offer, and he'd begun to think that nothing could ever surprise him.

But Lucy Tait, dressed to kill in a sexy black dress, with her legs looking at least seven miles long, with her hair piled sophisticatedly atop her head and her brown eyes made up and smoldering, had proven him wrong.

He'd expected her to arrive at the country club wearing something demure and functional. He'd expected he would have to use his imagination to see beyond her clothing to the woman he suspected was underneath.

She started toward him, and he felt his pulse kick into the double time of anticipation, which he immediately tried to squelch. He hadn't been thinking straight when he'd asked her to come to this party with him. It wasn't until he arrived and realized that he was the focus of covert—and some not so covert—attention that it occurred to him that, as his date, Lucy would be subjected to the same curious stares and speculation.

She didn't deserve that. He had to send her home before anyone saw them together.

That was why, when he first noticed her standing on the other side of the room, he didn't allow himself to react. He didn't even let himself do the double take he so desperately wanted to do.

But here in the darkness, away from all the prying eyes, Blue could do all the double takes he wanted.

Mercy.

She could have been the poster model for carnal desire. But as he gazed into her eyes, he realized that it was entirely possible that Lucy didn't know how incredibly sexy she looked. He could see hesitation in her eyes, and a kind of vulnerability that, combined with her incredible outfit, made her seem a curious mix of experience and innocence.

Blue couldn't remember the last time he'd seen a woman and wanted her more than the way he wanted Lucy right now.

He pushed himself up off the railing as she drew closer. The sexy black spike heels of her shoes made her nearly his own height and she gazed directly into his eyes.

"Seems I've been away from town longer than I thought," Blue said softly. He felt his body tighten as he dropped his gaze to her mouth to watch her nervously moisten her lips with the pink tip of her tongue.

"Twelve years," she murmured.

He nodded. "So...why aren't you married...settled down with a couple of kids and all?"

She crossed her arms, one dark eyebrow lifting slightly. "Why aren't *you?*"

"I never met someone I couldn't live without," he said bluntly. "I guess I'm picky that way."

Lucy lifted her chin challengingly. "And what makes you think I'm not?"

Blue had to smile. "Touché." With that defiant gleam in her eyes, she looked so like the girl he'd first met all those years ago—and so unlike her, all at the same time.

He could still remember the way fifteen-year-old Lucy had tried to hide her pain, even after the boys who had been beating on her had run off. Her nose had been bleeding slightly, and she was holding her side. Though Blue had seen one of the boys kick her savagely in the ribs when she was down on the ground, she never cried, and tried not to let on that she was badly hurt. But there was a sheen or perspiration on her face that had told Blue otherwise.

She'd sat on the grass, knees pulled in tightly to her chest, and he'd sat down next to her. "You all right, Yankee?"

"Yeah," she said, wiping the blood from her nose with the back of one hand. "Yeah, I'm . . . fine."

"You don't look so fine."

"I just . . . need to sit here for a minute."

"Okay," Blue said quietly. "Mind if I sit here for a minute, too?"

She shook her head. No, she didn't mind.

"Those boys give you a reason for kicking the bejesus out of you?" Blue asked.

"They don't think a girl belongs on the baseball team," Lucy said.

"Well, it *is* called the *boy's* baseball team," Blue commented.

Lucy's eyes flashed. "So where's the girl's team?"

Blue shrugged. "'Round these parts, girls try out for the cheerleading squad."

"The coach said I'm the best shortstop this hick town has ever seen," Lucy said flatly. "And from what I've seen, he might be right. He put me in the starting lineup and has me batting lead-off. And you want me to be a *cheer*leader?"

Blue hid a smile. "You're pretty sure of yourself, aren't you?"

"There are some things boys can do better than girls—like pee standing up," Lucy told him, her eyes narrowed dangerously, "but playing baseball is *not* one of them. I'm going to stick it in those creeps' faces by winning MVP this year—and accepting the award in a *dress.*"

Blue might have even laughed out loud at that, except a spasm of pain made Lucy wince. She closed her eyes and clenched her teeth. Her face looked so pale.

"How about I give your mama a call?" Blue asked.

Lucy shook her head. "She's working."

"You're hurt—"

"I'm fine."

Blue stood up. "She works in the office at the mill, doesn't she?"

"I said, I'm fine!" Lucy scrambled to her feet, and the effort made her sway.

Blue reached for her, holding her up. "You got a broken rib, Yankee. I'm taking you over to Doc Gray's."

"No, please!" Lucy's dark-brown eyes were wide, her voice beseeching as she gazed up at him. "It's only a crack. The doctor will tape me up and tell me I can't play ball for three weeks. By then I'll have been off the starting lineup for so long I'll have lost my place. I'll spend the rest of the season on the bench."

"Sometimes you gotta sit out."

"Not this time," Lucy said desperately. "If I sit out, those creeps will win. I can't let that happen."

Blue was silent.

"I'll tape myself up," Lucy had told him, chin held high. "It'll hurt, but I'm damned if I'm not going to play."

She *had* played, and sure enough, that year she'd won the coveted Most Valuable Player award for the junior-varsity team. She'd had one hell of a stubborn streak back then, and from the way she was holding her head at that same challenging angle, it seemed that she still had those same guts and grit now. Inside, she wasn't that different. It was the outer packaging that had changed some. A whole lot of some.

Blue let his gaze travel over Lucy's formfitting black dress and down her long, nylon-clad legs. "I guess what I really meant," he said, gazing back into her eyes, "was that I can't believe you're unattached. I can't believe you could walk into this place alone, looking the way you do."

"But I'm not alone," she said softly. "I'm with you."

Desire knifed sharply through Blue, and despite all his best intentions, he knew there was no way he could send Lucy home. Not unless he went, too.

But maybe he could go. In half an hour or so he could make his excuses to Gerry and Jenny Lee and bow out before dinner was served. Until then, he and Lucy could stay out here on the patio. No one would see them. No one would have to know.

Lucy held Blue's gaze, wondering almost desperately what he was thinking. And he *was* thinking. He was planning, deciding. There was more than sheer, hot, raw desire in his eyes—although there was plenty of that, too. She'd have to tell Sarah, she thought almost inanely, that her little black dress was a raging success.

"May I have this dance?" Blue finally said, his smooth Southern drawl like black velvet in the darkness.

Oh, yes. But... "Right here?" Lucy asked, breaking free from the magnetic hold of his eyes to glance around the deserted patio.

Blue smiled crookedly, just a slight lifting of one side of his mouth. "Yeah," he said. He hooked the rim of his hat over one of the posts of the cast-iron railing. And then he reached for her.

Inside the country club, the band was playing an old, slow, familiar tune. The music seemed to drift in the stillness of the night, distant and haunting and pure.

Lucy slipped her right hand into Blue's, resting her other hand on the solidness of his shoulder. She felt his arm encircle her waist, felt the warmth of his hand on her back.

Dear God, she was slow-dancing with Blue McCoy.

He was graceful and surefooted, and when his thigh brushed hers, she knew it was not by accident. Slowly and so surely he pulled her in, closer to him, until her breasts touched his broad chest, until their legs touched continuously. His hand moved upward, exploring the back of her dress, finding the round keyhole of exposed skin.

Lucy felt herself sigh, felt herself tighten her hold on Blue as his slightly work-roughened fingers caressed her back. Gently she pulled her fingers free from his and ran her hand up his arm and shoulders to meet her other hand at the back of his neck.

She could see satisfaction in the ocean-colored depths of Blue's eyes. He knew as well as she did that she was probably going to end up in his bed tonight. It was clear that pleased him. It was also clear that he desired her, too—she couldn't help but be aware of that from the way their bodies were molded together.

Any moment now, he was going to kiss her. Any moment now, he was going to lean forward and touch his lips to hers and they were both going to explode with passion. She could imagine them making a beeline for Blue's motel room, undressing each other as they climbed into the cab of her truck, barely making it inside before . . .

Lucy felt dizzy. This was moving much too quickly. Yes, she wanted to make love to this man. She'd come here tonight knowing that the clothes she was wearing sent a message, knowing that her mere *presence* was a loud and clear affirmative to Blue's unspoken sexual question. But she'd imagined them having dinner first—shoot, at least having a drink and a certain amount of conversation—before giving in to the animal attraction that flashed between them.

But polite conversation and small talk had no place in this relationship. Her body understood that, heat flooding her, readying her for what she really wanted—the most basic and intimate of acts.

Lucy didn't wait for Blue to kiss her. Pulling his mouth down to hers, *she* kissed *him*.

She felt more than heard his surprised laughter—laughter that lasted only a fraction of a second before he angled his head and returned her kiss with an urgency that took her breath away.

He pulled her with him deeper into the darkness of the shadows. His hands explored her body, covering her breasts, slipping down to cup her derriere, reaching for the edge of her dress and sliding up underneath the hem, pushing her miniskirt up along her nylon-smooth thigh. He discovered the edge of her thigh-high stockings and groaned, kissing her harder, deeper, as his fingers caressed the soft smoothness of her skin, as he found the silky lace of her panties.

They weren't even going to make it back to his hotel room. The thought flashed crazily through Lucy's head. But they had to. There were laws against making love in public. For God's sake, she was a police officer. She couldn't do this. Not here.

Lucy pulled back slightly. "Blue..."

"Come back to my room with me." His velvet voice was rough, hoarse, and out of breath.

She nodded. "Yes."

Blue kissed her again and she clung to him, shutting her eyes tightly against the regrets that were sure to come in the morning and all the rest of her tomorrows. But for the first time in her life, Lucy refused to think beyond the here and now. She lost herself again in his kiss.

He tasted the way she'd always imagined he would—sweet and clean and wonderful.

He broke away from her, taking her hand and pulling her toward the gate. "Come on."

"We're just going to leave?"

His eyes were blazing hot in the dim glow from the Japanese lanterns. "You bet."

"But..."

"Come on, Yankee. Let's go make all my dreams come true." His voice was low, vibrating with his desire as he tugged on her hand.

"Your brother will look for you." His brother and a hundred or so odd guests. "He'll wonder where you went."

"If Gerry caught sight of you walking into that country club, he'll know *exactly* where I went."

Lucy blushed. "I'm serious," she said, pulling her hand free from his grasp. "You know how small-town gossip can be. Everyone is going to think that you left because you couldn't stand watching Gerry with Jenny Lee."

"Me and Jenny Lee," Blue said, shaking his head. "That's ancient history."

Lucy could almost believe him. Almost. "That's not the way it's going to look," she said quietly. "No one is going to know that you left with me—no one has even seen us together."

"And I don't want 'em to," Blue said. "I don't want 'em talking about you, too."

Lucy smiled ruefully. "Whatever they'd be saying, it would probably be true, wouldn't it?"

He smiled, a tight, sexy, dangerous smile. "Well, yeah," he said, "if they say I took one look at you and lost control."

His soft words made Lucy's heart leap into her throat. But they were just words, she reminded herself. "I'd be willing to bet," she said, "that you don't ever lose control."

His eyes were unreadable, mysterious. "There's always a first time." His voice dropped to a nearly inaudible level. "All I know is, I'd do damn near anything to make love to you right now, Lucy."

"Well, shoot," Lucy said, crossing her arms and smiling to hide the way his words made her pulse race. "Maybe if I play my cards right, we can make that wedding on Saturday a double ceremony."

She was baiting him, watching to see if her words made him back off. "I said *damn near* anything," Blue said, smiling at her expression—she thought she had him retreating. So he called her bluff. "I guess getting married falls into that description. Sure. But why wait till Saturday? We can fly out to Las Vegas and get hitched tonight. Right now."

Lucy surrendered. "We both know you don't have to marry me to get what you want—what *I* want, too."

He stepped toward her. "Then what are we waiting for?"

She lifted her chin. "*We're* waiting for *you* to go inside and make your excuses to Gerry and Jenny Lee."

Blue smiled again—damn, he couldn't remember the last time he'd smiled and laughed so much. But this was fun. Lucy Tait was able to hold her own against him. She was a worthy sparring opponent, and he liked that. He liked it a lot.

He'd moved close enough to her to put his arms around her waist, close enough to lean forward for another long, sensuous kiss. But Lucy reached out for him first, sweeping her hands along the lapels of his jacket, lightly tracing the ribbons and medals he wore on his chest with one finger.

"Look at all these," she mused. "What are you, some kind of hero?"

"Just a SEAL," Blue murmured, mesmerized by the elegant curve of her lips, by the spattering of freckles that ran across her cheekbones and the bridge of her nose, by the delicate shell-like curve of her ears.

She leaned forward so that her lips were only a whisper away from his. "Go find your brother," she breathed.

He kissed her again—he couldn't resist—drowning in her softness, marveling how one woman could be such a complete montage of sweetness and spice. When he finally pulled away, his voice didn't sound like his own. "Don't go anywhere."

Lucy smiled. "I won't."

Chapter 3

Blue searched the country-club dining room for any sign of Gerry. The band was still playing in the corner, and couples were still out on the dance floor, but most of the crowd were starting to get seated at the round banquet tables that dotted half the room.

His sharp eyes finally picked Gerry out of the crowd. He was in the corner, having what looked like a serious discussion with R. W. Fisher, the Tobacco King.

Fisher had sold his tobacco farms and cigarette factories in Virginia and moved his massive fortune to Hatboro Creek about the same time Blue had moved to town with his mother. It had been more than twenty-five years since Fisher had earned his wages from growing and selling tobacco, but he would no doubt be known as the Tobacco King until the day he died.

Gerry was forever trying to work his way into R. W. Fisher's exclusive circle of friends and business acquaintances. Blue knew better than to disturb his stepbrother now.

On the other hand, Lucy was waiting for him out on the patio....

He could just as easily make his excuses for leaving to Jenny Lee, tell her that he'd talk to Gerry in the morning. Blue turned back to the table where he'd last seen his stepbrother's bride-to-be talking with several of her friends.

He worked his way across the room, and Jenny Lee glanced up. She rose to her feet, smiling a welcome, her cheeks dimpling prettily. Her friends were noticeably quiet, watching them both.

"Carter," Jenny said in her soft Southern accent. "We haven't properly said hello yet, have we?"

She held out her hand to him, and he reached for it automatically. Jenny Lee Beaumont. There had once been a time when he'd wanted this girl more than life itself. Her blond hair and blue eyes, her diminutive yet well-rounded figure, her lacy, frilly clothes had all seemed the definition of femaleness. It was funny, but now she seemed overdone—a caricature of the Southern belle, all peaches and sugar and girlish charm.

Funny, but somewhere during the past twelve years he'd developed a definite preference for spice. And for full-grown women.

Jenny Lee's fragrant scent enveloped him, cloyingly sweet and chokingly strong. Hell, he used to love the way she smelled. Now he had to fight a nearly overpowering urge to step back, away from her, to find some fresh air.

As she smiled up into his eyes, Blue felt nothing.

He *had* been afraid to see her again, he realized suddenly. He'd been scared that all the old wants and needs and hurts would come flooding back.

But he felt nothing.

Except an urge to get back out to that patio, where Lucy Tait was waiting for him.

"Jenny, I'm sorry," he said, gently disengaging his hand from hers, "but I can't stay for dinner. I've got to head out."

"Oh, dear. I was hoping to get a chance to talk to you."

As her smile faded, Blue could see lines of worry on Jenny's usually smooth face. And when she smiled again, he could see that it was forced and unnatural.

Blue glanced at the tableful of women, all still listening, as if they were watching an episode of "As the World Turns." Whatever Jenny had to say, she didn't want to say it in front of an audience.

"Of course, I really can't leave without at least one dance," Blue said, knowing that whatever was bothering her, she could tell him on the privacy of the dance floor.

Relief flashed through Jenny's eyes. "Of course," she said, letting him lead her out into the middle of the room. The women at the table were still watching, but at least they wouldn't be able to hear them.

"Is everything all right?" Blue asked. Dancing with Jenny was odd after he'd held Lucy in his arms. Lucy was nearly his own height, a perfect fit; Jenny was so much shorter. He felt awkward, as if he had to bend clear over to talk to her.

"I don't know what's going on," Jenny said. "Gerry has been acting so strangely the past few days...so worried and upset. I can't figure out why. Business has been better than ever. He just bought a new car, and the honeymoon plans he's made are *extravagant*.... It's not financial worries that have him down, that's for sure."

Her eyes were bright with tears, but Blue still felt nothing. Nothing more than brotherly concern for Gerry's future wife. She looked as if she was going to say more, so he waited.

"I just wonder..."

If she were Lucy, she would have spit out whatever was bugging her the moment they'd begun to dance. Lucy was straightforward and to the point. She said what was on her mind. It was refreshing, Blue realized. He liked it much better than Jenny Lee's approach, where every tiny piece of information had to be wheedled out of her.

"What is it, Jenny Lee?" he asked. "Just tell me."

She couldn't look him in the eye, embarrassment making her blush. "I just can't help but wonder if I haven't made a colossal mistake by inviting you here," she whispered.

Ten minutes stretched into fifteen, and all Lucy's doubts and reservations grew bigger and bigger.

What was she doing? Now that she was taking the time to think about it, the incredible power of the passion she felt from Blue's kisses scared her to death.

What if she did something really stupid? What if she fell in love with this guy?

Fell in love? Lord help her, she was already halfway over the edge. Could she really have sex with Blue, keeping the physical and emotional totally separate? Or would the physical intimacy send her into a tailspin from which she could never pull free?

Where *was* he? What was taking him so long?

Lucy had no questions, no doubts, when she gazed into Blue's eyes. She could move in no other direction but ahead. It was only when he wasn't around that she started to back away.

She opened the French doors and went back into the country club. Blue had probably gotten into some deep discussion with Gerry and couldn't get free. And she—she needed a drink, something with a kick to give her the courage to keep from running away.

Halfway to the bar, she saw him.

Blue was out on the dance floor, with Jenny Lee Beaumont in his arms.

Didn't it figure.

Lucy turned away, too disgusted with her own self to feel angry at Blue. Blue and Jenny Lee, ancient history? Lucy had almost believed it. That made her as big a fool as Blue.

She had to get away from here, fast, so she headed for the doors to the corridor. She was nearly there when the shouting started.

Lucy turned back, her police officer's training not allowing her to run from sounds of trouble. What she saw made her heart sink.

Gerry, his face livid, was standing in the middle of the dance floor, between Blue and Jenny. And even though he'd lowered his voice, he pushed at Blue repeatedly, clearly upset and angry.

Lucy could see from Blue's stance and from the way he held both hands in the air, palms out and facing his stepbrother, that he had no intention of letting this argument become violent. But Jenny was in tears, and Gerry pushed Blue harder and harder with every sentence he spoke. Lucy moved closer, wondering whether she should step in even though she wasn't on duty. Not that she'd had much luck settling this afternoon's disturbance....

The room was silent. Even the band had stopped playing. Sheldon Bradley, the chief of police, moved quickly to Gerry's side, and Lucy was glad. He had far more experience than she did, in addition to being one of Gerry's friends.

"I want him *out* of here." Gerry's voice started to get louder again. "Who the hell gave him permission to dance with Jenny Lee anyway?"

Was his speech slurred? He sounded funny, as if he were...

"Gerry, you're drunk," Jenny Lee said.

"It was *your* idea to invite him," Gerry shot back harshly, turning to berate his fiancée. "Stepbrother or not, I didn't think it was right to invite one of your ex-lovers to my wedding. But maybe you had some other kind of reason to want him here...?"

"When you sober up, brother," Blue drawled softly, "you're going to feel like a real idiot."

"Stay the *hell* out of my life," Gerry said, his eyes wild. "You're not my brother. I don't want you hanging around. I didn't when we were kids, and I sure as hell don't *now.*"

The flash of pain that appeared in Blue's eyes left so quickly that Lucy was sure she was the only one who'd seen it. But she *had* seen it. Gerry's bitter words had hurt Blue deeply.

"Come on now, boys." Chief Bradley tried to step between the two men.

"Besides, Jenny Lee is mine now." Gerry glared past Bradley at Blue. "You had your chance. You can't have her."

"She's not going to be yours too much longer if you keep this up," Blue said evenly, quietly.

"Is that some kind of threat? Because if that was some kind of a threat, I'm gonna . . ." Gerry swung at Blue.

Blue caught his hand effortlessly, stopping his stepbrother's punch midswing.

"Now, come on," the police chief said, "is this any way for brothers to treat each other?"

"He's not my brother." Gerry pulled his hand free from Blue's. "If my old man hadn't felt guilty for picking up and bedding Blue's white-trash mama—"

Blue reacted so quickly that Lucy didn't even see his movement. One moment he was standing several feet away from Gerry, and the next he had backed his stepbrother up against a support pillar and was holding on to the taller man by the lapels of his expensive tuxedo.

Chief Bradley looked as if he was thinking twice about getting on the wrong side of Blue. Still, he stepped forward. "Here now, boys. Let's not—"

Blue ignored Bradley, glaring into Gerry's eyes. "That time you went too far," he said softly. "I don't give a damn what you say about me, but you keep my mother out of this."

"Blue," the police chief said. "Son, I'm going to have to ask you to leave."

"You so much as breathe her name again," Blue continued, "and there'll be hell to pay, you understand me?"

Gerry nodded, finally silenced.

Chief Bradley wasn't used to being ignored. "Blue McCoy, I'm going to have to ask you to unhand your brother."

But Blue didn't move. "You apologize to Jenny Lee, and then you go on home and sober up," he said to Gerry, still in that same low, dangerous voice.

Gerry seemed to wilt, to sag, his arms going around Blue in an odd kind of embrace. He may have said something, whispered something in Blue's ear, but he spoke so softly Lucy couldn't hear it.

"As far as *I* can see, son, *you're* the one who needs to be making apologies and clearing on out of here." Chief Bradley looked around the room, searching for any kind of support. He spotted Lucy. "You on duty tonight, Tait?"

"No, sir. I'm here as—"

"Consider yourself on duty as of right now," Bradley said grimly. "I'm ordering you to escort Lieutenant McCoy back to his motel. See that he gets there without any more trouble."

"But..." Lucy glanced at Blue, who had let go of Gerry.

Blue turned to Jenny Lee. "I'm sorry," he said.

"I am, too," she said. She held her head high despite the tears that were in her eyes, and with a withering look at Gerry, she swept out of the room.

Blue turned and headed for the other door. Chief Bradley had pulled Gerry aside and was talking to him in a low voice. Lucy briefly considered waiting and voicing her arguments about being suddenly placed on duty during her night off, but she knew it wouldn't make any difference. Sheldon Bradley ran the Hatboro Creek Police Department according to his own set of rules. With a sigh, Lucy turned and followed Blue. She had to run to catch up with him.

"McCoy—wait!"

He turned and waited, his face impassive, his eyes expressionless. Together, they walked in silence out to Lucy's truck.

It wasn't until Lucy was pulling out of the country-club driveway that Blue spoke.

"I'm sorry about that," he murmured.

She glanced at him. He was watching her in the dim light from the dashboard. "You can't help the way you feel," she said quietly.

He shifted in his seat, turning so that he was facing her. "You don't think I was..." He stopped and started over. "Do you really think I would put the moves on Jenny Lee at the rehearsal dinner for her wedding to my stepbrother?"

Lucy pulled carefully up to the stop sign at the corner of Main Street and Seaside Road. "Everyone at that party was waiting for something to happen between you and Jenny Lee," she said, taking a left onto Main Street. "Everyone at that party saw you dancing with her and came to the same conclusion—that you're here to stir up trouble, that you want to win Jenny Lee back."

Blue's face was in the shadows, but she knew that he was watching her.

"Everyone at the party. Including you?"

She had to be honest. "Yes."

"And if I told you everyone at the party was wrong? That I feel nothing for Jenny Lee . . . ?"

"I'd have to assume you were only saying that in a last-ditch effort to get me to spend the night with you," Lucy said bluntly, pulling her truck into the motel parking lot and rolling to a stop.

"That's not true," Blue said quietly. "Yes, I want you in my bed, but I wouldn't lie to get you there. Come on, Yankee, let's just leave the past in the past." He reached out across the cab of the truck, gently touching her hair.

Lucy shifted away from him. "Don't."

"Lucy—"

She closed her eyes, trying to shut him out. "I can't do this," she said. "I thought I could, but I can't." She opened her eyes and looked at Blue. "I can't be a substitute for Jenny Lee."

Blue laughed, a flare of impatience in his eyes. "You're *not*—"

"Look, McCoy, I've got to go—"

"Why don't we go get a beer and talk about this?" he suggested. "Is that roadhouse—what's it called? The Rebel Yell. Is it still around? Why don't we go there?"

"No. Believe it or not, I'm actually on duty now. I've got to go back to the station and file a report."

"You know damn well you could do that in the morning."

"Yeah," Lucy said. "But I *want* to do it now."

Silence. Lucy stared out the front windshield, hoping and wishing that Blue would just open the door and climb out of the truck's cab. She heard him sigh.

"Damn Gerry to hell," he said tiredly. "I should have wrung his neck while I had the chance."

He opened the door and climbed out of the truck. "It was a genuine pleasure seeing you again, Lucy Tait," he said in his soft drawl. "I've got to tell you—I wish it could have been an even bigger pleasure. If you're ever in California, give me a call."

She turned to look at him—she couldn't help it. "Are you leaving town?"

His blond hair glistened in the cab's overhead light as he nodded. "I'm heading out on the next bus. I don't care where it goes, as long as it's a city big enough to have an airport."

He was leaving as soon as he could. Lucy looked away from him, afraid that he'd see the disappointment that surely crossed her face.

"Bye, Lucy," Blue whispered. He closed the cab door and was gone.

Lucy's phone rang well before dawn, waking her from a restless sleep.

It was Annabella Sawyer, the police dispatcher. "You better get down to the station," she said in her raspy voice, without any words of greeting. "All hell has broken loose. The chief is calling in all available manpower."

Lucy rolled over and looked at her clock. It was a few minutes after 4 a.m. "What's going on?"

"It started as a 10-65," Annabella said. "Jenny Beaumont called in at 2:11 a.m., reporting Gerry McCoy missing. He hadn't come home. Fifteen minutes ago, Tom Harper came across Gerry's motor vehicle by the side of Gate's Hill Road. Shortly after that, the 10-65 became a 10-54. At 3:56, Doc Harrington verified it. We've got ourselves a 187."

Lucy tiredly closed her eyes. "You mind translating that for me, Annabella?"

"The missing person became a report of a dead body," Annabella said. "We've got a homicide on our hands."

Lucy sat up. *"What?"*

"Gerry McCoy is dead," Annabella intoned. "He's been murdered."

Chapter 4

Lucy rushed into the police station, pulling her hair back into a ponytail and trying to rein in her growing sense of dread. Gerry McCoy was dead, and Lucy was almost positive that the tragedy wasn't over yet.

Officer Frank Redfield was behind the front desk, on the phone, but he nodded to her, holding up one finger, signaling her to wait.

"All right," he said into the telephone. His thinning brown hair was standing up straight, as if he'd rolled directly out of bed. "I understand, Chief. I'll get right on it." He hung up the receiver and turned to Lucy. "Hell of a situation," he said to her, taking a long swig of black coffee. "You been filled in on the specifics?"

"I've heard that Gerry McCoy's body was found up off Gate's Hill Road," Lucy said, pouring her own mug of coffee from the urn in the lobby. "I don't know any of the details. How did he die? Gunshot?" Nearly all the deaths in the county were gun related.

"Come on," Frank said, gesturing for her to follow him. "I've got to put out an all-points bulletin, but I'll try to bring you up to speed while I'm entering the info into the computer."

Lucy hurried down the hall after him. Frank was about four inches shorter than she was, and thin as a rail. But what he lacked in weight, he made up for in speed and good nature. It certainly wasn't his fault that, standing next to him, Lucy felt like some kind of Amazon. He was always friendly and respectful. In fact, Frank and his best friend, Tom Harper—tall and black and built like a defensive lineman—were the only men on the Hatboro Creek police force who hadn't muttered and complained about Lucy joining their previously exclusively male organization.

"First of all," Frank said in his thick South Carolina accent, "cause of death wasn't gun related. Gerry McCoy died from a broken neck."

"We're certain it wasn't accidental?" Lucy asked. "Sustained in a fall?"

"Gerry's body was found in the middle of a clearing," he said. "Unless he fell out of the sky, there was no way his injuries were accidental." He sat down at the computer desk, glancing up at her and grimacing. "Doc Harrington reported that his neck was broke clean through. Snapped like a twig." He shuddered. "Doc estimated time of death to be a little bit after eleven. We'll get a more accurate time when the forensics guy gets out here in the morning."

"Who's the APB for?"

"The stepbrother," Frank said, typing the information into the computer, fingers moving at his usual breathtaking speed.

Lucy's dread deepened. "Blue McCoy." Of course they were going to want to talk to Gerry's stepbrother—particularly since Blue was seen publicly arguing with the deceased hours before the estimated time of death. Family members were always high on the suspect list early on in a murder investigation. Statistically, most murders were committed by someone near and dear to the victim. Yet Blue wasn't a cold-blooded killer. He was a soldier, a warrior, but not a murderer.

Still, *damn Gerry to hell,* Blue had said. *I should have wrung his neck while I had the chance.*

Wrung his neck, he'd said. And now here Gerry was, dead—that very same neck snapped in two.

My God, was it possible . . . ?

No, Lucy couldn't believe it. She *wouldn't* believe it.

"We want to bring him in for questioning," Frank said.

"You don't need an APB for that," Lucy said. Questioning. Being brought in for questioning was marginally better than being brought in with charges already filed. "Blue McCoy is staying over at the Lighthouse Motel."

"Not any more," Frank said. "Chief just called in and reported that Gerry's brother checked out of the motel at around 1 a.m. Jedd Southeby over at the Lighthouse said Blue paid his bill and just walked out of there with some kind of heavy duffel bag over his shoulder." He looked up at Lucy. "In fact, now that you know as much as we know, you better get on the ball and join the search. A man on foot carrying a heavy load couldn't have gotten far."

What was it Blue had said as they were saying goodbye? *I'm heading out on the next bus. I don't care where it goes . . .*

Lucy picked up the phone and dialed information. "Yeah, I need the number of the bus station in Georgetown." She scribbled it on a piece of paper as Frank glanced over at her in barely concealed disbelief.

"There's no way in hell the stepbrother could've gone to Georgetown," he said. "It's nearly fifteen miles away. Use your head, Luce. This time of night the roads are quiet. He couldn't even get there by hitching. Nobody is around to pick him up."

"Georgetown has the nearest all-night bus station," Lucy said, dialing the number she was given. "And fifteen miles is an after-dinner stroll to a Navy SEAL."

"You're wasting your time," Frank said in a singsong voice.

After nearly seventeen rings, the phone at the Georgetown bus station was picked up. Lucy identified herself and was forwarded to the manager. "I need the schedule of all buses that have left or are leaving your terminal, starting at 3:00 a.m.," she said. It was unlikely that Blue had arrived in Georgetown that early, but she wanted to be safe.

"No buses left between 2:00 a.m. and 3:55," the bus station manager told her. "At 3:55, we had a departure for Columbia and Greenville. At 4:20, just a few minutes ago, a bus left for Charleston, and the next bus... Let's see—"

"Isn't there a naval base in Charleston?" Lucy asked Frank.

He nodded. "Yeah."

"That's the bus," Lucy said. It had to be the one Blue would take. He'd ride the bus to Charleston, and at the naval base he'd catch the next flight out of state, probably back to California. "Is there any way to contact the bus driver?"

"Not short of chasing him and flagging him down. The local buses aren't equipped with radios," the manager told her. "We can contact the bus depot in Charleston, but that's about it."

"What time does that bus get in?"

"It's not an express," the manager said, "so it stops in nearly every town along Route 17 from here to Charleston. It won't arrive at the final destination until 6:45 p.m. That's if they're running on time."

"Thank you," Lucy said, hanging up the phone. "I'm going to Charleston," she said to Frank.

"What you're going on is a wild-goose chase," he told her.

"Aren't my orders to join in the search to find Blue McCoy?" Lucy asked.

"Well, yeah, but—"

"I'm joining in," Lucy said, heading for the door.

"Chief is gonna get riled—"

"Tell the chief," Lucy said, "that I'll be back before eight o'clock—with Blue McCoy."

Blue was drifting in and out of sleep. It seemed incredible that he had spent most of last night hiking to the bus station in Georgetown. It seemed amazing that he had worked so hard just to get on this crummy old bus.

It seemed particularly incredible that he had worked so hard to leave Hatboro Creek, because for the first time in his life, Hatboro Creek was precisely where he wanted to be.

Because a woman named Lucy Tait was there, and try as he might, he couldn't get her off his mind.

She still lived in the same big, old house that she'd shared with her mother back when Blue had been in high school. Unable to sleep, he'd gone for a walk last night and found himself standing and staring at her darkened windows, wanting to go up to her door and knowing that he shouldn't.

He could have rung her doorbell, finagled an invitation inside. Once in Lucy's living room, it wouldn't have taken much to seduce her. He already knew that she found the attraction between them nearly impossible to resist.

He'd forced himself to turn around, to turn his back on the paradise that making love to Lucy Tait would bring. Why? He didn't know for sure, but he suspected his motivation was due to wariness. There was something inside that warned him that maybe, just maybe, this Lucy Tait was someone special. And Blue knew, plain as day, that he had no room in his life for anyone, particularly not someone who was special.

He knew from watching Joe Catalanotto, the commander of SEAL Team Ten's Alpha Squad and Blue's best friend, that finding someone special wasn't all hearts and flowers. Yeah, Joe seemed happy most of the time. Yeah, in general he smiled more and got irritated and frustrated less. But during the times when the Alpha Squad was on a mission, when it had been weeks since Joe had seen his wife, Veronica, and weeks, possibly even months, until he'd get a chance to see her again, Joe would grow quieter and quieter. Joe never complained, never spoke about it, but Blue knew his friend. He knew that Joe missed the woman he loved, and that he worried about her when he was gone for so long.

Blue didn't want that, didn't need that. No, sir—no, thanks.

So why was he sitting here on this bus, dozing and fantasizing about Lucy Tait, as if he could conjure her up just by wishing and wanting? When he pulled into Charleston, he'd look up one of the women he knew from back when he'd been stationed at the naval base, and...

"What the hell...?" he heard someone say. "Why are we pulling over here?"

"This stop ain't on the route," another voice said.

Blue opened his eyes. Sure enough, the bus was moving to the side of the road. Two men in work clothes, sitting across the aisle and several seats toward the front, were the only ones on the sparsely filled bus who were talking.

"Aw, hell," the first man said. "Driver must've been speeding. We're getting pulled over by a cop."

"If I don't get to Charleston by 7:00, I'm going to lose my job," the second voice complained. "I've been late too many times before."

Blue tried to see out of his window, but couldn't see a police cruiser, couldn't see anything, so he closed his eyes again. It didn't matter to him if this took five minutes or an hour. He'd get to Charleston when he got there.

He heard the hiss as the driver opened the door, heard the murmur of voices from the front of the bus.

"Oh, sugar," the first man said. "Come and arrest *me.*"

"Where do I sign up to get frisked?" the other man asked with a giggle.

"I've heard that one before," a third voice said, "so unless you can come up with something original, why don't you just keep your mouths shut?"

Lucy?

Blue opened his eyes, and sure enough, there she was, standing in the aisle, looking down at him.

"McCoy, you've got to grab your stuff and come off the bus with me," she said.

She looked tired, and her face had been wiped clean of last night's makeup. Her hair was up in a utilitarian ponytail, and her uniform shirt hid the soft curves of her body. Still, she looked *damn* good and Blue felt his mouth curve up into a smile of pleasure.

"Hey," he said, his voice rusty from sleep. He cleared his throat. "Yankee. Didn't think I'd see *you* again."

"Come on, we're holding these people up," Lucy said.

She wouldn't look him in the eye, as if she were afraid of the inferno of attraction he knew was burning there.

"Am I under arrest?" he teased, tilting his head so that she was forced to meet his gaze.

But she didn't smile. "No," she said. "Not yet."

Blue felt his own smile fade as he searched her eyes. She wasn't kidding when she'd said "not yet." Whatever Lucy was doing here, it wasn't gonna be good. "What happened?" he asked, suddenly concerned. Clearly she hadn't followed him halfway to Charleston because of their unconsummated, sizzling attraction to each other. "Something happened, didn't it?"

She gestured with her head toward the front of the bus. "Get off the bus and I'll fill you in."

Blue stood up and swung his duffel bag down from the overhead rack. He followed Lucy down the aisle and out the narrow stairs onto the dusty road. Something was going on here. Something *bad.*

As the bus pulled back onto Route 17, he dropped his duffel bag onto the street. "Spill it."

"Why don't you get into the car?" she suggested.

Blue didn't move. "Don't play games, Lucy. It's not your style. Just tell me what's going on."

"I've got bad news," she said tightly. "I'd like you to sit down."

Bad news.

Bad news meant death or the equivalent.

Last time Blue got "bad news," he'd been in the hospital, waiting with the rest of Alpha Squad for word about Frisco. For hours, they didn't know if he was going to live or die. And *I've got bad news* was what the doctor had said when he'd come out of surgery. Frisco was going to live, but he wasn't going to walk ever again.

That doctor knew about Navy SEALs. He knew that losing mobility, losing the ability to run and jump and even walk, was bad news akin to death.

And in a way, Frisco *had* died in Baghdad. The unsmiling man lying in that hospital bed with lines of pain around his eyes and mouth was nothing like the laughing, upbeat SEAL Blue had once known.

Bad news.

Someone had died. He could see it in Lucy's eyes. But who? Blue didn't want to guess. He just wanted her to tell him.

Lucy felt a rush of relief as she looked at Blue. He was gazing into her eyes as if he were trying to read her mind. He honestly didn't know what she was about to tell him. He didn't know—he honestly didn't know that Gerry was dead. He couldn't possibly be the killer. No one was that good a liar.

"I don't need to sit down to get bad news," Blue said in his soft drawl.

Lucy knew that she was just supposed to tell him that his stepbrother was dead. That way she could gauge his reaction, further verify that he didn't know anything about the killing. But it seemed so cruel, so heartless. Although recently Blue and Gerry hadn't been on the best of terms, they *had* been friends in their youth.

"Come on, Yankee," Blue said softly. "If it's gonna hurt, do it fast, get it over with."

Lucy nodded, moistening her lips. "Gerry is dead."

Blue squinted slightly, as if the sun were suddenly too bright for him. "Gerry," he said, looking out over the farmland that stretched into the distance as the muscle in his jaw clenched again and again. "Dear God. How?"

"He was killed sometime last night," Lucy said.

Blue turned to look sharply at her, his blue eyes neon and intense in the morning light. "Killed," he repeated. "As in...murdered?"

Lucy nodded. "His neck was broken."

Blue swore under his breath. "Who would've done that to him—three days before his wedding?"

"We don't know yet. The homicide investigation has just started."

Something changed in his eyes and his entire body became stiffer, more tense. "Am I a suspect?"

"Right now everyone in town is a suspect," Lucy told him. "As a family member, you just happen to be up a little higher on the list."

"I can't believe he's dead." Blue shook his head. "Gerry. When I was a kid, I thought he was immortal. One of the gods." He laughed, but it held no humor. "The last thing I said to him I said in anger, and now he's dead." He fixed Lucy with his brilliant blue gaze, and she caught her breath at the depth of the pain she saw in his eyes.

"I loved him," Blue said simply. "He was my brother. I wouldn't kill my brother."

Chapter 5

"I believe him," Lucy said.

Sarah gazed back at her silently for several long moments from her prone position on the couch. "Richard told me that Gerry's neck was broken cleanly," Sarah said. "He said that in order to do that, a man either had to be a martial-arts expert or have extreme upper-body strength." She paused for a moment, pushing herself up on one elbow to take a cooling sip from a tall glass of orange juice. "Speaking of upper-body strength, didn't you tell me something about Navy SEALs being able to bench-press three or four hundred pounds or something like that?"

Lucy shook her head. "I know what you're getting at," she said. "Yes, you're right. Blue McCoy probably has the strength and ability to break a man's neck the way Gerry's was broken. But I don't think he did it."

"Have they arrested him?" Sarah asked, her hazel eyes sympathetic.

"No," Lucy said. "They don't have enough to hold him. The fact that he was—quote, unquote—'fleeing the scene of the crime' is only circumstantial evidence."

The phone rang jarringly loudly, disrupting the calm of Sarah's living room. Lucy jumped and Sarah winced, making a face in apology. "Richard got a ring amplifier for the phone," she explained. "He was afraid he'd sleep straight through some medical emergency because he wouldn't hear the phone ringing in the middle of the night. I tell you, it's tough being married to a small-town doctor." Her smile turned impish. "Or maybe it's just tough being married to Richard. Excuse me for a sec." Sarah reached out and took the cordless phone from its resting place on the coffee table in front of her. "Hello?"

Lucy gazed around Sarah's living room. It wasn't until the baby was well on its way that Sarah and Richard had gotten around to furnishing their new house. For nearly a year, there had been almost nothing in the living room. But now everything was finally out of boxes. The house was filled with furniture that was toddler friendly. There were no sharp edges or breakable surfaces; everything was softly rounded, designed for being bumped by small heads and grabbed by tiny fingers. Yet despite its functional furnishings, the living room was tastefully decorated. Sarah wouldn't have had it any other way.

"No," she was saying into the phone. "I'm still waiting for this baby to decide that it's time to be born." She laughed. "Don't worry, you'll get a call." She paused, glancing up at Lucy. "Yes, she's here. Do you want to talk to her?"

"Who is it?" Lucy mouthed.

"Tom Harper," Sarah mouthed back. "Oh, okay. I'll give her that message. Consider her on her way." She laughed. "Sure, Tom. Thanks. Bye." Sarah pressed the off button, looking up at Lucy. "Tom was calling with a message from the chief. You're wanted down at the station. Immediately."

Lucy drained the last of her orange juice. "Did he happen to say why?"

Sarah smiled. "He mentioned something about Chief Bradley putting you in charge of the entire investigation since you did such a good job tracking Blue McCoy down."

Lucy nearly dropped her glass. *"Me?"*

"I don't understand," Lucy said vehemently, climbing into her truck. "Every other person on this police force is better qualified to handle this investigation. Why *me?*"

Blue stowed his duffel bag under his feet and calmly closed the passenger door, locking it with his elbow. "Because every other person on this police force thinks that I killed Gerry."

"And since when does Chief Bradley let the prime suspect select the officer in charge of the investigation?" she sputtered.

"Drive this thing, will you?" Blue said, squinting as he gazed out the front windshield. "I want to get out of here."

It was clear that he wasn't going to answer any of her questions until she put her truck in gear and pulled out of the parking lot.

It wasn't until she was on Bluff Drive, heading down toward the beach, that Blue started to talk. "Bradley doesn't know that *I* chose you," he said in his soft drawl. "He thinks *he* did. He was trying to get me to sign a confession and he claimed that the case against me was gonna be open and shut. Even though they don't have enough evidence to hold me today, the chief said this one was so easy that even the dumbest, greenest rookie on the force would be able to collect the necessary evidence to send me to jail within forty-eight hours. I took the opportunity to maneuver him into standing by his claim."

"And I'm that dumbest, greenest rookie," Lucy said dryly.

"You're green, Yankee," Blue said, "but you're not dumb. And you're not going to overlook any evidence that supports my innocence in your zeal to hang me."

Lucy was silent for a moment. "What if I only find evidence that will help convict you?" she finally asked.

Blue pointed toward the beach parking lot. "Pull in," he said. "Please."

Lucy did. At this time of the late afternoon, the parking lot was almost empty, the last of the beachgoers heading home. She pulled up to the big boulders that lined the lot and turned off the engine. When she was in high school, this was where kids had come at night to park and make out. She'd never gone, but she was willing to bet that Blue had brought Jenny Lee here plenty of times.

Blue turned in his seat to face her. "I have a gut feeling," he said slowly, "that you're only going to find evidence that points to my guilt." He held up one hand, stopping her before she could speak. "Something about this whole thing reeks of setup. Whoever killed Gerry wants it to look like I'm the murderer. I don't know who's involved, or how far they're willing to take this. Until I do know there's only one person I'm going to trust in this town, and that's you."

Lucy stared at him in disbelief. He was serious. Out of all the people he could have turned to for help, he'd turned to *her.*

But as the officer in charge of the investigation, her job wasn't to play favorites with a suspect. Her job was to find the killer—no matter who that killer turned out to be.

Lucy rested her head on her folded arms atop the steering wheel. "What if I decide you're guilty?"

"I believe you already decided that I'm not."

Lucy lifted her head. "I need to question you," she said. "you need to tell me where you were at the time of Gerry's death."

"I don't have an alibi," Blue told her. "I was by myself."

Lucy took her notebook out of her pocket and opened the truck door. "Let's walk on the beach," she suggested.

Blue nodded. "I'd like that," he said, following her out of the truck.

The sand crunched beneath Lucy's shoes. Blue had kicked off his sandals, she noticed, and his feet were now bare. He had nice feet. They were strong looking, with high arches and long, straight toes.

Lucy held her questions until they reached the edge of the water. They headed south along the coast in silence, watching the play of the early-evening sun on the ocean.

"We're in an interesting position here," Lucy finally said. It wasn't easy, but she had to be honest with him because she *needed* him to be honest with her. "Last night we were on the verge of a...certain kind of relationship, but today that relationship has to be something entirely different."

Blue was quiet, just listening, so she pushed on. "I'm going to ask you a whole bunch of questions, and you've got to answer them honestly, do you understand?"

Lucy moved away slightly so that a wave rushing up to shore wouldn't get her shoes wet. Blue let the water wash over his bare feet. It soaked the hem of his pants, but he didn't seem to notice or care. He glanced up as if he felt Lucy watching him, and nodded. Yes, he understood.

"Okay." Lucy exhaled a burst of air. She hadn't realized it, but she had been holding her breath. "I dropped you off at your motel room around 8:30 p.m.," she said. "Tell me everything you did from then till the time you checked out."

Blue narrowed his eyes, thinking. "I went inside the room, took a shower and changed out of my dress uniform. I got some fried fish and a salad to go from the Grill, went back to my room and watched part of a movie on cable while I ate dinner," he said. "It wasn't very good—the movie, not the food—so I turned it off before the end. It was probably around ten at that point. The air conditioner wasn't working real well, and I was...restless, so I went outside, for a walk."

Restless. Lucy had been restless last night, too. She knew he was watching her, so she kept her eyes carefully on her notebook. "Where did you go? It's possible someone saw you while you were out."

"I went down Main and cut over some back lots to the marina," Blue said. "I sat down there for a while—I don't even know how long." He paused. "And then I walked up toward Fox Run Road."

Lucy couldn't keep from turning and looking at him. Her house was on Fox Run Road.

"That's right," he said. "I went to see if maybe you were still awake, like me."

She had been. She'd been awake last night until well into the early hours of the morning. She'd stared at the shadows on her ceiling, wishing that she had been reckless and bold, wishing that Blue were there with her. But even as she'd wished for his presence, she knew that what she *really* wished for was some kind of fairy-tale ending, for him to kiss her and confess that he couldn't live without her, that his only hope of finding true happiness was there in her arms.

She'd told herself all along that she was walking into a short, hot, love affair, a one-night stand. She'd tried to convince herself that that would be enough. But all along, she'd hoped—secretly, even from herself—that something magical would happen and Blue would stay in town.

Lucy stared down at the neat lines of notes in her pad, but her eyes were unfocused, and the notes looked more like the tracks of seabirds in the sand than words. Blue *was* going to stay in town, but the something that had happened was far from magical. It was evil and deadly.

If Blue hadn't killed Gerry—and he was right; she didn't believe that he had—then the real killer had long since disappeared or, worse, was somewhere out there, watching and waiting, biding his time.

Lucy glanced up to find Blue still gazing at her, a smoldering fire in his eyes. "There wasn't a light on in your house," he said, "but even if there had been, I wouldn't have knocked. You made it clear when you dropped me off at the motel that you didn't want me around."

That wasn't true. She *had* wanted him around. But it just got way too complicated when she'd seen him holding Jenny Lee in his arms out on the country-club dance floor.

"I don't know why I even walked over to your place," Blue continued, glancing away from her, out at the ocean. "I guess maybe I hoped I'd find you out dancing naked on your back lawn or something."

Lucy had to laugh. "I don't spend much time dancing naked these days," she said.

"Too bad," he said, looking back at her with a slow smile.

Too bad. It *was* too bad that Blue hadn't knocked on her door last night. And it was too bad that Lucy had turned down his invitation to come into his hotel room earlier. "If I'd spent the night with you, you would have had an alibi," she noted.

Blue met her eyes, the heat in his gaze suddenly dangerously high. "That's right," he said softly.

Lucy looked away, scanning her notes again, knowing without a doubt that it was time to get into the sticky questions, the ones she'd been avoiding asking. She needed to know about Blue's conversation with Jenny Lee and the ensuing argument with Gerry. That would keep them from drifting into these dangerous waters.

"Let's backtrack a bit," Lucy said. "Last night, at the country club..."

"I arrived at the club a little before six-thirty," Blue said. "See, I'd called Gerry's office in the afternoon, after I'd checked into my room at the motel. His secretary said he would be in meetings all day and that he'd said he would see me at the party, that I should come early to talk to him."

Lucy stopped walking. "What did you talk about?"

"He never showed." Blue drew a line in the wet sand with his toe and watched as a gentle wave erased all but part of it. "I watched for him until after seven, but the first I saw of him was when he and Jenny Lee made their grand entrance."

Blue had been looking for his stepbrother at the country club last night, Lucy realized. He hadn't been watching and waiting for her as she'd thought. Disappointment washed over her, and she forced herself to ignore it. There was no room for such emotions in their current relationship as investigator and suspect.

"Any idea what he wanted to talk to you about?"

Blue raked his fingers through his thick, blond hair, pushing it back from his face. The breeze immediately made a wavy lock fall forward again. It danced lightly about on his forehead. "I thought it was just a casual meeting," he said. "You know 'Hey, how are you? How's it goin'?

Whatcha been up to in the past two years since I last saw you?' Catching up. That stuff."

"But . . . ?"

Again Lucy saw that glimmer of hurt on his otherwise expressionless face. If she hadn't seen it before, she might not have noticed it. He started forward down the beach and she walked backward, in order to watch his face as he spoke.

"After that little show on the dance floor," Blue said. "I'm thinking Gerry was originally intending to give me his 'get lost' speech in private, before the party started."

"You can't blame him for being jealous," Lucy remarked. "You *were* dancing with his fiancée." She caught herself, turning away, facing forward now, as if she were intent on reading her notes. She wasn't here to give her opinions on the situation. She was supposed to be gathering facts. "Okay, I know where you were from seven-fifteen until a few minutes before eight."

"I remember that part pretty damn clearly, too," Blue said.

Lucy knew that if she glanced up, she'd find him gazing at her, so she kept her eyes carefully locked on her notebook. "You went inside to talk to Gerry," she said. "Apparently you didn't find him."

"He was in the middle of a business conversation with Mr. Fisher," Blue told her. "So I gave my regrets to Jenny Lee."

"By asking her to dance?" Lucy couldn't keep the incredulousness from her voice. God, she sounded like a jealous girlfriend. She immediately backpedaled. "I'm sorry. Please continue. What happened then?"

But Blue didn't continue. He stopped walking and looked at her, studying her face and her eyes, his gaze probing, searching. The sensation was not unlike being underneath a microscope.

"You didn't believe me when I told you that the only thing between Jenny Lee and me was ancient history," Blue finally said. "When you saw me dancing with her—that's what changed your mind about spending the night with me, wasn't it?"

"That has nothing to do with this investigation—"

"Come on, Yankee," Blue drawled. "I'm answering all *your* questions honestly. The least you can do is answer one of mine."

Lucy lifted her head and looked him squarely in the eye. "Yes," she said. But it was only half the truth. The real answer was yes *and* no. Seeing Blue with Jenny Lee had somehow broken the spell he'd cast over her. Seeing him with her made Lucy remember that she didn't do things like sleep with sailors who were in town for only a few days.

Blue was watching her. His eyes matched the brilliant blue of the ocean. He moved a step toward her and then another step. Lucy found herself immobilized, unable to back away. He reached out and gently tucked a loose strand of her hair behind her ear.

"Let's get back to Jenny Lee," Lucy said desperately. The mention of Blue's former girlfriend was successful, as usual, in dissolving the odd power he had over her.

"When I told her I was leaving the party," Blue said, "she told me that she wanted to talk to me." He crouched and picked up a smooth rock from the beach, wiping the sand off it, weighing it in the palm of one hand. "She seemed really worried, really upset about something. It was clear that she wanted the conversation to be private, and since pulling her off into some secluded corner of the room seemed inappropriate, I asked her to dance."

Blue straightened up and flung the rock out into the ocean, past the breaking waves. It skipped several times before it vanished. "You probably won't believe me," he said, his voice still matter-of-fact. "But what I'm gonna tell you is God's own truth, Lucy."

Lucy nodded, her pen poised to take notes.

Blue wiped the remaining sand from his hands, glancing at her notebook. "You don't need that," he said. "This doesn't have anything to do with the case." His gaze was steady. "I just wanted you to know that the entire time I was dancing with Jenny Lee, I was wishing it was you in my arms."

Lucy closed her eyes. My God! Was it possible Blue still thought he had a chance with her? Was it possible that he didn't realize that their current roles didn't allow for any type of romantic interaction whatsoever? And, really, did he honestly think she was so naive she would believe he'd prefer her over Jenny Lee Beaumont?

"Let's stay focused on the case," she said. "I'd rather hear God's own truth about what Jenny Lee said to you while you were dancing."

Lucy didn't believe him. Blue hadn't really expected her to. But now, perhaps, was not the best time to convince her otherwise.

"Jenny Lee told me that she was worried about Gerry," Blue said. "He was acting strangely, as if he was under a lot of stress. She told me that she believed she'd made a mistake in inviting me to the wedding. Apparently it was her idea to ask me to be best man. She thought Gerry liked the idea—if he didn't, he didn't tell her otherwise. But over the past few days, Jenny Lee was starting to wonder if Gerry's upset was caused by my coming back to town, considering my and Jenny's history." He paused. "In short, Jenny asked me to leave."

Lucy nodded, scribbling in her notebook, lower lip clasped gently between her teeth in concentration.

Blue couldn't help but remember how soft those lips had felt, how delicious Lucy's mouth had tasted, how willing she'd been to take that kiss to a more intimate level. Before he left town again, he was going to find a way back to that moment they'd shared. And when he did, the attraction that ignited between them like rocket fuel was going to launch them past the point of no return. It was going to be good. It was going to be very, *very* good.

It was also going to be good to track down the son of a bitch who'd killed Gerry, to see him brought to justice. Although Blue and Gerry had had their disagreements in the recent past, and despite Gerry's harsh words to Blue last night, Blue couldn't forget the friendship he'd shared with his stepbrother during his childhood and adolescence. And he still couldn't believe that Gerry was really dead. The thought that he'd never see Gerry's upbeat smile again made him feel empty.

"I'd like to take a look at the body," Blue said. "See if there's anything that the police might've missed."

Lucy shook her head. "The state medical examiner's office is performing an autopsy. It's required on all suspicious deaths. If everything goes smoothly, the body will be returned to town on Friday for Saturday funeral services."

"Who's taking care of the funeral arrangements?" Blue asked.

Lucy looked up from her notebook. "Jenny Lee is."

Jenny Lee. Hell, whatever pain Blue was feeling at Gerry's death, it surely was amplified hundreds of times over for poor Jenny Lee. Instead of marrying Gerry on Saturday, she was going to be burying him.

"How's Jenny holding up?"

"As well as can be expected, I guess," Lucy told him. As always, when Jenny Lee's name came up, her dark eyes were guarded. The shadows were getting very long, and she turned, looking back down the beach in the direction they had come. "We'd better head back."

"This whole thing stinks," Blue said in a low voice.

Lucy glanced at him again, compassion in her eyes. "This must be hard for you," she said. "Everyone has been so busy making accusations. No one has offered you condolences on your stepbrother's death."

"It doesn't matter."

"Yes, it does," Lucy said. "At times like this, you need to know that people care."

Blue smiled. "I know *you* care, Yankee," he said. "And that's all I need."

Chapter 6

Lucy dropped Blue off at the Lighthouse Motel, then swung back onto Main Street, heading for the Grill. It was well past suppertime, and she was far too exhausted to cook. She pulled into a parking spot on the street in front of the tiny restaurant, dreaming about a cheeseburger and French fries and knowing that she'd end up ordering vegetable soup and a salad.

She hadn't been inside and sitting at a booth by the window of the crowded Grill for more than five minutes, when the door opened and Blue McCoy came in.

All conversation stopped.

Blue headed for the only empty table—the one next to Lucy's. Giving Lucy a nod hello, he dropped his duffel bag on the floor and sat down. He glanced around the still-silent room, as if noticing for the first time that he was the center of attention. Some people were downright rude as they stared at him, hostility in their eyes.

Iris came out to Blue's table. The normally friendly waitress wasn't smiling. In fact, she looked worried. "I'm sorry," she said to Blue, and it was clear that she was. "But that table is reserved for someone else."

Lucy knew it damn well wasn't. Tables at the Grill had always been, and would always be, first come, first served.

Blue knew that, too, but he reached down under the table and picked up his duffel bag.

"Why don't you come sit with me, McCoy?" Lucy called out. "I've got this big booth all to myself." She looked up at Iris challengingly. "Unless *it's* suddenly reserved for someone else, too."

Iris flushed, but she faced Lucy and then Blue. "I feel real bad about this, but I'm going to have to ask you to leave," she said to Blue. "I can't risk trouble getting stirred up inside my establishment, and you, sir, are trouble."

The crowd murmured its agreement. "Get him out of here," said a voice, as Iris disappeared into the back.

"Yeah." Travis Southeby stood up, light glinting off his police badge. "Eating dinner with Gerry McCoy's killer in the room is gonna give me gas."

Lucy raised her voice to be heard over the sudden din. "Whatever happened to innocent until proven guilty?" she asked, looking directly at Travis. "Blue McCoy hasn't been convicted of any crimes—he hasn't even been *charged.*"

From the other side of the room, a chair scraped across the floor as it was pushed back from a table. Leroy Hurley stood up and Lucy's heart sank.

"Whatever happened to the good old days," Leroy asked the crowd, "when a town didn't have to pay millions of dollars to convict a cold-blooded killer? Anyone remember back then? My granddaddy used to tell me about those times. They didn't need no judge or jury. No, sir. They just needed the townfolk, the guilty man and a sturdy length of rope."

Travis Southeby grinned. "It sure saved the taxpayers a heap of money."

As Blue watched, Lucy pushed herself to her feet. She was spitting mad. Her cheeks were flushed and her brown eyes were alight with an unholy flame. Her teeth were clenched and she had one hand on the handle of her sidearm. He was glad as hell that she was on *his* side.

"Are you talking about a *lynching?*" Her voice was low and dangerous. She turned to glare at the stocky police officer. "Shame on you, Travis, for making light of this. You should know better than that." She turned back to Leroy. "How about it, Hurley? Shall I run you in for attempting to incite a riot, or shall I charge you with attempted murder? Because times have changed since your dear old granddaddy was allowed to run amok in this town. These days we've got another name for a lynching, pal. It's called first-degree murder." She looked around the room. "Are you all clear on that? Does anyone have any questions? I wouldn't want to leave anyone confused about this matter."

Leroy Hurley stomped out of the Grill, and the rest of the customers turned back to their food. Travis Southeby still stood, a pink tinge of anger on his puffy face.

He gestured toward Blue. "If I was in charge of this investigation, *he'd* be locked up by now."

"Well, you're not in charge," Lucy said tartly. "So just sit down and finish your dinner, Travis. If you have any complaints, take them to Chief Bradley."

Travis threw down several dollar bills and left the Grill, his dinner barely touched.

Before Lucy could sit down, Iris appeared from the kitchen, carrying a big paper bag. "It's enough for both of you," she said, looking from Lucy to Blue and back. "And it's on the house." She moved to the front door and opened it wide. "As long as you take it outside."

Lucy shook her head. "I'm disappointed in you," she said to Iris.

Blue silently slipped his duffel bag over his shoulder as Iris said, "Last time there was a fight in here, that big plate-glass window broke. Insurance company wouldn't cover it, and we were paying off the debt for three months straight. Billy Joe and me, we've got a kid in college now, Lucy. We can't afford that again. You know that."

Blue went out the door first and Lucy followed. "I'm sorry," Iris said again as she shut the door tightly behind them both.

"I'm sorry about that, too," Lucy said to Blue.

"People get passionate," he said quietly. "They don't always stop to think."

She looked at the heavy bag he was still carrying over his shoulder. "Why didn't you leave your stuff in the motel?"

He shook his head. "I'm not staying over there."

"There's nowhere else in town to stay," Lucy said. "What are you going to do? Sleep outside?"

Blue shrugged. "Yeah," he said. "I guess."

She looked closely at him, her eyes narrowing. "What's going on?"

He gazed at her several long moments before answering. "Jedd Southeby informed me that there are no vacancies at the motel at this time," Blue finally said.

Lucy's mouth got tight, and she flung open the driver's-side door to her truck with more force than necessary. "Get in," she said.

Blue climbed into the truck and watched with interest as she jammed the key into the ignition, revved the motor much higher than necessary and threw the truck into reverse.

"There are *never* no vacancies at the Lighthouse Motel," she said grimly. "That's total bull. I know for a fact that there are at least fifteen rooms unoccupied right this very moment."

It took less than a minute to drive to the motel. Lucy came to a halt with a squeal of tires.

"Jedd Southeby, what is wrong with you?" she fumed, marching into the motel office lobby. "No vacancy, my foot!"

Jedd didn't even get out of his chair. "He's not welcome here," he said coldly, motioning to Blue with his chin. He was small and angular, in contrast to his brother Travis, who was small and beefy.

"That's illegal," Lucy said, crossing her arms. "You can't discriminate against—"

"I most certainly can," Jedd told her smugly. "I reserve the right to turn down any paying guest if I have justifiable reason to believe he will cause injury to my property, himself or my other paying guests. Considering Blue is suspected of killing his stepbrother, I'd have to say that I have a damned good justifiable reason, wouldn't you?"

Lucy was aghast. "So where is Blue supposed to stay?" She shook her head. "Chief Bradley told him not to leave town. If you won't rent him a room . . ."

"There's room in the town jail," Jed said. He looked at Blue and smiled nastily. "You might as well get used to sleeping in a room with bars on the windows, McCoy."

Lucy took a deep breath and forced a smile. "Jedd." She carefully kept her voice steady, reasonable. "Your own brother is on the police force. I'm sure he's told you that no one gets any sleep at the station at night. The lights are always up, it's noisy, the TV is on and—"

"Blue shoulda thought of that before he killed Gerry, huh?"

"What if it rains tonight?" Lucy asked, slapping her hand down on the counter as she lost her cool. "Are you going to sit there and tell me that you're going to make this man—who, I might point out, has not been accused of *any* crime—sleep out in the rain?"

"I don't give a flying fig where he sleeps." Jedd turned back to his television set.

"Dammit!" Lucy turned away, pushing open the glass door and stepping out into the muggy heat of the night. Giving in to her urge to slap Jedd Southeby's smug smile off his face wouldn't do Blue or her career any good. *"Dammit!"*

"I'm a SEAL. I've slept in the rain before," Blue said calmly. He looked up at the sky. "Besides, it's not gonna rain."

"Get in the truck," Lucy fumed, climbing back into the driver's seat of her Ford.

Blue looked at her through the open passenger's-side window. "Where are we going?" he asked. "Because I'd honestly rather sleep out in the rain than spend the night in the Hatboro Creek jail house."

"Don't worry, I'm not taking you to the jail," she said. She took in a deep breath, then let it slowly out in an attempt to calm herself down. This was not the best solution, but it was the only one she could think of at the moment. "You can spend the night at my house."

Blue opened the door and climbed into the truck. "That sounds like the best idea anyone has had all day."

Lucy shot him a dangerous look. "In one of the spare bedrooms."

He smiled back at her. "Whatever you say."

Lucy's house was a great big, rambling old thing on top of the hill off Fox Run Road. It had been built sometime around the turn of the century, Blue guessed. He knew that it had stood empty for a few years before the Taits had moved into town. No one had wanted to buy it—it would have cost way too much to keep up—and Lucy's mother had gotten it for a song. Of course, the Taits had spent every weekend and most weekday evenings scraping paint and sanding and painting and repairing the old monster. When they finished with the inside, they started in on the outside.

Even in the eerie glow of twilight, Blue could see that all their hard work had paid off. The big, old house was gorgeous. They'd painted it white, with dark green shutters and trim. It looked clean and fresh and as if it might even glow in the dark.

"Place looks great," Blue said.

"Thanks."

"Still as big as ever."

"Yep. Too big since my mom died." She snorted. "Too big before that, too."

"Maybe you should sell it," Blue said.

Lucy looked up at the house as she climbed out of the truck. "I could. Betty Stedman over at the real-estate agency makes me an offer on the place every few months or so. It's just . . . It's the reason I'm still here in town," she admitted. "If I sold it, I'd have to find someplace else to go."

"There are about a million choices out there," Blue said dryly, pushing himself up so that he was sitting on the hood of her truck, "and in my opinion just about every one of 'em is better than Hatboro Creek."

"You *were* in a big hurry to get out of this town, weren't you?" Lucy asked, gazing up at him.

"I made a promise I'd get my high-school diploma. I knew I needed it to get where I wanted to go in the navy," Blue said, "or I would've left town the day I turned sixteen."

"If you had, I never would've met you," Lucy mused. "I would've had the devil kicked out of me, or worse—remember that day the boys from the baseball team tried to beat me up?"

Blue nodded. "Yes, ma'am." He leaned forward slightly to see her face in the darkening twilight. "What do you mean, 'or worse'?"

"Nothing really." Lucy hefted the paper bag that Iris had handed her. "What do you say we sit on the porch and eat some of this food?"

Blue slid down off the hood of the truck, following her up the path to the house. "You wouldn't have said 'or worse' if you meant nothing." He caught her arm before she went up the stairs. "Lucy, what did those boys do to you? Did they ever come near you again?"

Her eyes were wide as she looked down at where he was holding on to her arm, but he wouldn't let go.

"They just . . ." She sighed. "They were jerks. They told me that if I stayed on the baseball team they'd take me out in the woods and show me the only thing a girl was good for—and I don't think they had cooking and cleaning in mind. I was too embarrassed to tell you—or anyone—about their threats."

She gently pulled free from his grasp and went up the stairs and onto the porch.

"Did they . . . ?" He could hardly get even that much of the question out as she sat down on a porch swing.

"They never touched me again," Lucy said. "Not after you did your superhero imitation. They thought I was high up on your list of friends." She glanced up at him, a smile playing about the corners of her mouth. "Of course, I helped perpetuate that myth by telling them how Blue McCoy was going to take me fishing, or how I was helping Blue

McCoy fix up his boat.... I had quite the little fantasy world going, and they bought into every word of it."

When Lucy smiled at him like that, Blue forgot about everything—about Gerry's untimely and tragic death, about the murder charges looming over him, about how the people in this town had turned their backs on him yet again. He could only think about Lucy—about the way she'd had that same sparkling smile back when she was a high-school freshman, back when she'd had a crush on him.

If he had known then what he knew now, things would have been mighty different for him. He probably wouldn't have left town with his heart stomped into a thousand pieces. No, he would have left Lucy with *her* young heart trashed and broken, instead. But that really wasn't more appealing than the way things *had* worked out. Of course...maybe...if Lucy Tait had been his girlfriend back in high school, Blue wouldn't have left town at all.

Now, where the hell had *that* thought come from? Blue had wanted to leave Hatboro Creek from the first moment he'd pulled into town at the tender age of five. Even if things had turned out differently between Blue and Jenny Lee, even if she had truly loved him rather than tried to use him to reach Gerry, he *still* wouldn't have stayed in town. And if Jenny Lee Beaumont, with her considerable charms, couldn't keep Blue from leaving town, what made him think Lucy Tait could have done otherwise?

"It looks like Iris packed a couple of burgers, a vegetable soup, some of her fish chowder, two turkeys on whole wheat, an order of fries and some onion rings," Lucy said, spreading the feast out on the porch railing. "There are even plastic spoons. I've got dibs on the veggie soup, but everything else is up for grabs."

Blue picked up the waxed cardboard soup bowl that held the fish chowder and pried off the lid. He gave the fragrant soup a stir with one of Iris's plastic spoons, then sat down next to Lucy on the porch swing. He sensed her stiffen, and knew the words were coming before she even spoke.

"I'd appreciate it if you didn't sit quite so close."

"Come on, Yankee. You know you've got to have two on one of these swings to get the proper balance."

Lucy didn't look up at him. She wouldn't meet his eyes. She just stared down into her vegetable soup as if it held the answers to all the questions in the universe.

And when she finally did speak, she surprised him again with her frankness. "I know you're probably thinking about me as a sure thing," Lucy said. When he started to protest, she held up one hand, stopping him, her dark eyes serious. "I mean, here we are at my house. I brought you home to spend the night, right? Sure, I said you'd have to sleep in the spare bedroom, but you're figuring I probably didn't mean it. How could I mean it after last night? We nearly went all the way on the patio outside the country club. And if we had gone straight to your motel room from that patio, things would have turned out really different than they did."

She set her soup down on the railing and turned to face him. "Yes," she continued. "In some ways you're right. Yes, we came very close to having sex last night. You wanted to. I wanted to. And if we'd been anywhere but out in public, we most likely would have. Even though it's not something I'm comfortable admitting, and even though I've never done anything so reckless in my life before last night, I can't deny that.

"It puts a very odd spin on our relationship today—because today if there is one thing that I absolutely, positively *cannot* do, it's engage in sexual activity with you. I'm the investigator. You're the suspect. If I were to allow us to have sex, I'd be breaking every rule in the book and then some."

She took a deep breath. "So there, I've said it."

Blue nodded, trying to hide his smile. Damn, but he liked this girl. She didn't play games. She just laid the facts out straight, just lined 'em all up on the table in full view. "No chance of changing your mind?" he asked.

She didn't realize he was kidding. She shook her head. "No way. I'd lose my job. *And* my self-respect."

"Well, all right," Blue said. "I guess there's only one thing we can do."

Lucy was watching him, her eyes nearly luminous in the porch light.

He *wanted* to kiss her. Instead, he stood. "We start with me easing back a bit. We don't want any spontaneous combustion," he added. "Then we wake up tomorrow morning, bright and early, and work our butts off to find a way to eliminate me from the list of suspects. And tomorrow night... we can take it from the porch swing."

Lucy sighed, closing her eyes briefly. "I wish it were that simple."

Blue tossed his empty chowder bowl into the empty brown paper bag. "It *is* simple."

But Lucy didn't look convinced. She looked tired and wistful and very weighed down by responsibility.

Blue wanted to put his arms around her and ease her burden. But right now he knew that would only make it harder to bear.

Chapter 7

Lucy's alarm clock rang at 5:45, pulling her up and out of a deep, dreamless sleep. She'd finally fallen asleep sometime after midnight. Before that she'd lain awake in her bedroom, listening to the familiar quiet noises of her house, straining to hear any hint of Blue moving around upstairs in the guest bedroom.

She'd heard the thump of the pipes as he turned on the shower, and the hum of the pump and the hissing of the water as it was pushed up from the deep well. Several minutes later, she'd heard another thump as the water was turned off, but then . . . nothing. Silence. No footsteps. No noise.

Not that she'd expected to hear anything. Blue was Alpha Squad's point man. She'd asked, and he'd told her that last night, after she'd shown him to the guest room and gotten several clean towels down from the linen closet.

"I lead the squad in combat or clandestine situations," he said.

Blue didn't know it, but Lucy already knew what a point man was. A point man could lead his team of SEALs silently right up to an enemy encampment without being discovered. A point man could lead his squad single file through a mine field without a single injury. A point man moved silently, carefully, always alert and watchful, responsible for the safety of his men.

Lucy already knew all this because she'd read every book about SEALs that she could get her hands on. She'd read the first book in high school because she'd been thinking about Blue, and had heard through the local grapevine that he'd been accepted into the SEAL training program.

She'd read the rest of the books not because of Blue, but because the first book had fascinated her so thoroughly. The concept of a Special Forces team like the SEALs intrigued her. They were unconventional in every sense of the word. They were trained as counterterrorists, taught to think and look and act, even *smell,* like the enemy. Due to the special skills of individual team members in areas such as language and cultural knowledge, they were able to lose themselves in any country and infiltrate any organization.

They were tough, smart, mean and dedicated. They were a different kind of American hero.

And Blue McCoy was one of them.

Every man in a SEAL unit was an expert in half a dozen different fields, including computers, technical warfare, engine repair, piloting state-of-the-art helicopters and aircraft. Each SEAL in the elite Team Ten was an expert marksman, intimately familiar with all types of firearms. Each was an expert scuba diver and extensively trained in demolition techniques—both on land and underwater. Each could parachute out of nearly any type of aircraft at nearly any altitude.

They seemed superhuman, strong and rugged and very, very dangerous.

And Blue McCoy, already her hero, was one of them.

She was attracted to him. There was no point in denying that. And Blue had made it quite clear that the feeling was mutual. He'd told her that he'd thought about her as he'd danced with Jenny Lee at the country club.

That was a hard one to swallow—Blue McCoy thinking about Lucy Tait while he was dancing with Jenny Lee Beaumont.

Still, he'd told the truth about his conversation with Jenny. Lucy had read Jenny Lee's statement about the events leading up to the time of Gerry's death. The statement had included a description of Jenny's conversation with Blue at the country club. Jenny's version was identical to Blue's.

But there was no way to verify exactly what Blue had been feeling when he'd danced with Jenny, holding her in his arms.

Lucy knew that Blue wanted to make love to her. She saw that truth in his eyes every time he looked in her direction. The power of his desire was dizzying. But she was brought down to earth quickly enough by the thought that Blue probably only wanted her because Jenny Lee was not available.

Lucy moved quietly into her bathroom and took a quick shower before pulling on a clean uniform. She brushed out her hair, leaving it down as it dried, grabbed an apple from the kitchen and left the house. She'd be back before Blue even woke up.

Blue saw Lucy's truck pull away from the house as he finished his morning run.

He'd slept only two hours last night. He'd gotten up well before sunrise, wide awake and alert, filled with a restless kind of energy and anticipation he'd felt in the past before going into combat situations. This time, however, it was laced with an undercurrent of sexual tension that sharpened the feeling of anticipation, giving it a knifelike edge.

He had run five miles before dawn, another five as the sun rose, and still the edginess wouldn't go away.

He watched the dust rise as Lucy's truck pulled out of the driveway. She looked as if she had on her uniform, and he was willing to bet she was heading down to the police station. She was probably going to fill the chief in on all that Blue had told her yesterday and find out if anything new had come in from the autopsy report.

Blue climbed the stairs to the porch and tried the kitchen door. It was locked. He'd left his bedroom window open all the way up on the third floor. He knew he could get in that way; still, there was bound to be another window open a bit closer to the ground.

The ground-floor window over the kitchen sink was open, but the sill was lined with plants being rooted in jars of water. He spotted an open window on the second floor, recognizing it instantly as Lucy's room by its location.

He climbed easily up the side of the porch and was outside the window in a matter of moments. There was nothing to knock over inside, just a filmy white curtain blowing gently in the morning breeze.

He unfastened the screen and slipped into the house.

Lucy's room was big—at one time it had no doubt been a front parlor or a sitting room. She'd put her bed in an offset area, surrounded on almost three sides by big bay windows. Her bed was unmade, her sheets a bold pattern of dark blues and reds and greens. A white bedspread had been pushed off the bed onto the highly polished hardwood floor. A white throw rug was spread on the floor. It was unnecessary in the summer heat, but it would be nice in the winter when the bare floors would be cold.

The walls were white, with a collection of framed watercolors breaking up the monotony. The pictures were mostly seascapes with bright-colored sailboats out on the water or beach scenes. There were only two framed photographs, and they sat on a dresser. Blue recognized Lucy's mother in one, smiling through a hole in the half-finished wall of the kitchen. The other was a photo of Lucy, her arms around a tall, thin man he didn't recognize. The man had his arms around Lucy's shoulder, and the two of them were laughing into the camera.

Who the hell was he? What did he mean to Lucy that she should keep this picture in her bedroom? Was he a former lover? A *current* lover? If so, where was he? Did he live across the street, or across the country?

Lucy hadn't mentioned having a boyfriend. She hadn't acted as if she had one, either. But on the other hand, Blue had no right to feel these pangs of jealousy. He wasn't looking for commitment, just a night or two of great sex. If

Lucy had some kind of steady thing going on the side, that was her problem, not his.

So why did the thought of Lucy laughing like this as she leaned forward to kiss this other man leave such a bad taste in Blue's mouth? Why did he have this compelling urge to tear this photograph in two?

Blue headed for the door, suddenly very aware that he was invading Lucy's privacy. But he turned and looked back over his shoulder before he headed for the stairs up to his bedroom and the third-floor shower.

It was a nice room, a pleasant room, spacious and as uncluttered as the rest of the house. Lucy wasn't the sort of person who had to fill every available space with doodads and souvenirs. She wasn't afraid of a clean surface or an empty wall. Yeah, he liked this room. He hoped he had a chance to see it again—from the perspective of Lucy's bed.

"Lucy!"

Lucy turned to see Chief Bradley jogging down the corridor toward her.

"Hey, glad I caught you, darlin'," he said, out of breath. "I see you picked up a copy of the autopsy report. Good. Good. Did you also get the message from Travis Southeby? He just happened to be talking to Andy Hayes over at the Rebel Yell last night and found out that Andy saw Blue McCoy leave his motel room at about ten o'clock on the night of Gerry's murder."

Lucy nodded. "Yes, sir," she said. "That fits with what Blue told me as to his whereabouts that evening."

Sheldon Bradley nodded, running his fingers through his thinning gray hair. "Did he also mention that Matt Parker was just in, not more than a few minutes ago, saying how he thought he saw someone who looked just like Blue McCoy arguing with Gerry at around 11 p.m., up in the woods near where the body was found? He saw them there just twenty minutes before the established time of death."

"Matt *thought* he saw someone who looked like Blue?" Lucy allowed her skepticism to show. "No, I didn't get that message. I'll make a point to go over and talk to both Matt and Andy this afternoon."

"Let me know what else you come up with," the chief said.

"I'll have another report typed up and on your desk by the end of the day," Lucy told him. She opened the door, but again Bradley stopped her.

"Oh, and one more thing," he said. "Leroy Hurley mentioned that he saw Blue McCoy here in town with a automatic weapon."

"Chief, it wasn't a real—"

He held up his hand. "As a result, it came to my attention that as of yet no one has confiscated whatever weapons McCoy might have—and I've heard some of those Special Forces types walk around carrying an arsenal."

"Without a warrant, I'm not sure we have the right to—"

"Actually, we do," Bradley told her. "It's an old town law, dates back from Reconstruction, from when folks ran a little wild. The Hatboro Creek peacekeeping officers have the right to gain possession of any individual's personal weapons until that individual crosses back over the town line. We never did get around to amending that law. It was brought up at a meeting a few years back, but then Hurricane Rosie came through, knocked it off the town agenda."

"I'll ask him if he has any weapons—"

"You'll search the son of a bitch," the chief told her. "Or you'll bring him down here so that we can search him, if you're not up to it."

Lucy lifted her chin. "I'm up to it. But you should know that the gun Hurley saw him with was just a plastic toy."

"Either way, I won't have him running around my town with an Uzi or the likes," Bradley said. "Whatever he's got, I want it locked up in my safe by noon, is that clear?"

Lucy nodded. "Yes, sir."

"And get a move on with this investigation," Bradley added, heading back down the hallway. "I want Blue McCoy locked up, too, before sundown tomorrow."

* * *

Lucy pulled her truck into her driveway, unable to shake the feeling of dread in her stomach, dread that had started with the chief's news that someone had allegedly seen Blue arguing with Gerry near the murder site. Matt Parker. He was an upstanding citizen. He'd recently had his share of bad luck, though. He'd even been the cause of one of Annabella's 415 dispatches earlier in the summer when he and his wife got to fighting about his recent unemployment just a little too loudly. But other than that, he wasn't one of the town troublemakers or one of Leroy Hurley's wild friends. Parker stayed mostly to himself, kept up his house and yard and showed up at church every Sunday without fail.

Why would Parker lie about what he'd seen the night of Gerry's murder?"

And if he wasn't lying, did that mean Blue was?

No. Blue had looked her in the eye and told her that he wasn't the one who had killed his stepbrother. Lucy believed him. He wasn't lying. The air of calm that seemed to surround him, his definite tone of voice, his steady eye contact all reinforced her belief.

Lucy got out of the truck and walked up the path to the house. It was only 9:30 in the morning, and already she felt as if she couldn't wait for the day to end.

She had to search Blue McCoy for concealed weapons. That was going to be fun. Lucy rolled her eyes. She couldn't get within three feet of the man without risking third-degree burns. How on earth was she supposed to *search* him? She was going to have to make him assume the classic body-search position, arms stretched out in front of him, legs spread, hands against the wall. Because God help her, if he simply held out his arms while she patted him down and she happened to glance up and into his eyes... What was it that Blue had said last night? Spontaneous combustion. It was an accurate description of the way she'd felt at the country club when he'd held her in his arms and she'd kissed him. What a kiss that had been.

God, maybe she *should* take Blue down to the station, let Frank Redfield or Tom Harper search him. But that would be admitting that she wasn't "up to it," as Chief Bradley had said.

Lucy unlocked the kitchen door. She'd picked up a bag of doughnuts and two cups of coffee at the bakery in town, and she put them on the table. The house was quiet. Was it possible Blue was still asleep?

Then she saw it. There was a note on the kitchen table. Blue had written a message to her on a paper napkin. He'd taken care to write neatly, printing in clear block letters: "Seven a.m. Went to scout out woods off Gate's Hill Road. C.M."

C.M.?

It took Lucy a moment to realize that C.M. were Blue's initials. His real, given name was Carter McCoy. Why hadn't he signed the note Blue? Did he think of himself as Carter? Or was he just so used to initialing navy paperwork that the C.M. had come out automatically?

Either way, he was already up and out, doing *her* job. Lucy grabbed the doughnuts and coffee, locked the kitchen door behind her and went back to her truck.

Chapter 8

Lucy didn't find Blue up in the woods by Gate's Hill Road. Blue found Lucy.

He just sort of appeared next to her. One minute she was alone at the edge of the clearing where Gerry's body had been discovered, and the next Blue was standing right beside her.

She'd been expecting him to do something like that, so she didn't jump. At least not too high. She handed him a paper cup of coffee, instead.

"Hope you like it black," she said.

He nodded, sunlight glinting off his golden hair. "Thanks."

The day was promising to be another hot, muggy one. Blue was still wearing his army fatigue shirt with the sleeves cut off, but he had it unbuttoned most of the way, allowing Lucy tantalizing glimpses of his rock-solid, tanned chest.

She handed him the doughnut bag. "I also hope you like jelly doughnuts," she said, wishing that it were winter and thirty degrees so he'd have to wear a parka zipped up to his chin. "I ate all the honey glazed. That's what you get for coming out here without me."

Blue smiled. "Serves me right. What's the latest news down at the station?"

"The autopsy report is in." Lucy took a sip of her own coffee, leaning back against a tree as she gazed at him. His blue eyes were clear, his face unmarked by fatigue. He'd probably gotten eight hours of dreamless, perfect sleep, damn him. He didn't look as if he'd tossed and turned for one moment last night, distracted not a whit by the thought of her sleeping several rooms away.

Lucy had tossed and turned enough for both of them.

"The cause of Gerry's death was definitely a broken neck," she continued, "but we already knew that. It *was* a clean break, though, and the medical examiner found some slight bruising on his head and neck, indicating some kind of stranglehold. Whoever killed him knew what he was doing. It wasn't accidental, and apparently the bruising wasn't severe enough to indicate a long, passionate struggle. The killer knew exactly what he intended to do before he even got his hands on Gerry."

Blue looked away, swearing softly.

"The good news is that Gerry didn't feel it," Lucy said quietly. "He probably didn't even know."

"Yeah, I know that." His mouth was tight as he looked up at Lucy again. "What else was in the report?"

She shook her head. "I just skimmed the first few paragraphs. I'll read it more thoroughly later. You can look at it, too, if you want." She sighed, knowing that she had to tell him about what Matt Parker allegedly saw.

"You've got more bad news," Blue said, reading her face. "What is it?"

"A couple of witnesses have surfaced," Lucy said. "One of them places you up here, arguing with Gerry, about twenty minutes before his established time of death."

Blue didn't say a word. His lips just got tighter.

"Either this witness is lying," Lucy continued, "or he saw someone or something up here that could give us a lead to finding out what really happened."

"Someone was up here, all right," Blue said. He set his coffee cup and the bag of doughnuts down on a rock and headed out into the center of the clearing, motioning for Lucy to follow.

"Gerry's body was found right about here," he told her, pointing at an area where the weeds were trampled flat. "I didn't expect to find anything new. Too many people, both police and paramedics, added their footprints before a proper investigation could be made." He straightened up. "What I did this morning was search the clearing and the woods, moving out in circles away from the place where Gerry was found."

He headed into the woods, and Lucy followed him through the thick underbrush.

"I don't think the police searched out this far from the murder site," Blue said over his shoulder as they walked for what seemed like half a mile. "But I didn't have anything better to do this morning, so I just kept going."

He stopped at a trail that was cut through the dense growth. It was little more than two tire paths, ruts worn into the side of the hill for a truck or Jeep to get through.

Blue crouched, pointing at the damp earth. "Tire tracks," he said. "*Big* tires. Wider than your average truck tires by a good four inches. And whatever it was those great big tires were attached to, it was big and heavy, too."

Sure enough, the tracks sank deeply into the dark soil. The mud was starting to dry. Whatever had left this track had been here directly after the last rain—probably around the time of Gerry's death.

"Was it some kind of monster truck?" Lucy mused, crouching next to him.

"That or an all-terrain vehicle," Blue said.

"The tires look new," Lucy remarked. "The tread is barely worn. God, we can take a print of this and make an easy match, find out who else was up here that night—if they're still in town."

"And look over here," Blue said, standing up and pointing farther down the trail. "Whoever drove this thing left in one hell of a big hurry."

Lucy straightened too, wiping her hands on her pants. "This is great! Let's go back to my truck and radio for assistance. I'll have the crime team take some photos and make a mold of these tire tracks." She grinned. "McCoy, I think you may have just saved your own neck."

Blue smiled at her enthusiasm as he followed her toward the main road, where she'd parked her truck. "Careful, or folks are going to say that this isn't an unbiased investigation."

"Yeah, well, it's not," Lucy admitted.

When she glanced over her shoulder at him, he could see a healthy dose of that simmering heat that could turn his blood boiling hot in less than a blink. But he could also see admiration shining in her eyes. He could see admiration and respect and something akin to hero worship.

And in that instant, Blue realized that Lucy still had that old schoolgirl crush on him—no, not on him, but on some larger-than-life heroic image of him. He was a superhero who'd saved the day, chasing away her attackers twelve years ago. He was a member of the elite Navy SEALs—and he knew from the shelf of books about the navy and the SEALs that he'd found in Lucy's living room that she'd read all about the legendary heroism and patriotism and loyalty of the SEAL units. To Lucy, he was a living legend.

And that made him attractive to her—probably more attractive than any normal, mortal man she'd ever known.

The truth was, Lucy didn't really know Blue at all. Because he *was* mortal. But all her powerful attraction, all her respect and admiration, was based on some idea of how he *should* be. It was based on an image of the way she *thought* he was.

Still, what did he expect? Since he'd arrived, he'd done nothing to straighten her out. He'd told her none of his secrets, shared none of his feelings. As a matter of fact, Blue could count the people he'd shared his feelings and secrets with on the fingers of one hand.

Frisco was one. But it had been years since Blue had really talked to the injured SEAL. He'd gone to see him in the Veterans' Hospital and the rehab center a few times right after he'd been wounded. But Frisco didn't want to talk. And Blue finally stopped going to see him.

It was hard to visit. It was hard to handle the guilt of knowing that he, Blue, could stand up and walk out of the hospital, while Frisco never would. It was hard to smile and offer hope in the face of Frisco's pain. And now it had been so long since Blue had visited Frisco, he wouldn't know what to say to the man.

But Blue could still talk to Joe Catalanotto, the commander of Alpha Squad. And Daryl "Harvard" Becker, Alpha Squad's chief. But that was it. Hell, forget his fingers. These days, Blue could count the people he let in to his life on his thumbs.

He watched the sunlight play in Lucy's long, brown hair as she opened the door to her truck and took out the microphone attached to her CB radio. She smiled at him—a flash of white teeth and sparkling brown eyes.

What did he care that she wanted to sleep with him because of some overblown heroic image she'd been carrying around in her head for a dozen years? The key part of that sentence was that she wanted to sleep with him. Everyone had motives. Jenny Lee's motive back in high school had been to hang around Gerry's house to catch the attention of Blue's elder brother. The women he'd had relationships with since then had had their motives, too. They wanted to break away from the boredom of their lives, live on the edge for a while, go the distance with a good-looking stranger who was going to slip out of their lives in a day or two. So what if Lucy's motive was that she wanted to sleep with Superman?

Of course, she wasn't entirely convinced that she should sleep with anybody. She had a solid streak of good girl running through her that had been overpowered by emotions and lust and the pull of the full moon the other night at the country club.

Blue watched Lucy radio in the information about the tire tracks he'd found. She was so alive, so animated. Even though she was speaking to the dispatcher over the radio, she talked with her hands, gesturing, shrugging, moving, smiling. He was struck again by just how beautiful she was.

It wasn't the kind of beauty that would draw stares or whistles when she walked down the street. In fact, dressed as she was right now in her police uniform, most men wouldn't give her a second glance.

But Blue knew better. He knew the encompassing warmth of her smile; the powerful draw of her fresh, funny, upbeat personality; the dazzling sparkle of her eyes. And he knew the seductive taste of her kisses and the unforgettable feel of her incredible body against his.

As he watched, her body language changed, subtly, slightly. He tuned himself in to her words.

She glanced at her watch. "I realize the time," she said. "I know it's almost eleven, but this is more important than—"

"The chief says he'll send someone out right away," a woman's scratchy voice said over the radio, "but you better get your rear end back here to the station before noon with whatever weapons McCoy is hiding, or there'll be hell to pay."

Whatever weapons McCoy is hiding?

It wasn't really that much of a surprise. Blue had figured it was going to come sooner or later. They'd search him, hoping to find and take away whatever gun he had on him, hoping to make him less dangerous.

Lucy was doing her best to postpone the inevitable. "Annabella—"

"The chief is yelling for me, Lucy. I can't stay on and argue with you right now," the dispatcher said. "Do your job. This transmission is over."

"No, Annabella..." Lucy swore sharply, leaning into the truck to adjust the radio. "She turned it off." She hooked the microphone back into its slot and looked at Blue. "She actually *turned off* the police station's citizens-band radio."

"You know, Yankee, if there's something you have to do back at the station, I can hang here and wait for the crime team to show up," Blue volunteered.

Lucy shook her head. "That won't work," she said. "Because *you're* what I have to do."

Blue smiled. "While I truly like the way that sounds," he drawled, "I've got a feeling that's not exactly what you meant."

Lucy felt her face flush. Still, she forced herself to look into his eyes. "I have to confiscate your weapons, McCoy," she told him. "I need to search you. And then we have to go down to the station so you can fill out the paperwork to get your property back when this is over."

Blue nodded slowly. "This is easy," he said. "You're not going to find any weapons on me. We don't have to go anywhere. You can just radio that information in."

He hadn't said he didn't have any weapons. He'd said she wouldn't *find* them. Lucy held his gaze. "Look me in the eye and tell me you're not carrying," she said softly.

"I'm not carrying," he said, his eyes steady.

The rush of disappointment that went through her almost knocked her down. "Well, damn," she said. "I guess now we've established that you *will* lie to me."

Blue didn't say anything. He just watched her.

Her eyes blazed fire as she looked up at him again. "You want to try that one more time?" she asked.

He didn't bat an eyelash. "I'm not carrying."

Blue thought for a moment that Lucy was going to haul back and punch him in the stomach. Instead, she crossed her arms. "Hands against the truck, and spread 'em, mister."

"Lucy, it's not going to do any good—"

"Because I won't find anything?" she finished for him. "You want to make a bet on that?" She gestured to the truck. "Come on, move it, McCoy. Assume the position."

"This isn't necessary."

Lucy exploded. "You're a SEAL, dammit," she said, slapping the side of her truck with one opened hand. The sound echoed in the stillness. "*I* know you didn't come into town unarmed, and Chief Bradley knows you didn't come into town unarmed, either. He's not stupid and I'm not stupid, and—"

"And *I'm* not stupid, either." Blue caught her chin in one hand, pulling her head around so that she was forced to look into his eyes. In one swift movement he was standing close to her, penning her in against the side of her truck. His thigh was pressed against hers, the sensation nearly making him forget everything but his enormous need to feel her lips against his again. Nearly. Somehow he centered his focus and returned to the task at hand.

"You're right," he whispered. "I'm a SEAL. And I can't forget that somebody out there killed Gerry. I'm not walking around unarmed—virtually *naked*—with a killer on the loose. And if that means I have to lie to you, Yankee, then I'm gonna have to lie to you. It's not personal. Don't think that it is. There's not a SEAL alive who wouldn't lie to Mother Teresa herself to stay armed in a potentially dangerous situation like this one."

Lucy tried to pull away from him, but he held her tightly.

"You look me in the eye," Blue continued, "and you tell me that if I admitted to you that I was armed you wouldn't insist on confiscating those weapons." His eyes were like blue steel, hard and unrelenting. "You tell me that you'd simply say, 'Well, thank you very much, Blue. Thank you for telling me the truth. I know how much having that sidearm and that knife on your person means to you, so I won't include that information in my report to Chief Bradley.'"

Lucy was silent.

"Can't tell me that, huh?" Blue nodded. "In that case, I'll say it again. I'm not carrying."

Lucy lifted her chin even higher. "And *I* said, hands against the truck and spread your legs, mister."

Blue had to laugh. She was so clearly overpowered, so obviously in a position of being dominated, yet she wouldn't give in. She refused to back down. As annoying as that was, he had to like her for it. And he did. Mercy, he did like her.

"Are you going to let go of me and do as I say, or do I have to haul you to jail first?" Her brown eyes were flashing again, her mouth trembling slightly in anger. It was all that Blue could do not to kiss her. Dear, sweet Lord, he wanted to kiss her something fierce. He wanted to, and dammit, he was going to.

"Come on, Yankee," he said softly. "Let's not fight. We're on the same side here, aren't we?"

She glared at him. "I'm not so sure of that anymore."

"Yes," he said definitely. "We *are* on the same side. So let's just kiss and make up."

Lucy's eyes widened as he leaned forward, lowering his mouth to hers. His lips grazed the softness of her sweet lips and he was milliseconds from sheer, total paradise when she spoke.

"Don't," she breathed. "Please, Blue—don't."

He didn't. He didn't kiss her. He pulled back. Out of all the tough things he'd done in his life, it was quite possibly the toughest.

"I can't do this," Lucy whispered. "Remember? Until I'm through investigating Gerry's murder, you're a suspect, and I cannot do this."

"It's just a kiss." His voice sounded raspy and strained in his own ears.

Lucy shook her head. "No," she said. "It most definitely is not just a kiss." Somehow he'd lost his ability to hold her, and she broke free from his arms, pushing herself away from the truck and moving a safe distance away from him. She turned to face him. "It's not *just* a kiss, and you know that as well as I do."

Her hand shook slightly as she pushed her hair back behind her ear, and she folded her arms tightly across her chest as if she had to hold herself steady. Her eyes looked big and almost bruised, and she clasped her lower lip between her front teeth. But still she gazed directly at him, her chin held high.

"Either way, it's totally inappropriate," she added. She took a deep breath, exhaling it quickly in a loud burst of air. "So let's just get on with it, then, okay?"

Was she talking about . . . ?

Son of a bitch, she still intended to frisk him. Blue swore under his breath.

Lucy tried to slow her hammering heart, waiting and watching as Blue slowly turned back to the truck. The muscles in his powerful arms flexed as he used them to support most of his weight, his feet planted and his long legs spread.

He turned his head and looked at her over his shoulder. The heat in his eyes was unmistakable.

Not quite a minute ago, he'd been about to kiss her, and now she was supposed to frisk him, patting him down all over his body to make sure he had no weapons concealed underneath his clothing. Or concealed *in* his clothing, she realized, looking at the big, metal buckle of his belt. Still, this was weird. Too weird.

"Well, come on," he said. "Don't keep a man waiting."

Lucy stepped forward, uncertain exactly where to begin. Blue was watching her with one of those slow, lazy half smiles on his handsome face, though, so she started with his back. It seemed a whole hell of a lot less dangerous than the long, sturdy lengths of his legs or, Lord help her, his perfect, athletic rear end.

Or *was* it less dangerous? As she ran her hands down the soft, worn cotton of his shirt, she could feel the ridges and bulges of his muscles. It was only his back. How could he have so many muscles in his *back?* But she wasn't supposed to be looking for muscles. She was looking for any kind of concealable weapon. A handgun. A knife. Who knows, maybe even some kind of grenade. He was carrying something, and despite what he said, she was going to find it.

Lucy could feel a bead of sweat dripping down her own back as she slid her hands around to his sides.

Jackpot. He was wearing a shoulder holster under his left arm. Triumphantly, she slipped her hands up underneath his shirt, only to find the holster was...empty?

"Where's the gun, McCoy?" she asked.

"I told you," he said. "I'm not carrying."

"Yeah, right," she said. She was standing there with her hands inside his shirt, the back of her fingers resting against the smooth warmth of his skin. She moved her hands quickly away. "I'm supposed to believe you wear the holster empty because you're so used to wearing it you'd feel off balance if you didn't have it on, gun or no gun. Right?"

"Exactly," Blue said with a smile. "I couldn't have said it better myself."

Lucy humphed, searching through the contents of his shirt pockets, trying hard not to touch his satiny-smooth skin again. In his right-hand shirt pocket she came up with a Swiss Army knife.

It was Blue's turn to humph. "That's no weapon," he scoffed. "I use the knife on that thing to spread peanut butter on my sandwiches."

"From what I've read about Navy SEALs," Lucy said, "a *shoe* could be a weapon."

"I'm not wearing shoes," Blue drawled. "Although if I were, you'd want to be sure to check for the secret SEAL submachine gun that's hidden in the soles."

"Just be quiet and let me get this over with," Lucy muttered, bending to pat his right ankle, her hands moving slowly up his leg. He had disgustingly nice legs.

"Get this over with?" Blue murmured. "Shoot, I thought you were enjoying this. *I* sure as hell am. I figure if you want to touch me all over, and I mean *all* over, well, that's more than fine with me. I'd sure prefer it if we'd do it back in the privacy of your bedroom, though, instead of out in the open like this. But... whatever turns you on."

Lucy tried to move her hands over the hard muscles of his legs quickly and impersonally, until she realized what he was doing. He was purposely trying to fluster her, to keep her from taking her time. There was something here that he was trying to hide.

Her hands moved up one strong thigh, all the way to the juncture of his legs. But then she hesitated. Dear Lord, how exactly did a woman search a man thoroughly without embarrassing them both? And then there was the question of his belt....

"Don't stop there, honey," Blue drawled.

And Lucy suddenly knew that he only said that because he *wanted* her to stop there. He was trying to freak her out, make her back away.

Well, fine. She'd play it his way—but only for a while.

She went back to his left ankle, working her way up, again, to the top of his thigh. Again she stopped short.

She patted his rear end and hips rather gingerly—to make him think he was winning the game.

"Nice belt," she said, continuing with the ineffective patting around his waist. Then she dropped her bomb. "A big, metal buckle like that must set off all the bells and whistles at the airport, huh? I bet airport security makes you take that belt off and walk back through the metal detector without it on all the time."

Blue shrugged "It's happened once or twice," he said.

"You don't mind if I take this off and have a look at it," Lucy said, unfastening the buckle. "A much *closer* look?"

She had to hand it to him. He didn't react as she pulled his belt free from the belt loops on his pants. He didn't show his surprise. He didn't sigh, didn't groan, didn't even clear his throat in acceptance of his defeat. And he *had* to know it was coming.

He just said, very matter-of-factly, "That belt holds up my pants."

"Looks like it does more than that," Lucy said, examining the inside of the buckle. Sure enough, hidden inside the buckle, and extending down through part of the thick leather of the belt, was a short but very deadly looking switchblade knife.

Blue glanced at both her and the knife over his shoulder, but still said nothing.

"What you use this one for?" Lucy asked, putting the knife back into the belt buckle. "And don't tell me it's the grape-jelly knife."

He met her eyes steadily. She could see no remorse on his face. "I guess I underestimated you," he said, starting to straighten.

Lucy stopped him. "We're not done," she said, smiling sweetly. "As long as you've got your belt off, maybe you want to unfasten your pants and give me that gun I know you're hiding in your shorts."

He smiled. Then he laughed. And then he called her bluff. "You *think* I'm hiding something there," he said. "But you're wrong. 'Course, feel free to check and see for yourself."

He knew she wouldn't do it. No, he *thought* he knew—but he was wrong again.

The worst that would happen was that Lucy was mistaken and she'd end up briefly handling a man she'd daydreamed about since she was fifteen. Of course, if she *was* mistaken, he'd probably never let her live it down.

But she *wasn't* mistaken. She couldn't be. God only knows where the gun from his shoulder holster had gone. Still, Blue had surely had a second gun tucked into the small of his back. It wouldn't have taken too much to push it down into his shorts and then wriggle it to a place where most women wouldn't search very carefully—if at all.

Praying that she was right, she reached for him and her fingers found...

Metal.

"Ouch," Blue said. "Careful. Please."

"Sorry," Lucy said sweetly. "You want to get that thing out of there, or should I? Of course, God forbid that it's loaded and I accidentally knock the safety off and—"

Blue scowled at her, reaching into his pants. He pulled the tiny handgun out.

And aimed it at her, dropping into a firing stance. "Hands up," he shouted, and she raised her hands in alarm.

Stepping away from him, Lucy tripped over a tree root and went down in the dirt right on her rear end.

Blue popped the safety back on and helped her up with one hand while handing her the gun with the other. "Dammit, Lucy," he said. "You ID'd a weapon on my person, and you had me get it out myself? That's damned stupid. If I were the bad guy, I would've come out shooting and you'd be dead right now. Next time you're in a similar situation, you aim your own firearm at the guy's head and order him to drop his pants *and* his shorts, and let his weapon fall on the ground. Whereupon *you* pick it up. Do you understand?"

Lucy nodded. Her heart was still pounding, adrenaline surging through her veins. This was one lesson she was never going to forget. But she had one to give him, too.

"If you ever," she said coolly, "*ever* aim a gun at me again in the course of this investigation, I will arrest you and hold you on charges of threatening a police officer. Do *you* understand?"

Down the road she could spot a police cruiser heading in their direction. It was Frank Redfield and Tom Harper. They'd come out to take photos and a plaster casting of the tire tracks.

Blue looked from the cruiser to Lucy and nodded. "Sounds fair to me," he said. Then he smiled. "Provided you can catch me and contain me after I do it."

Lucy didn't smile. She just stared coldly at him. She'd triumphed by finding two weapons he hadn't thought her capable of finding, but he'd kept the upper hand by making her look a fool.

"Stick my gun and my belt in your lockbox," Blue told her. "We just have time to take these guys out to see the tire prints before we have to head into the station and surrender my gear."

Lucy picked Blue's belt with the knife hidden inside it up off the ground, praying that she wasn't about to become an even bigger fool. Instead of holding on to the belt, she handed it back to him.

"You said you needed this to hold up your pants," she told him. She pulled her keys out of her pocket and unlocked the heavy steel box that was attached to the bed of her truck. She stashed Blue's gun and the Swiss Army knife inside and locked it back up. "I know you said never to assume," she added, turning to look at him, "but in this case, I'm assuming that the occupant of your shoulder holster isn't too far away. Otherwise I'd give you the gun back, too. Too bad I can't complete the scenario by thanking you for telling me the truth."

Blue hadn't moved. He stood staring at her, just holding his belt. There was an odd mixture of surprise on his face—surprise and something else that she couldn't quite pinpoint. Whatever it was, it was clear he hadn't expected her to break any rules on his account.

Lucy walked past him, heading toward where Frank had parked the patrol car. She glanced over her shoulder at Blue. "I guess you did underestimate me," she said.

Blue didn't say a word, but the expression in his eyes spoke volumes.

Lucy helped Tom and Frank lug the heavy equipment and supplies they needed to make a plaster casting of the tire tracks up through the woods. The three of them huffed and puffed and sounded like an entire army crashing through the thick growth. Only Blue managed to move silently despite the fact that he carried at least as much—and maybe even more—gear.

They were halfway up the hill, when Blue held up a hand, stopping them.

There was a sound in the distance. It was little more than an odd buzzing, a midrange-pitched whine.

It wasn't until Blue turned and began to run toward the tire tracks that Lucy realized what that sound was.

Dirt bikes.

It was the sound of a group of dirt bikes. With very little effort, the dirt bikes could obscure the tire tracks on the trail, bringing the investigation back to square one.

Lucy dropped the bucket of dried plaster she was carrying and ran after Blue. She shouted over her shoulder for Frank and Tom to follow.

Blue was moving so quickly through the trees it was nearly impossible to keep up with him. Still Lucy tried, leaping over rocks and roots as leaf-filled branches slapped her in the face and arms.

The sound of the dirt bikes grew louder and then more distant, and when Lucy saw Blue just standing up ahead, she feared that the worst had happened. She slowed, and he surely heard her approaching, but he didn't turn around. He just stood, looking down at the trail.

The imprint of the big tires had been totally flattened and erased. There was nothing worth saving, nothing they could use to get a match on the vehicle that had been here the night of Gerry's murder.

Blue's face was tight, expressionless, and when he glanced at her, his eyes were cold.

"I should have stayed up here," he said softly. "I should have guarded the tracks until the casting was done. This was my mistake."

"Mine, too," Lucy whispered. "Oh, Blue, I'm sorry."

Blue was silent as they drove back to her house. He was silent as she did a cursory search of his duffel bag, silent as they drove down to the police station and turned in one of his guns to Chief Bradley.

It wasn't until they'd left the station that he spoke.

"Sheldon Bradley is involved," Blue said.

Lucy turned to look at him in surprise. "Involved in what?"

"This setup," he said. "This frame. And probably in Gerry's murder."

"You think the chief of police," Lucy repeated skeptically, "murdered Gerry and is trying to pin it on you?"

"I didn't say that," Blue said. "I said I think Bradley is somehow involved. Bradley or someone else on the police force."

"Look, I know you're upset about this," Lucy said. "It was bad timing that those dirt bikes were up on that trail—"

"I thought the timing was pretty damn perfect myself," Blue interrupted. "You radio in to the station, tell Bradley about the tire tracks, and not forty minutes later dirt bikers ride on that very same trail, erasing the evidence?"

Lucy sighed. "You're right," she admitted. "It does seem a little too coincidental. But it doesn't mean that the chief is involved. Anyone listening in on channel nine could have heard that we found those tracks." She pulled her truck up in front of the Grill. "What do you say we get some lunch?"

Blue took a five-dollar bill from his wallet. "Better get mine to go," he said, handing it to her.

Lucy nodded. "I'll be right out."

The Grill was crowded, as usual, but Lucy caught Iris's eye and quickly gave her an order for a couple of sandwiches. Sarah waved at her from a table in the corner, and Lucy walked over.

"Hey," she said, sitting down across from Sarah.

Sarah made an obvious point of looking out the window, out at Lucy's truck, where Blue was sitting. "Can't he come in and order his own lunch?" she asked. "Or does he have too many Y chromosomes to do that?"

Lucy sighed. "Last time he was in here, we almost had a riot," she said. "Most of the town has already found Blue guilty of murder."

"Not you, though," Sarah said, watching her friend.

"No, not me," Lucy agreed.

"Are you sure you're not getting in too deep with this guy?"

Lucy forced a smile. "Can we talk about something else?" she asked.

Sarah hesitated. She clearly had more to say on the subject.

"Please?"

"Okay," Sarah said evenly. "Here's something new—some good news. Remember that demo tape I sent to the Charleston Music Society? They want me to be part of their winter concert series as a featured artist. They've asked me to do a program of French art songs."

Lucy smiled at her friend, her eyes alight with pleasure. "That's great! Did they give you a date?"

"Sometime in December," Sarah said. She made a face. "That's assuming I've had the baby by then."

Lucy had to laugh. "That's six months away. No one has ever been pregnant for fifteen months."

"Not yet, anyway."

"Lucy," Iris called out. "Your order is up."

Lucy stood. "Congratulations," she said.

"Thanks," Sarah said. "Call me later, okay?" She leaned forward and lowered her voice. "Lucy, I've got to ask you if it's true what I've heard—that the superhunk is staying at your place? With you?"

Lucy closed her eyes, swearing silently. She sat back down at Sarah's table. "You heard that?" she asked.

Sarah nodded. "People are talking," she said, "and what they're saying isn't very nice."

"Jedd Southeby wouldn't give Blue a room at the motel," Lucy said. "What was I supposed to do, make him sleep in the jail?"

Sarah nodded. "Yes," she said. "It's a shame, but... yes."

Lucy shook her head, standing up again. "I can't do that," she said. "Thanks for telling me, but..." She shrugged. "I guess people are just going to have to talk."

"Lucy, he *could* have done it, you know." Worry showed in Sarah's hazel eyes. "You're opening your house to a man who could very well be a killer. I know you probably don't see it that way—he's a man you've always respected and admired. Don't let that cloud your good judgment."

"I appreciate your concern," Lucy said. "I really do."

"But..."

"I'll talk to you later."

Lucy could feel Sarah's eyes on her as she paid Iris for the lunch and carried the paper bag of food with her onto the sidewalk. She started for her truck and stopped.

Blue was gone.

This time she didn't swear silently. She turned around, did a complete three-sixty, searching for any sign of where he might have gone.

Tom Harper's police cruiser went past, moving faster than usual, and on a hunch, Lucy climbed into her truck, tossed the bag with the sandwiches onto the passenger seat and followed.

Tom's patrol car pulled up in front of the vacant lot next to the gas station, several blocks down Main Street.

Sure enough, there was Blue. He was facing off with three men, looking as if he was intending to fight them all simultaneously. One of the men had a chain and another had a length of two-by-four, but Blue was the one advancing. A small crowd had gathered to watch.

As she jumped out of her truck and ran toward them, Lucy could see that one of the men was Merle Groggin. Another was Matt Parker. And the third was Leroy Hurley.

Matt's nose was bleeding, Merle had what appeared to be the start of a black eye and Leroy was hot and sweaty. Blue didn't even look ruffled. Just mad as hell.

"All right, break it up," Lucy called out, Tom Harper just a step behind her.

"You call *him* off," Merle said, gesturing to Blue. "He's the one threatened to tear us limb from limb."

"You jumped me," Blue drawled. "Remember?"

"McCoy, back off," Lucy said sharply.

He glanced at her, and she could see anger in his eyes. Real, hot, molten, deadly anger.

"These boys just came back from a joy ride on some dirt bikes," he told her. "Shiny, brand-new dirt bikes. Who do you suppose gave them those bikes? They tell me they found 'em, that they fell off a truck that went past on the state highway. I figured they needed a little encouragement to tell me the real story—like who called them and told them to take that ride on that trail over by Gate's Hill Road—so I asked them to think a little harder. That's when they jumped me."

"He's crazy," Leroy said. "It's the truth that we found those bikes. The packing crates are still up there on Route 17. We'll show you where, if you want. We didn't think it would do 'em any harm to take 'em for a test drive."

Blue's voice was low, dangerous. "You are so full of garbage. You and your 'buddy' Merle just happened to be out for a stroll along the state highway? Or maybe you were the one who found 'em and you thought, 'Gee, maybe I should give Merle a call, see if he wants to take a ride.' Never mind the fact that two days ago you were threatening to *kill* him."

Leroy brandished the two-by-four he was holding. "Are you calling me a liar?"

"Hell, yes." Blue's eyes were shooting fire. "You're a liar and a drunk and a son of a bitch, and I aim to get the truth out of you if it's the last thing you do."

Leroy bristled. "Call me a liar again, and I'll—"

"You want to hit me with that stick, go on and do it, you lying sack of—"

Leroy sprang, the two-by-four slicing down through the air.

But Blue had moved. He was no longer where he had been standing. He spun, kicking as he turned, his foot connecting solidly with Leroy's arm. The piece of wood went flying, and there was a loud crack that had to be the sound of breaking bone.

Leroy screamed.

Lucy threw herself in front of Blue, grabbing his arms, trying to hold him back. "Stop it," she hissed. "Right now!"

Leroy was curled up on the ground, moaning and holding his arm.

"Tell me who gave you those bikes," Blue demanded.

Leroy spit on the dirt.

Blue looked at Lucy. His eyes were wild and he was still breathing hard. "I can make him tell me," he said.

She shook her head. "No, you can't," she said.

"Radio for medical assistance," Tom told her. "We better bring 'em all in."

Lucy was angry at Blue.

Her anger was a palpable thing that filled the inside of her truck, surrounding them both. She was angry as she pulled out of the police-station parking lot, angry as she drove down Main Street. She was still angry as she took the right-hand turn onto Fox Run Road and skidded to a stop in her gravel driveway.

She climbed angrily down from the truck cab and stalked up the front walk and onto the porch. She unlocked the kitchen door and pushed it open.

"I want you to go inside," she said tightly, "and I want you to stay there until I get back."

Blue's own temper sparked. "Since when did you start telling me what to do?"

"Since *you* started acting like an idiot," Lucy said. "God Almighty, McCoy, what were you thinking? Did you honestly figure you could beat up Leroy Hurley, make him tell you what you wanted to know and *not* risk imprisonment?

I had to talk rings around Chief Bradley to keep him from locking you up." She pushed her hair off her face in frustration as she stalked into the kitchen and paced back and forth across the floor. "I don't know how it works in the SEALs, but in this part of America, you just can't go around terrorizing people because you're mad. Lord, I expected more from you."

I expected more from you. Her words pushed Blue over the edge, sending him down into a spiral of emotion and anger that he couldn't pull out of. He tried, but it enveloped him completely, and he lost his temper.

"If you expected more from me," Blue exploded, "that's *your* problem, Yankee, not mine. Because guess what? I'm not perfect. I never have been."

The force of his words pushed Lucy back against the kitchen counter. He could see shock in her eyes, alarm on her face, but once he'd started, he couldn't stop.

"You see me as some kind of damned hero, but I'm not. I'm flesh and blood, and just as capable of screwing up as the next guy.

"Guess what else?" he continued. "I yell sometimes. I *like* to yell. I *like* to fight. But I don't always win, because I'm *not* a hero. I'm *not* always right. I'm *not* always in control. I make mistakes, sometimes *stupid* mistakes. I get angry. I get hurt. I get scared. And right now I'm all *three* of those things." His voice got softer, and he looked away from her, out the kitchen window. "Only I can't tell you that, can I? Because... you expect more from me."

The silence that surrounded them seemed almost unnatural, artificial. Blue could hear the hum of the refrigerator, the almost inaudible ticking of the clock. Outside, a breeze blew and a tree branch bumped the house.

He heard Lucy take a step toward him and then another step, and then he felt her hand on his back. It was a touch meant to give comfort. Blue didn't know what he wanted from her, but he was almost certain it wasn't comfort. Still, when he turned and saw the sheen of tears in her eyes, he knew without a doubt that he was going to take whatever she had to offer. And maybe even then some.

She went into his arms, holding him as tightly as he held her, and the longing that welled up inside him was sharp and painful as hell. This wasn't comfort; it was torture.

"I'm so sorry," she murmured.

He felt her hands on his back, in his hair, meant to soothe and calm. It wasn't working.

"Lucy, I want you," he whispered, "and I don't think I can stand it anymore."

He felt her stiffen at his words. She lifted her head and he gazed directly into her eyes.

"Blue—"

He touched her lips with one finger, silencing her.

"I'm not what you think I am," he said. "You think I'm some kind of gentleman. You think all you have to do is tell me 'no,' and 'don't,' even though you damn well want it as much as I do. You think that because I'm some kind of hero I'll keep both of us from going too far. You think you can look at me with these big, brown eyes, not bothering to hide how much you want me, too. You think you can put me upstairs in some guest room, while you sleep one flight away, with your bedroom door unlocked and open, as if I'm strong enough to keep us apart. But guess what? You leave that door open and unlocked tonight, and I'm going to take it as the invitation that it is—because I'm *not* strong enough. I don't want to be strong enough anymore. I'm not a hero, Lucy, and I'm tired as hell of playing one."

She was trembling, actually trembling, in his arms. "Blue, I can't. You're right. Part of me wants to be with you that way, but I can't—"

"Maybe you can't, but I sure as hell can."

Blue kissed her. He covered Lucy's mouth with his and drank her in. She tasted sweet and hot and she so absolutely set him on fire. If she resisted his kiss, she resisted for all of a half a second. And then her tongue welcomed him fiercely, pulling him into her mouth, harder, deeper.

The power of her answering passion took his breath away. He kissed her again and again, trying desperately to get even closer, to fill his senses with her, to have more, *more*.

He reached for her shirt, yanking the tails up and out of the waist of her pants. He found the softness of her skin and moaned at the smooth sensation beneath his fingertips.

And still he kissed her and she kissed him. It was wild, incredible, amazing. He couldn't get enough, would never get enough. Her hands were in his hair, on his back, on the curve of his rear end, pulling him closer to her.

She could surely feel him pressed against her, fully aroused. He was so hard he hurt.

Blue picked her up and her legs locked around his waist. He was dizzy, delirious with the knowledge that he was going to have her. Right here and right now, he could take her and she wouldn't refuse.

He pulled his shirt off over his head and quickly unbuckled his shoulder holster, then tossed it onto the kitchen table. Lucy's hands were everywhere, skimming across the muscles in his shoulders and chest and back, touching him, caressing his skin, just lightly enough to drive him totally insane.

I can't.

Blue's eyes opened. Lucy hadn't spoken. She was still kissing him. She hadn't given voice to her protest again. But still, it echoed in his head, over and over and over.

I can't.

If they didn't stop, she'd lose her job and her self-respect, just as she'd told him.

And if they did stop, he'd lose his mind. After all, he was no hero.

But even so, how could he willingly do something that would destroy her?

As if she felt his hesitation, Lucy lifted her head, staring with sudden shock into Blue's eyes.

"Oh, my God," she said. "What are we doing? What am *I* doing? Blue, I can't do this. . . ."

Blue gently set her down, away from him, on the kitchen counter. He had to look away from her—she looked too damn good with her hair messed and her clothing askew. He picked up his holster from the table and his shirt from the floor, keeping his eyes averted.

"I'll be outside," he said, barely getting the words out through his clenched teeth, "getting some air."

Chapter 9

When Lucy came home from the police station, the sun had already set. Her house was dark. There were no lights on, and she climbed out of her truck filled with trepidation. Where had Blue gone this time?

She'd told him to stay here, but that didn't mean he'd be here.

Hoping she'd find another note on the kitchen table, Lucy wearily climbed the stairs to the porch, searching for her key in the darkness.

"It's unlocked."

Lucy jumped. My God. Blue was sitting out on the porch in the dark.

"You're here," she said inanely.

"You asked me to stick around."

As her eyes adjusted to the darkness, she could see that he was on the porch swing, rocking slightly, just watching her.

"And you told me you were going to do what you wanted."

"Not entirely," he said softly, his meaning clear. He was referring to this afternoon—to when they had almost made love.

Lucy sat down on the steps. It was as far as she could get from him and still be on the porch.

"I'm sorry about before," he murmured.

She turned to look at him. From this distance, she couldn't quite make out his features in the darkness. "Which part of before?" she asked bluntly. "The part where you yelled at me, or the part where we almost had sex?"

"I'm sorry for yelling."

"But not for the other."

He chuckled. "I'm sorry about that, too—but only that we didn't get to finish what we started."

Lucy was silent for several long minutes, just looking up at the stars. Another man probably wouldn't have admitted that. Another man would have pretended to apologize.

Of course, another man wouldn't have blithely lied about the fact that he was carrying three different concealed weapons. Another man wouldn't have egged on an angry man holding a two-by-four.

Blue McCoy wasn't a hero. He was a man, with a man's strengths and weaknesses. Until his outburst, Lucy hadn't allowed herself to see past the comic book-perfect facade she'd constructed for him. She hadn't allowed him to have any real human emotions or fears. But he did.

The moon came out from behind the clouds. It was still quite full, and it lit the yard and made the white paint of the porch seem to glow.

"Are you really afraid?" Lucy asked.

She heard him sigh. "Normally, I wouldn't admit something like that more than once a decade," he said. "But, yeah, Yankee. I'm scared."

She turned to face him, leaning back against the banister, tucking her knees in to her chest and holding them with her arms. "You don't act like you're afraid of anything."

"I'm not afraid of fighting," he said. "I know what to do when it comes down to violence. I know how to respond to that. I know I'm good at it. The thought of getting hurt doesn't frighten me, either—I've been hurt before. Pain ends. Bodies heal. I'm not afraid of dying, either." He looked up at the moon, squinting slightly as he studied it. "I've got my faith," he added quietly.

He turned to gaze at her, and his eyes reflected the moon's silvery light, making him appear otherworldly.

"But I'm terrified of getting caught in a legal system that's corrupt—and possibly controlled by the people who are trying to frame me. I feel like I'm in the middle of a war that I don't know how to fight."

He closed his eyes briefly, and Lucy knew that this wasn't easy for him.

"I'm afraid of going to jail, Lucy. It damn near scares me to death. I won't let them lock me up. I swear, I'll run before that happens."

Lucy sat forward. "But don't you see? That'll make you look guilty."

"I already look guilty as hell," Blue said flatly. "Everyone in town thinks I did it."

"Well, *I* know you didn't kill Gerry," Lucy said fiercely, "and I'm going to make damn sure that you don't go to jail for something you didn't do."

She could see an odd play of emotions cross his face in the moonlight.

"You still believe in me," he said. He sounded faintly surprised.

"Of course."

"Even though I'm not . . . some kind of superhero?"

The truth was, Lucy liked him better this way. The human Blue seemed so much warmer, so much more real. Realizing he had imperfections and weaknesses added a depth and dimension to her image of him. He was still outrageously attractive—maybe even more so, because she knew now that he was human, with a full array of human emotions. His vulnerabilities contrasted with his strengths, giving him a sensitivity she hadn't realized he'd possessed.

"What does that have to do with whether I think you killed your stepbrother?" she asked evenly.

"I don't know," he admitted. He paused. "I guess maybe I misunderstood your reasons for wanting to help me."

Lucy laughed softly. "I assure you my reasons are only pure," she said. "The pursuit of justice. The defeat of evil. Things like that. Whether you can leap tall buildings has nothing to do with it."

Blue was silent. She knew he was thinking about Gerry. In Gerry's case, evil had won. And Lucy knew that if she didn't come up with some new evidence exonerating Blue, Chief Bradley was going to bring charges against him. With Matt Parker's damning testimony and without the hard proof of the tire tracks they'd seen, it was only a matter of time. She'd talked to Matt Parker today. He insisted that Leroy's story about finding the dirt bikes on the side of Route 17 was true. And he swore it was Blue he saw up in the woods on the night Gerry had died.

"Maybe you should call someone," Lucy said. "Get a lawyer."

Blue shifted his weight, making the swing rock slowly.

"I tried calling Joe Cat this afternoon—Joe Catalanotto. He's my commanding officer in the Alpha Squad. And he's my friend," Blue told her. "I figured he'd know how to proceed, maybe even get me a good navy lawyer, get this mess cleared up. But I found out that Alpha Squad is out on a training mission until further notice. And SEAL Team Ten's normal liaison, Admiral Forrest, is suddenly unavailable." His normally relaxed voice sounded tense, tight. "I spoke to some pencil-pushing commander from Internal Affairs, who says he's handling all of Alpha Squad's paperwork and messages until further notice. IA does this every few years when it's time for budget cuts. This commander is looking for dirt—for reasons to get rid of Alpha Squad. I didn't dare tell him I wanted to talk to a lawyer. If he found out that one of the members of Alpha Squad was going to be up on murder charges . . ." Blue shook his head. "I've got to get through this on my own."

"But you're not on your own," Lucy said softly. "You've got me."

Across the porch, Blue tried to smile. "Thanks, Yankee, but . . ."

"I'm not part of Alpha Squad," she finished for him.

He nodded. "We've been trained to work as a team," he tried to explain.

"I know," Lucy said. "I know how the SEAL teams operate. And from what I've read about Alpha Squad, some of you guys have been together since basic training."

Blue nodded. "Joe Cat and I went through BUDS together more than ten years ago. We were swim buddies. Still are."

Swim buddies. That meant that all throughout BUDS—Basic Underwater Demolition/SEAL training—Blue and his friend Joe Cat had stuck together like glue. Where one went, the other had to follow. They had no doubt formed a bond that went way beyond friendship, based on respect and determination and an unswerving responsibility toward each other and Alpha Squad.

"I've read about Hell Week," Lucy said, resting her chin in the palm of her hand as she gazed up at him. "It sounds awful. Was it true that you had only four hours of sleep all week?"

"Yeah," Blue said with a smile. "Both Cat and I were hallucinating before it was over. Fortunately, when I was seeing sea monsters he took charge. And when *he* was the one foaming at the mouth I was able to grab him and set him back on track. That was one hell of a week. I guess that's why they call it that."

"Will you tell me about it?" Lucy asked.

Blue gave the porch swing another push with his foot and it creaked rhythmically as it swung back and forth. He gazed at her, his expression unreadable for many long moments.

"Please?" she added.

"'You gotta want it badly enough,'" Blue said.

For a second, Lucy was confused. But then he explained.

"That's what one of the SEAL instructors used to shout at us, and it's the single most lucid thing I remember about Hell Week."

The moon slipped back behind a cloud, taking its silvery light with it. Blue became a dark outline on the other side of the porch, but his voice surrounded her, as warm and smooth and completely enveloping as the darkness.

"The instructors would shout at us over these bullhorns," he said. "It was relentless. They would ridicule and torment us all the time as they hit us with surf torture or made us run endless laps on the beach or do sugar-cookie drills. But there was this one bastard—his nickname was Captain Blood—and he was the meanest, toughest instructor of them all. He was out for blood, literally. But one of the first things he ever said to us through his megaphone was 'You gotta want it badly enough.' "

Blue laughed softly. "It must've been on the first day. We were in the water. It was *cold* water, less than sixty degrees. We had to lock arms and just sit in the surf and try not to freeze our asses off. They called it surf torture and it was designed to see how much we could endure, the thought being that someday we'd find ourselves swimming for hours in the ice water off Alaska.

"Anyway, we were in the freezing mother of an ocean for about an hour, when the first man quit. It was so damn cold. I'd never been that cold before in my life. All around me I could hear other guys complaining. What were we doing this for? Why did we need to do this? What were the instructors trying to prove?"

The clouds covering the moon thinned and then broke apart and Blue paused. Lucy gazed up at him. She could picture him sitting in the freezing water, silently enduring the cold, his handsome face tight, his teeth clenched.

"As I sat there," Blue continued, "these other guys started to give up. Just like that. It got too uncomfortable, too tough, too painful, so they just up and quit. But I wasn't going anywhere. And I looked at Joe Cat, and I knew he wasn't going anywhere, either. I could tell from the expression on his face that he was thinking the same thing I was thinking—'You gotta want it badly enough.' And we did. We wanted to make it through, get our SEAL trident pin."

Blue smiled down at her, and Lucy found herself smiling almost foolishly back at him. His eyes seemed to caress her face and he shook his head slightly, as if he were bemused. "You *are* pretty, aren't you?" he asked softly.

Lucy had to look away. Everyone was pretty in the moonlight.

"You sure you don't want to sit up here on the swing, next to me?" Blue added.

She met his eyes evenly. "You know I can't."

"I know you *won't*," he countered.

"Either way," she said. "I better stay where I am."

"We could just hold hands," Blue said. "Like sweethearts. Nothing more. It'd be real innocent."

Lucy had to laugh. "You don't have a single innocent cell in your body, McCoy. You know as well as I do that holding hands would lead to a kiss, and we both know where *that* would go."

Blue's eyes turned hot. "Yeah, I sure do," he said softly. "I spent most of the evening fantasizing about it."

Lucy stood up. "I think it's time for this conversation to end."

Blue sat up. He didn't want her to go. More, even more than he wanted to make love to Lucy, he wanted her company. Her smile and her beautiful midnight eyes kept all his demon fears at bay. "You sure you don't want to hear more about Hell Week?" he asked.

He'd never talked so much in his entire life. He'd never told his stories, recounted his past the way some of the other guys in the squad did over and over again. It wasn't that he didn't have good tales to tell—he just always preferred to listen.

And he and Joe Cat didn't talk that much. They knew each other so well that they shared each other's thoughts, communicating with a look or a nod.

His friendship with Daryl Becker—nicknamed Harvard because of his Ivy League college education—was filled with talk of books and philosophy, of science and art and technology and anything—you name it and they'd touched on it. But Harvard did most of the talking, thinking aloud, rattling off ideas before they'd even become fully formed. Blue kept his thinking to himself, carefully forming his opinions before he spoke. As a result, his comments were always short and sweet.

But tonight, even though he was nearly hoarse from doing so much talking, he was willing to keep going if it meant Lucy would stay with him just a bit longer.

Lucy was still standing by the steps, her arms crossed in front of her. "Are you going to let me sit over here?" she asked warily.

He nodded. "Yeah."

She sat down, just gazing at him expectantly in the moonlight.

It took Blue a minute to remember he'd promised to tell her more about Hell Week. Except he was damned if he could think of a single thing to say.

"I'm not sure what you want to hear about," he said lamely.

Lucy shifted, getting more comfortable on the hard wood of the steps. "I've read about something called 'rock portage,'" she said. "Did you have to do that in basic training?"

"Yeah. Halfway through Hell Week we had to do a nighttime coastal landing in our IBS—our rubber life raft." Blue nodded again, glad she had given him something to talk about. Or had she? The night his BUDS team had done rock portage was a nightmare blur. He hesitated. "I don't remember much about it," he admitted. "I remember wondering how the hell we were going to get safely ashore with our boat intact. The surf was rough and the coast was nothing but a jagged line of rocks. It wouldn't take much to crush a man between the rocks and our boat." He looked down at his hands, wondering what else he could tell her. "We were exhausted and freezing and some of our boat crew had injuries. I can't really tell you exactly how we got ashore, just that we did."

Blue glanced up to find Lucy still watching him. She was listening, her dark eyes luminous and warm in the moonlight. And he knew then what he could tell her. He could tell her the truth.

"I remember being scared to death while we were doing it," he added quietly. "I felt like such a coward."

His words hung in the air. He'd never admitted that to anyone before. Not Joe Cat, not Frisco or Harvard. He'd barely even admitted it to himself. The sounds of the night surrounded him as he gazed into Lucy's eyes, wondering what she would do with this intimate truth that he'd shared with her.

She smiled. "You weren't a coward," she said. "A coward doesn't keep on doing something that scares him to death. A coward quits. Only a very strong, very brave person perseveres in the face of fear."

Blue nodded, smiling back at her. "I know that now," he said. "But I was younger then."

"I bet a lot of guys quit during rock portage," Lucy said.

"Our boat crew's senior officer did," Blue told her. "He took one look at those rocks and checked out of the program. We made our landing that night without a senior officer—just us grunts, getting the job done."

Lucy was fascinated, hanging on his every word. Blue knew that as long as he could keep talking, she'd stay there with him. And he wanted her to stay.

"By the end of the week, only half the class was left," he continued, the words flowing more easily now. "We were running down the beach and my entire boat crew was limping—we were a mess. Like I said, our senior officer had quit on us, and Joe Cat and me, even though we were grunts—just enlisted men—we took command. Someone had to. But by this time, Cat was really hurting. Turned out he had a stress fracture in his leg, but we didn't know it at the time."

"He was running on a *broken* leg?"

"Yeah." Blue nodded, watching all of Lucy's emotions play across her face. She gazed up into his eyes, waiting for his response, one hundred percent of her attention focused on him. He had to smile. He quite possibly had never had a woman's total, undivided attention before—at least not while they both had all their clothes on. Maybe there was something to this storytelling thing after all.

"Anyway, Cat was damned if he was going to get pulled because of his injury," Blue said, "so we hid him from the instructors. We carried him when we could, surrounded him, held him up, dragged him when no one was looking. But Captain Blood finally spotted him and started in on how Cat was slowing us up, taking us down with him. He shouted into his damned bullhorn how we should ditch him, just leave him behind, toss him into the surf."

Blue grinned. "Well, Joe Cat and me, we'd both about had enough. This was day seven. We were sleep deprived. We were psychologically abused. We were hurting. Cat was in excruciating physical pain, and I don't think there was a single part of me that didn't ache or sting. We were cold and wet and hungry. And Cat, he gets really annoyed when he's cold and wet and hungry. But I get mean. So I tell Captain Blood to go to hell, going into detail about just exactly what he should do with himself when he gets there. Then I order the rest of the boat crew to put Cat up on top of our IBS. We'd carry him on the life raft.

"But as we're doing that, Captain Blood realizes that Cat is hurt worse than he thought, and he orders him out of the line. He's gonna pull him because of his injury, and he starts calling in for an ambulance. I look up at Cat, sitting on top of that raft, and he's got this expression on his face, like his entire world has come to an end. There are five hours left in Hell Week. Five lousy hours, and he's gonna get pulled.

"So I get in Captain Blood's face and I interrupt that phone call. I tell him that Joe Cat's leg is fine—and to prove it to him, Cat will do a mile lap down the beach. The captain knows I'm full of it, but he's into playing games, so he tells me, fine. If Cat can run a mile, he can stay in till the end."

The moon went behind the clouds again, plunging the porch into darkness. But Blue could hear Lucy's quiet breathing. He heard her shift her weight, saw her shadowy form. He could feel the power of her attention as if it were a tangible thing, as if she were next to him, touching him.

"Cat is ready to jump down off that IBS to try to do a five-minute mile right then and there," Blue continued.

"But I know he'll never make it. Just putting his weight on his damned leg is enough to make him start to black out. So I put Joe Cat's arm around my shoulder. I'd figured we could run down the beach together, kind of like a three-legged race, with Cat staying off his bad leg. But he was hurt worse than I thought, so I ended up picking him up and carrying him on my back."

Blue heard Lucy's soft inhale. "You *carried* him for a *mile?*" she whispered.

"We were swim buddies," Blue said simply. "Cat is no lightweight—he's about five inches taller than me and he's built like a tank—so about a quarter mile in, I'm starting to move really slowly. But I'm still running, 'cause I want it badly enough, and I know Cat does, too, and I'm not gonna let him get pulled. But I start to wonder how the hell I'm going to find the strength to do this. And then I look up, and the rest of our boat crew is running right next to me. Me and Cat, we're not alone. Our crew is with us. Crow and Harvard and all the rest of the guys. They're all hurting, too, but they're with us. We all took turns carrying Cat that entire mile down the beach. It was no five-minute mile—it took more like a half an hour.

"But when we were done, Captain Blood looks at Cat and he looks at me, and then he nods and says to our boat crew, 'You boys are secure.' Just like that, four and a half hours early, Hell Week was over for our entire crew. We'd made it—all of us. And I swear to God, Captain Blood turned and gave us a salute. An officer, saluting a bunch of enlisted men. That was a sight to see."

Lucy had tears in her eyes and goose bumps on her arms. She sat hugging her knees to her chest, glad for the darkness that hid her emotional response to his soft words. It was an amazing story. And Blue had told it so matter-of-factly, as if he didn't realize how rare and moving his loyalty to his friend truly was.

She knew that Blue's loyalty had to be a two-sided thing, and she knew that if this Joe Cat hadn't been on a training mission, he would be on his way here to Hatboro Creek. Lord knows Blue could use some help. Lucy was doing the best that she could, but she knew without a doubt that her best wasn't enough. She didn't have the experience to pull this investigation off.

And the one thing she did know how to do, she couldn't. She couldn't let herself love Blue—not on the physical level that he so desperately wanted, and not even on an emotional, spiritual level. She couldn't fall in love with him; she couldn't allow herself to feel more than dispassionate compassion for him.

But she did. She felt far more than that. She ached at his pain, suffered his worries, felt the cold of his fears.

She couldn't fall in love with him . . . but that was exactly what she was beginning to do. Right here, in the darkness, with the echo of his velvet voice in her ears, she was sliding deeper in love with Blue McCoy.

It was ironic. Until this afternoon, until Blue's outburst had jolted her, she would have labeled her feelings for Blue as a crush. It had been a very surface-level mixture of awe and admiration and lust—mere hero worship.

But then, with his actions and his words, Blue had stripped off his superhero costume, revealing the imperfections of the flesh-and-blood man underneath.

The hero could only be worshipped.

But the man could be loved.

It was crazy. Even if she succeeded in clearing his name, Blue would be gone in a matter of days, probably hours. How could she let herself fall in love with a man who would never love her in return?

But the point was moot. She couldn't let herself love him. She had to stop herself from falling. Because right now her hands were securely tied by her responsibility to the murder investigation.

"Try calling Joe Cat again in the morning," she said. Her voice was husky with emotion, and she cleared her throat. "If he's not there, try again in the afternoon."

"I will," he said. "Sooner or later he'll be back."

She stood up, and she felt, more than heard, him tense.

"Lucy," he said softly. "Don't go inside yet. Please?"

She could hear loneliness in his voice and knew how much he wanted her to stay, how much it had taken him to ask her not to go.

But she couldn't stay. Every word he spoke brought him a little deeper into her heart. She wasn't strong enough to resist him. Even here in the darkness, six feet apart, she found the sexual pull, the animal attraction between them, alarmingly strong. And the emotional pull that she felt was overpowering.

But she couldn't tell him that.

"I'm sorry, I'm exhausted," she said. She crossed the porch and opened the kitchen door. "I'm going up to take a shower and then go to bed."

She could feel his disappointment, but he didn't try to change her mind.

"All right," he said quietly. "Good night."

The screen door closed after her, and she was halfway through the kitchen before she heard Blue's soft voice.

"Lucy?"

She stopped, but she didn't turn around. She heard him move so that he was standing on the other side of the screen.

"Lock your door tonight," he said quietly.

Lucy nodded. "I will."

The clouds that covered last night's moon brought a dismal, gloomy rain to the day. It was an appropriate backdrop for Gerry's funeral.

Most of the town had been there, many of the people slanting dark looks in Blue's direction.

He had sat alone in a pew toward the front of the church, wearing his gleaming white dress uniform. Only Jenny Lee Beaumont spoke to him, and just briefly, as she was led from the church, following Gerry's gleaming white coffin out to the waiting hearse.

This was supposed to be Lucy's day off, but she'd gone into the police station intending to carry on with the investigation into Gerry's murder. Except, when he saw her there, Chief Bradley had taken the liberty of temporarily assigning Lucy to the task of directing the funeral traffic. She now stood in the rain, halting traffic and giving the right-of-way to the funeral procession heading out to the cemetery.

Blue had borrowed Lucy's truck and he met her eyes briefly through the windshield as he pulled out of the church parking lot. Lucy had gone into the church for the ceremony and had seen that he clearly wasn't welcome at his stepbrother's funeral. He hadn't been asked to carry the casket. He'd been virtually ignored. The minister of the church hadn't even mentioned Blue in his short eulogy to Gerry's life.

Lucy's heart ached for Blue. As she stood getting wetter with each drop of rain that fell, she prayed for a break in the case.

Today wouldn't be a good day to talk to Jenny Lee Beaumont, but maybe tomorrow Lucy could go over to the house that Jenny and Gerry had shared. If she wanted to find Gerry's killer, maybe she should start by looking for a motive. Why would someone want Gerry dead? Did he have any enemies? Was he in the middle of any fights, any business disputes? Maybe Jenny would know.

And if Jenny didn't, someone in town had to know. Lucy was going to start out on Gate's Hill Road, near where the murder had taken place, and work her way through town, knocking on doors and asking questions. Somebody saw or heard something that night. Somebody knew who really killed Gerry McCoy.

And then there were Leroy Hurley and Matt Parker. Blue was right about them. Their story about finding the dirt bikes by the side of the road was ludicrous. Someone had paid them off to obscure those tire tracks. And it was possibly the same someone who was paying Matt Parker to say he'd seen Blue up in the woods with Gerry.

The last of the cars pulled out of the church lot and Lucy watched their taillights vanish as they made a left at the corner of Main and Willow.

Turning, she pushed her wet hair out of her face, adjusted her soggy hat and headed for home. It was nearly three o'clock, and she wanted to change out of her soaked uniform and have something to eat. She'd make herself a salad and actually sit down at her kitchen table to eat it. And in order not to feel as if she were wasting time, she'd take the opportunity to really read over Gerry's autopsy reports.

It was three-fifteen before she got home, three-thirty before she got out of the shower and nearly four o'clock before she sat down with her salad at the kitchen table. She'd pulled on a short pair of cutoff jeans and a tank top, and brushed out her wet hair.

She skimmed through the autopsy report, then went back to read it more carefully. It wasn't until the third time through that she saw it.

There was almost no alcohol present in Gerry's blood.

No alcohol?

She checked the numbers again, and sure enough, according to these figures, Gerry couldn't have had more than one beer all evening long on the night he died.

That had to be wrong.

She'd seen Gerry's drunken behavior with her own eyes. He had looked and acted inebriated at the party at 8:15, yet had been dead at 11:06, not quite three hours later, with only the slightest trace of alcohol in his blood.

It didn't make sense. Either the autopsy report was wrong...

Or...

Was it possible that Gerry's drunken behavior had been an act? Had he been stone sober at the country club, only pretending to be drunk? And if so, why? What purpose could it possibly have served? He'd embarrassed himself and Blue *and* Jenny Lee. Why would he have done that intentionally?

It didn't make sense.

Lucy had to tell someone. She had to ask questions, talk to Jenny herself, find out if Gerry had seemed sober or drunk earlier at the party. And R. W. Fisher. Blue said he'd seen his stepbrother talking to the Tobacco King right before Gerry's outburst. Lucy had to talk to Fisher, see if he'd noticed anything odd about Gerry during their conversation.

Lucy stood up, stuffed her feet into her running shoes and grabbed her raincoat from its hook by the kitchen door. She was out on the porch before she realized that she didn't have her keys—or her truck.

Okay. That was okay. She'd take a few minutes, go inside, change out of her shorts and into a pair of jeans. As hot as it was with the humidity from the rain, it wouldn't do her any good to appear at the police station in shorts.

Lucy took the stairs to her room two at a time and quickly kicked off her sneakers. She wriggled out of her shorts and pulled on her jeans. She fished her cowboy boots out from under her bed and pulled them on, too.

She was reaching for the phone, about to call down to the station, looking for a ride, when she heard the kitchen door open and shut.

Blue was back.

Lucy clattered down the stairs and into the kitchen, stopping short when she realized that Blue was taking off his dripping clothes right there in the doorway.

But his clothes weren't just wet, she realized. They were also muddy and torn. And smeared with blood. *His* blood.

Blue had been in a fight.

He'd taken off his jacket and the shirt he wore underneath. His arm was bleeding, his fingers dripping with blood. Lucy got a glimpse of a nasty cut across his biceps before he pressed his shirt against it, trying to stop the flow of blood.

Fear welled up in her. He'd been out there, in town, all alone, without her. He could have been badly hurt. Or even killed. "Are you all right?"

He met her eyes briefly as he stepped out of his muddy pants. "I could use a first-aid kit," he said. "And I'll need some ice for my leg."

Lucy saw that he had the beginnings of a truly dreadful-looking bruise on his left thigh.

Silently she moved to the cabinet and took out her first-aid kit, with its vast array of bandages and gauze. As she set it on the kitchen table, she saw that Blue was still standing in the doorway, awkwardly holding his filthy clothes.

"I don't want to get your floor any dirtier," he apologized.

"Just put them down," she said, hoping he wouldn't notice how her voice was shaking. "The floor can be washed."

He nodded, setting his clothes on the floor.

"What happened?" Lucy asked, since it was clear he wasn't going to volunteer the information himself. She filled a wash basin with warm water and set it on the table next to the first-aid kit.

"Fight," Blue said, gingerly lowering himself onto one of the kitchen chairs.

Lucy took a soft washcloth from the shelf, throwing him an exasperated look over her shoulder. "You want to be a little more specific there, McCoy?"

She handed him the washcloth, then went to the freezer to get an ice pack for his leg.

"No."

His knuckles and hands were torn up, and he had a scrape across his left cheekbone. It was still bleeding, and he tried futilely to blot the blood with the back of his hand.

Lucy's cold fear turned hot with frustration. "No," she repeated. She wrapped the ice pack in a small towel and crossed toward him.

"It was nothing I care to issue a complaint about," he said. He lifted his wad of shirt from the cut on his arm, and it welled with blood. He quickly covered the wound with the soapy washcloth, applying pressure.

"Issue a complaint?" Lucy stared at him. "I asked you what happened. I didn't ask you if you wanted to file a complaint."

"I'm not trying to start another fight here," Blue said, glancing up at her. His eyes were startlingly blue. "It's just... you've been careful about remaining in your role as a police officer at other times, I figured what happened to me this afternoon was something you wouldn't want to know."

Lucy was shocked. "Is that all I am to you, a police officer?"

"I thought that was your choice," Blue said, rinsing the washcloth in the basin, then using it to reapply pressure to his slashed arm. "I thought you were the one who set those limits."

"I can't be your lover," Lucy told him. "*That's* my limit. But I thought at least I was your friend."

He looked up at her again, his eyes sweeping down the length of her body and back up before settling on her face. "My friends don't look that good in their jeans."

"I suppose you don't have a single friend who's a woman."

"No, I don't."

"You do now," she said grimly. She crouched next to him, not certain of the best way to put the ice pack on his leg. The bruise looked incredibly painful. It was turning all sorts of shades of purple, with a long, darker welt in the center, as if... "My God, were you hit with a pipe?"

He briefly met her eyes again. "Yeah. I think that's what it was." He took a bottle of antiseptic spray from the first-aid kit and sprayed it on his arm. It had to sting, but he didn't even blink.

"God, Blue, if they'd hit you with this much force on your head..." Lucy sat back on her heels, feeling sick to her stomach. He could have been killed.

"They didn't," he said. "I was careful not to let them do that."

"Please tell me what happened." Slowly, carefully, trying to be gentle, Lucy lowered the ice pack onto Blue's leg. He didn't wince; he merely clenched his teeth a little tighter at the contact.

"I stayed behind at the cemetery," Blue said, using a roll of gauze to wrap up his arm.

"Do you want me to do that?" Lucy asked, interrupting him.

He sent her a tight smile. "No," he said. "Thanks. It's tricky doing it with only one hand, and that's keeping my focus off my leg."

"It must really hurt."

"Like a bitch," he agreed.

"It could be broken," Lucy said, worried.

"It's not," Blue said. "I've felt broken before and it's not."

He was sitting in the middle of her kitchen, wearing only a pair of red briefs, Lucy realized suddenly. Even battered and bruised, he was drop-dead gorgeous. Every inch of him was trim and fit and muscular and tanned a delicious golden brown.

"I hung back to visit my mother's grave," he was saying, continuing his story.

Lucy forced herself to pay attention to his words, not his body.

"I thought everyone had gone home from Gerry's burial, but apparently I was wrong. I was walking back to your truck, and I was jumped."

He'd rinsed the washcloth clean and was now using it to wipe rather ineffectively at the cut on his cheek. Lucy pulled another chair over and took the cloth from his hand, leaning across him to wash the cut for him. She had to use her left hand to push his hair back from his face. It felt thick and soft underneath her fingers. She tried not to think about it, tried not to think about his mouth, only inches away from hers.

"Did you see who it was who jumped you?" she asked evenly.

"My old friend Leroy Hurley was there," Blue said. "And Jedd Southeby. He was the owner of the pipe, I believe. I'm not sure who else was at the party. There were an awful lot of 'em."

Lucy pulled back slightly so she could look into his eyes. "How many?"

"I don't know."

She searched his eyes. Did he really not know, or was he keeping the truth from her? "Make a guess."

"More than fifteen, fewer than twenty."

Lucy's mouth dropped open. "*That* many?"

"Most of 'em weren't a real threat," Blue said. "When it was clear that I wasn't going to curl up into a little ball and die, most of 'em ran away."

Lucy's gaze dropped to the bandage on his arm. "Who exactly was the owner of the knife?" she asked.

"We weren't introduced," Blue said, "but he'll be the gentleman checking in the county hospital with a broken hand."

Lucy laughed. She had to laugh, or she would start to cry. Still, her eyes welled with tears.

"Hey," Blue said softly. He gently touched the side of her face with the tips of his fingers. "I'm okay, Yankee. It's the other fifteen guys who don't look so good right now."

"More than fifteen guys attack you, and *they're* the ones who don't look so good?" Lucy laughed again, and this time the tears escaped, flowing down her cheeks. "What if one of them had had a gun?"

"Someone probably would've been shot," Blue said, gently running his fingers back through her hair. "But there wasn't a gun. No one was badly hurt."

Lucy almost couldn't help herself. She almost put her arms around Blue's neck and held him close.

He could see it in her eyes, she knew, because his eyes grew hotter, more liquid. Other than that, he didn't move a muscle.

Lucy made herself back away, wiping her face free of tears with her hands.

"I have to go down to the station," she said, taking a tissue from a box on the kitchen counter and blowing her nose, trying desperately to break the highly charged mood that lingered in the room. She emptied the basin of water and rinsed out the washcloth. "I read the autopsy report and found something odd. Gerry had almost no alcohol in his bloodstream when he died."

Blue frowned. "It must be a lab error," he said. "Gerry was corked that night."

"Was he?" Lucy asked, turning to face him. "Or was he only trying to make you *think* he was? Did you actually smell alcohol on his breath?"

Blue was silent, trying to remember. "I don't know," he finally admitted.

"I was thinking about that whole incident," Lucy said, leaning back against the sink, "and it occurred to me—I've never asked what Gerry whispered to you before you left the country club. Do you remember?"

Blue nodded, the muscle working in his jaw. "He said, 'I'm sorry, but you have to leave town.' You know, I thought he was referring to Jenny Lee—that he didn't want me around stirring up the past during his wedding. But now..."

"What if he knew something bad was going to happen?" Lucy asked. "What if he staged that whole drunk scene because it was the only way he could communicate with you?"

Blue stared down at the ice pack on his leg. "That was one hell of a way to communicate," he said. "Why wouldn't he just pull me aside and talk to me?"

"Maybe he couldn't," Lucy said, excitement tingeing her voice. "Maybe he knew he was in danger. Maybe he knew someone was going to kill him."

"Why wouldn't he tell me about it?" Blue asked, looking back up at her, his frustration vibrating in his own voice. "I could've helped him. I could've kept him safe."

Lucy shook her head. "I don't know," she admitted. "But the first thing I've got to do is talk to some of the people who were at that party—people who interacted with Gerry. And I'll have the lab double-check the results of the autopsy blood test. I want to find out for sure if Gerry *was* sober that night."

She picked up her raincoat from where she'd thrown it over the back of a chair. "I'm going down to the station right now," she said. "Will you be all right alone?"

He smiled. "I'll be fine."

Lucy started for the door, but then turned back. "My bathroom has a Jacuzzi in it," she said. "Maybe it would help your leg to sit in it for a while."

Blue shook his head. "That's all right. I don't want to invade your personal space—"

"Please," she said. "Use it. I'll be back as soon as I can."

Chapter 10

Sheldon Bradley sat behind his big, oak desk and stared at Lucy. "That's ridiculous," the police chief said. "Whether or not Gerry McCoy was drunk at a party has nothing to do with the events that transpired nearly three hours later—events that led to his death."

"I think it does," she said, stubbornly holding her ground. "I intend to talk to the people who were there—people who spoke to Gerry before his outburst. R. W. Fisher had a long conversation with Gerry—"

"No," Bradley said, rising to his feet. "Absolutely not. This has gone too far. I'm taking you off this case. In fact, I'm temporarily suspending you from the force."

Shocked, Lucy stood up, too. "What?"

"I've had word of your inappropriate behavior concerning Blue McCoy," the chief said. "Clearly, your judgment is skewed."

He sat down again, opening a file—her personnel file, Lucy realized. "Sir, I have done *nothing* that could be considered inappropriate."

Bradley looked up at her, eyebrows raised. "Do you deny then that the chief suspect in this case is sharing your house with you? And before you perjure yourself, darlin', be warned that neighbors *have* seen McCoy come home with you at night and leave with you in the morning."

"He needed a place to stay!"

"So naturally, you offer him your bed?"

"I did no such thing—"

"Officially, the charge would be sexual misconduct," Bradley told her, "and the punishment would be dismissal, not mere suspension. But you're young and you're new, and I give everyone here one mistake. This one is certainly yours."

"But, sir—"

"I suggest you keep your mouth closed, Ms. Tait," Bradley said, "because I am going to say this only once, *and* this matter is *not* negotiable. I'm suspending you for at least one week, your return subject to my approval. You'll turn in your badge and your sidearm." He held up his hand. "However, I'll record the suspension in your permanent file as an unpaid vacation. There'll be no further questions asked, no more talk about this matter and no ugly blot on your record. Unless, of course, you raise a racket about it."

Lucy shook her head. She felt numb. "But I did nothing wrong."

"I'm not asking you for a signed confession," he said. "Like I said, as of this moment, there will be no more questions asked—"

"Yet I'm suspended."

"Yes, you are."

"Because you think I had sex with Blue McCoy."

Bradley winced at her lack of delicacy. "I don't wish to discuss the details—"

"But I'm telling you that I *didn't.*"

"Other individuals have expressed their concerns and suspicions, fearing that you have allowed yourself to...shall we say, fall under the suspect's...influence." Bradley closed her file. "I have no desire to attempt to judge exactly who is right or wrong in this matter—"

"But you are," Lucy said. "By suspending me, you're finding me guilty of something that I did *not* do."

"Are you telling me that your opinions about this case are one hundred percent impartial?"

Lucy couldn't answer that, and she knew her silence damned her.

Bradley leaned forward. "Do yourself a favor, Lucy," he said. "Take a vacation. Leave town for a few days—at least until this mess is over."

"I can't do that," Lucy said. She was so angry her voice shook.

"Don't make this worse than it has to be," Bradley said. "Don't make me have to fire you."

"If you're charging me with sexual misconduct, I want to be officially charged."

"If I charge you," Bradley said tightly, "the penalty will *not* be suspension. As I said, you will be removed from the force."

"*If* I'm found guilty," Lucy said.

Bradley had had enough. "Fine," he said. "I find you guilty. Hearing closed. You're fired, darlin'." He tossed her personnel file into the garbage can. "Leave your badge and your gun on my desk and get the hell out of my office."

"If that's your idea of a fair hearing, then I don't want to work for you. You can't fire me—I quit!"

She nearly threw her badge and her gun down onto Bradley's desk.

"I'll pass along your reports on the investigation to Travis Southeby," the chief said.

Travis Southeby? "You're letting Travis take over the investigation?" Lucy was aghast.

Travis Southeby, whose brother Jedd had been among the group of men who'd attacked Blue just this afternoon. Travis Southeby, who'd stood up in the Grill because he didn't want to eat dinner in the same room as Gerry's "killer."

Travis Southeby? Impartial investigator?

Not even close.

Frustration and anger bubbled inside Lucy, and she left Chief Bradley's office, slamming the door behind her.

* * *

Blue closed his eyes, leaning back in the tub and letting the water gently massage his aching leg.

When Lucy had first told him about the Jacuzzi in her tub, he'd imagined it was one of those little tiny ones. Instead, it was a great big hot tub with room enough to throw a party.

He tried to imagine Lucy serving champagne and wine as she and a bunch of her friends sat laughing and talking in this tub. But he couldn't picture it. It seemed too out of character. He tried to imagine her sitting in this tub with the man in that photo on her dresser, having a very, very private party. That picture came far too easily, and he shook his head, trying to clear his mind of that image. He didn't want to picture that.

He tried to imagine her, instead, coming back from the police station. He could picture her clearly, dressed in those sinfully snug-fitting blue jeans and those black cowboy boots, black tank top clinging to her curves, her shining hair loose around her shoulders. She'd lean in the doorway for a moment, watching him with the temperature in her dark-brown eyes soaring way past that of the hot tub. Then she'd straighten up and pull her shirt up and over her head and—

Blue opened his eyes at the sound of the kitchen door opening. Lucy was back. He heard her toss her keys down onto the kitchen table. The refrigerator door opened.

"Blue, you want a beer?" he heard her call out.

He didn't have to think about it. "Yeah. Thanks." Damn, he would have accepted an offer of hemlock if it meant she'd bring it up here to him.

He heard the thump of the refrigerator door as she closed it. A drawer opened in the kitchen and she fished around, looking for something. Then he heard the sound of bottle caps being removed, a thud as she put what had to be a bottle opener down on the table and two smaller thuds as she tossed the caps into the trash.

Then he heard her climbing up the stairs. Mercy, just the thought of Lucy walking in here had made him hard as rock. He forced himself to keep breathing, to relax. She was bringing him a beer. Nothing more. But maybe if he wasn't shooting pheromones into the air, if he could look as if he didn't want to gobble her up, maybe then she'd sit down and talk to him awhile.

That was really what he wanted. True, he'd give damn near anything to have sex with this woman, but he wouldn't risk scaring her away. Because he needed her company tonight—her smile, the sound of her husky laughter, the warmth of her eyes and maybe most important her patient and unswerving belief in him. He needed all that more than he needed sexual relief.

And then she was standing in the doorway.

Blue could sense her tension. He picked up her undercurrent of anger and frustration before she even spoke.

"I hope American beer is okay," she said, handing him the dark-brown bottle. She turned to pull the shade down on the window. "It was on sale and—"

"It's fine," he said. Her hands were shaking and her voice was unnaturally tight. But she was working so hard to hide it from him, he wasn't sure if he should ask her what was wrong. "How'd it go in town?" he asked instead, keeping the question neutral, his voice light.

"Well, it went," she said, taking a long pull of her beer. "It went straight to hell in a handbasket." She turned and gazed directly into his eyes. "Mind if I climb in there with you?"

Blue's heart stopped. And then it jump-started in double time. "No," he somehow managed to say.

Lucy leaned against the sink to pull off her boots and socks. She tossed them into the bedroom, then unzipped her pants.

As Blue watched, she wriggled out of her blue jeans. Her legs were longer and even more shapely than he remembered. Her panties were bright white against her tanned skin. Mercy. He was going to die.

She didn't look at him as she peeled her shirt up and over her head and threw it down on top of her jeans. Her bra was also white, and she unfastened the front clasp as if she casually stripped naked in front of a man every day of her life.

Her breasts were beautiful, so full and firm, with dark-brown tips that tightened under his gaze. Her body was exactly as he'd imagined it. She was slender, yet she had some real muscle in her arms and legs and torso, giving her body shape and definition. Her stomach was flat, her hips curving softly out.

He was going to explode, Blue realized. Out of all the ways he'd imagined that this evening would end, he hadn't considered the possibility that Lucy would throw all her cautions and reserves to the wind and make love to him. He'd fantasized about it, but he never believed it could possibly happen. Just last night she'd locked her door tightly against him. He knew she'd locked it—he'd tried the knob.

So what had happened between then and now? What had happened between now and just a few hours ago, when Lucy had maintained that they stay friends instead of lovers?

Lucy slid her panties down her legs and moved up the steps to the top edge of the hot tub. She paused for a moment, looking down at him, boldly meeting his eyes. "You seem to have run out of things to say," she said.

She slid down, letting the water slowly cover her body. She sat, a full half circle away from him. Closing her eyes, she let her head fall back against the side of the tub.

"I'm just trying to figure out when I died and went to heaven," Blue said.

Lucy opened her eyes. "You're not in heaven, McCoy—at least not yet."

Blue had to laugh. This was just too much. He couldn't have written a better script for a sexual fantasy himself. "Lucy, I'm confused as hell," he admitted. "What's going on here?"

"I decided I'd come home and seduce you." Her eyes suddenly looked uncertain, vulnerable. Her voice got very soft. "Am I doing it wrong?"

"Oh, no," Blue said quickly. "No, you're doing it perfectly. I just don't understand *why* you're doing it."

"I was suspended from the police force," she said in that same low voice. "For sexual misconduct."

"But—"

"I had no real hearing and no chance to challenge the charges," she said, her voice growing stronger. There was a spark of anger in her eyes. "Bradley removed me from the investigation and gave me a one-week suspension, disguised as a vacation. I argued—he fired me—I quit."

Blue swore. "This is my fault."

"You didn't do anything wrong," Lucy said. "And I didn't, either. But I figured as long as I've been tried, convicted and I'm serving sentence for breaking a rule I didn't break, well, hell, I might as well break that rule, right?"

Blue didn't know what to do, what to say. She wasn't here because she honestly wanted to be. She was here in some kind of knee-jerk reaction to her altercation with Chief Bradley.

With any other woman, Blue wouldn't have hesitated. With any other woman, he would have already been on the other side of the hot tub, performing a seduction of his own. She'd taken it this far; he could easily see it through to its climax, so to speak.

But... Lucy was his friend. She had been right earlier today. Something had developed between them that could only be called friendship. And as much as Blue wanted her, he didn't want her this way.

So he kept his distance and waited for her to answer her own question.

"But this really isn't me," she finally said. "I mean, I don't...do things like this. I've never tried to seduce someone before...."

"Yankee, I do believe you're a natural," Blue said with a slow smile.

Lucy laughed, covering her face with her hands. "I'm feeling pretty stupid."

"Don't be," he said. "I'm in serious pain."

"Then why are you sitting way over there?"

Her soft question made the bathroom seem suddenly very, *very* quiet. Blue could hear his watch ticking from underneath the pile of clean clothes he'd brought into the room. He moistened his dry lips. Damn, he couldn't remember ever being this nervous with a woman before. "Do you want me to sit next to you?" he asked.

Her eyes were wide and a bottomless shade of brown as she gazed at him. "I don't know what I want," she admitted.

Blue took a deep breath, trying to slow his raging pulse, trying to lower his soaring blood pressure. "When *you* know," he said, "then you let *me* know."

She was silent, just staring at him. "I can't believe you're turning me down," she said at last.

"I'm not turning you down, because you haven't made me a real offer," Blue said quietly. "You make me an offer, Lucy, and I assure you, I will not turn you down."

There was wonder in her eyes, wonder and the sheen of tears. "You told me you weren't a gentleman," she said.

"I'm not."

Which was why he had to get out of there. Right now. Blue stood, water sheeting off him. He climbed up the stairs and out of the tub, trying not to limp. He could feel Lucy's eyes on him, skimming over his nakedness, and he wrapped his towel around his waist. She couldn't have missed his state of arousal. Even though he'd tried his best to calm his raging libido, he could have sat in the tub forever and still it wouldn't have completely gone away.

"What do you say we go downstairs and I cook us both some dinner?" Blue said. He didn't wait for her to say no. "Throw some clothes on and meet me in the kitchen."

It was nearly ten o'clock before dinner was over.

Lucy had gone into the kitchen with some trepidation, but Blue did or said nothing to remind her how foolishly she'd behaved up in the bathroom.

He made her set the table and then sit and do nothing but watch as he cooked up a fragrant pot of spaghetti sauce and pasta.

As he cooked, and then as they ate, he told her the story of how his friend and swim buddy, Joe Cat, had met his wife, Veronica. She was a seemingly prim-and-proper media consultant who worked for European royalty. He was a rough, tough Navy SEAL from a bad part of New Jersey. According to Blue, it was love at first sight—only, both Joe Cat and Veronica stubbornly refused to acknowledge it.

"Do you really believe in love at first sight?" Lucy asked Blue as he began washing up the dishes.

"Yeah," he admitted. "I know it sounds corny, but, yeah, I do. I saw it happen with Cat. Something just grabbed him and wouldn't let go. It scared the hell out of me. One day everything was normal, and the next Cat was totally out of control."

Lucy was silent. She understood. She was falling in love with Blue, and it was way, way beyond her control.

"Cat and Veronica both tried to run away from what they felt," Blue said in his slow Southern drawl. "But you can't run away from something that's inside you. I saw that first-hand. Cat was miserable without Veronica."

And Lucy would be miserable without Blue. But why force herself to be miserable *with* him, too? She *could* have him—even if only for a few days, even if only on a physical level.

She knew Blue wanted their relationship to be a sexual one. Even though he'd gallantly turned her down up in the hot tub, he'd made that more than clear. She could have his body. All she had to do was ask. It was more than nothing, and it would have to be enough.

Why should she refuse herself even just an hour or two of happiness and pleasure? Yes, Blue was going to leave. No, Blue wasn't in love with her. Yes, she'd probably be just a substitute for Jenny Lee Beaumont. But Lucy didn't have to think about that. She didn't have to make herself miserable. She had the entire rest of her life to do that. She deserved at least a day or two of happiness now, even if it was only false happiness.

But how was Lucy supposed to tell him that she finally knew what she wanted—that she wanted to make love to him?

Another seduction attempt? The thought made her squirm.

Make me an offer, he'd said. That kind of offer seemed so unromantic, so calculated and cold.

Maybe instead of an offer, she could issue an invitation.

Lucy stood. "I'm going to head upstairs," she said. "Unless you want me to help clean up?"

Blue glanced at her over his shoulder and then at his watch. It was still early, and he was clearly disappointed that she was leaving. "No, that's all right," he said. "I'm almost done down here."

"Good night, then," she said, and started out of the room.

"Lucy."

Lock your door. He didn't have to say it aloud. "I know," she said. Heading up the stairs, she smiled.

Blue tried calling California from the telephone in the kitchen as he finished up the dishes. Yes, Lieutenant Joe Catalanotto was still out on a training mission. Yes, Admiral Mac Forrest was still not available.

He hung up the phone, fighting a feeling of dread.

Lucy was no longer in charge of Gerry's murder investigation. Travis Southeby was. Blue figured it was only a matter of days, maybe even hours, before Southeby found what he felt was enough evidence to lock Blue up. Tomorrow Blue very well might be in jail.

And today Blue had had heaven in his hands, and like a damn fool, he'd let it slip away.

It was still early—before midnight, anyway—and he was feeling way too restless to sleep. His leg hurt too badly to go for a run, but a walk might do him good.

He headed upstairs to get his gun and...

The door to Lucy's room was unlocked and open a crack.

Her room was dark inside, but the door had definitely been left open.

Dammit, he wasn't strong enough for this. He'd turned her down once tonight, but there was no way he could handle twice. He knocked loudly on her door. "Hey," he said crossly. "Yankee. You forgot to lock up."

"No, I didn't." Her voice was soft, but very certain.

The meaning of her words crashed down around him, and Blue had to hold on to the door frame for a moment to keep his balance. She'd left the door open. Intentionally.

"May I . . . come in?" he asked.

He heard her husky laugh. "How many invitations do you want, McCoy?"

Blue pushed open the door. The dim light from the hallway spilled all the way across Lucy's room, falling onto her bed. She was sitting there, wearing an old extra large T-shirt and a pair of panties and quite probably nothing else.

Her hair was down around her shoulders and she had no makeup on her face. She looked clean and fresh, and as she smiled hesitantly at him, he couldn't believe how utterly beautiful she was.

She held out her arms, shrugging slightly, her smile turning almost apologetic. "This is me," she said, laughing self-consciously. "What you see right now is really me. No negligee. No borrowed little black dress or spike heels. No fancy hairdo. No hot-tub seduction. Just an old University of South Carolina T-shirt and a pair of cotton underpants. White. No frills. Just like me. If you decide to . . . accept my . . . invitation, this is what you get."

Blue knew instantly that this was what he'd been waiting for. She had no police badge to hide behind, no hesitation, no more doubts. She'd worked their relationship down to the simplest equation: she wanted him and he wanted her.

And oh, how he wanted her. He'd had his share of women wearing fancy negligees and seductive clothing, but none of them looked even half as sexy as Lucy Tait did in an old university T-shirt with her hair tumbling down her back, her face clean of makeup. No frills, she'd said. Maybe not. Maybe just one hundred percent pure woman.

Blue sat down on the bed next to Lucy and gave her his answer in a kiss. Despite all the fire surging through his veins it was a sweet kiss—the sweetest he'd ever known. He felt her fingers on his chest, unfastening the buttons of his shirt and he put his hand over hers, stopping her, slowing her down.

"We've got all night," he whispered, pulling back to look at her.

He closed his eyes as she ran her fingers through his hair. It felt sinfully, deliciously, good.

"Then you won't mind if I just sit here and do this for about an hour," Lucy said.

"Not as long as I can kiss you, Yankee," Blue murmured, pressing his lips to hers.

He pulled her back with him onto the bed, and their legs intertwined, and still he kissed her. He gave her long, slow, deep kiss after long, slow, deep kiss, until her breath grew short, her hands gripped him tighter and her body strained against his.

Deftly, he removed her T-shirt, pulling it up and over her head in one quick motion. And then all of her smooth, sleek skin was his to touch, to caress, to kiss.

Lucy was delirious. She'd known that making love with Blue was going to be an extraordinary experience, but she'd never imagined that his hands could be so gentle. She'd never dreamed that he could kiss her so slowly, so completely.

She'd imagined a frantic, urgent joining, not this languorous, sensuous worship of her body. She clung to him as he brought his lips down first to one breast and then the other, laving her tender nipples with his tongue, drawing them slowly into his mouth.

She tugged at his shirt and he slipped it off, tossing it onto the floor along with his shoulder holster. As she ran her fingers across the satiny skin of his back, careful of the bandage on his arm, his mouth journeyed downward, to her stomach, stopping to explore the softness of her belly button.

Heat pooled through her, sending liquid fire through her veins. Her love for this man seemed such a tangible thing that Lucy was almost certain he could see it.

"You're so beautiful," he whispered, meeting her gaze and smiling as he slid her panties down her legs. The heat in his eyes was more than lust. It was more powerful, more pure—almost transcendental, making the blue of his eyes seem luminous and soft.

For the first time in her life, Lucy felt cherished.

She knew it couldn't possibly be so. In reality, Blue didn't love her. He would never love her. But she fought that reality, allowing herself the complete illusion tonight. Tonight, she would be cherished.

He kissed the inside of her knee, parting her legs as he slowly moved his mouth down toward the sensitive skin of her thigh. And farther. Lucy gripped the bed as he touched her, kissed her, first gently, then harder, deeper.

The sensation was beyond pleasure, beyond ecstasy, beyond anything she had ever felt or known before. And that, in tandem with her love for this man, catapulted her up and over the edge.

She heard herself cry out as he held her tighter, as a sudden and unexpected release cannonballed through her, seeming to rip her apart with wave upon wave upon unending wave of sheer, excruciatingly wild pleasure.

Finally, *finally,* it came to an end. She reached for Blue, pulling him up and across her. He was laughing, real delight in his eyes.

"Hoo-yah," he said.

"Oh, man," Lucy gasped.

"Do you do that all the time, Yankee?" he asked, smoothing her hair back from her face.

"No," she breathed. "Never. Not like that."

His smile grew broader, satisfied. "Good."

He kissed her, slowly, tenderly, but that wasn't what she wanted. She deepened their kiss and reached for his belt, unbuckling it.

"Mercy." Blue pulled back, laughing again. "You want *more?*"

"Yes." Lucy unzipped his pants, tracing his length with her fingers. There was so much of him. She ached to feel him inside her. "Please." She reached down into his shorts, touching him, encircling him with her hand as she kissed him fiercely.

She heard him groan, felt him pull away as he pushed and kicked his pants from his legs. She tried to help, but she suspected she only made the process more difficult. Still, she wanted to touch him, to run her hands along the lengths of his long, muscular legs—

Oh, shoot, she'd forgotten all about his injured leg. She pulled back. "Oh, Blue, have I hurt you?"

He just laughed at that, catching her mouth with his and kissing her, hard. She felt herself melt against him, opening herself to him in every possible way. She reached down to touch him again and found he'd already ensheathed himself with a condom he must have taken from his pocket.

He kissed her again, a kiss of fire and passion, and she felt something shift, as if the powerful kick of their rocket fuel–powered attraction was ready now to ignite. She knew instantly that this phase of their lovemaking would be neither slow nor languorous.

Blue felt Lucy arch her hips up toward him, seeking him, and he felt the first tier of his ragged control start to crack. He needed to feel her surrounding him. Now.

He plunged into her, hard and fast…and mercy! He had to slow down, take care. He didn't want to hurt her.

Yet she was anything but hurt. "Yes," she was murmuring into his ear, "yes," pulling him closer, meeting each of his thrusts with a dizzying passion.

This was too good. No one should ever be allowed to feel this good. The thought made him laugh aloud and he kissed Lucy again, spinning with the joy and exhilaration of knowing he was exactly, precisely, where he wanted to be.

He rolled over onto his back, pulling her with him so she sat straddling him. She flicked her hair back out of her eyes, moving hard and fast, the way he liked it. She grinned down at him, her eyes sparkling and dancing with sheer pleasure, and more of his precious control crumbled.

He reached for her, his hands covering her breasts, and she arched her body, pressing herself more fully into his palms. She threw her head back, her smile fading, and Blue felt her body tense and tighten. She cried out his name, her voiced ecstasy music to his ears. Her release was as powerful as before, only this time she took him with her.

Never before had his pleasure been so perfect. Never before had the rush of his passionate explosion sent him soaring quite so high, quite so far. Never before had he wanted to take a moment in time and freeze it for all eternity.

But it wasn't the moment of mind-blowing, raw sexual pleasure that he'd freeze. It was this moment afterward, as he held Lucy tightly against him, his face buried in her hair, their two hearts still beating wildly as they drifted slowly back to earth. This was the moment he wanted to save and keep forever. Because never before had he felt such peace, such completeness.

His chest ached and his eyes burned, and he wanted to speak, wanted to tell her something, but he didn't know what to say. He didn't know what words he could use that could possibly describe this feeling. So he kissed her, instead, sweetly, gently, hoping she'd understand.

Chapter 11

Blue woke up several hours after dawn. He stretched and yawned, feeling oddly rested. He hadn't slept this well in a long time and...

He opened his eyes.

He was in Lucy's bed. She was lying next to him, still sleeping peacefully, the sheets tangled around her.

Memories of last night came roaring back to him in a rush, and for a moment he could barely breathe, barely think. The things they'd done, the things he'd felt...

Mercy.

But the sun had crept up above the tree line, and it was shining in Lucy's windows. The night had ended and it was morning.

Morning. The time of regrets and recriminations. The time of awkward silences and uncomfortable conversations. Like some broken spell, the magic of the night before always shriveled and died in the morning light.

A night of sex was understood by all to be nothing more than a good time. But when breakfast was added to the equation, that night of sex became something else entirely. It became a relationship. It became a possibility, an expectation, a future commitment. Blue had long since learned to clear out of a lady's bedroom well before dawn.

This time he hadn't. This time the spell he'd been under had held him in its power and he'd slept the dreamless sleep of the enchanted. But now he eased himself up and off the bed. There was still time to make his escape.

Lucy remained asleep. But as he looked at her lying there, his eyes followed the exposed curve of her derriere, the gentle swell of her breast as she lay on her stomach, her arms tucked up underneath the pillow. He felt an unexpected surge of desire.

The few times he'd stayed with a woman until the morning, he'd awoken with his lust abated, his sexual attraction fading fast. Aided by the harsh morning light, his lover's slept-in and smudged makeup, disheveled hair and usually bloodshot eyes left him wanting nothing more than to leave, and leave quickly.

But Lucy looked like some kind of angel in the early-morning light. Her skin seemed to glow, it was so smooth and perfect. He wanted to reach out and touch her. He wanted to feel her softness beneath his fingers again. Her hair was messed, but on her it looked sexy. And her face...

She was impossibly beautiful. Her lashes were long and dark and they lay against cheeks that had been kissed by the sun. Her mouth was open very slightly, and her lips looked so moist....

Lucy stirred slightly and Blue ran, noiselessly leaving her room before her eyes opened. He ran because he'd always run away before.

"'Morning," Blue said, clearly ill at ease, not quite meeting Lucy's eyes as he opened the refrigerator and took out the pitcher of orange juice.

Lucy had been down in the kitchen for nearly an hour before he'd appeared. As she watched, he helped himself to a glass from the cabinet and poured the juice, still not looking at her.

The last of Lucy's hopes shattered into a million tiny pieces.

She was a fool. She knew when she'd awakened to see Blue making his clandestine escape from her room that he was most likely regretting their lovemaking. Of course, he might have been leaving to replenish his supply of condoms. But when he didn't return even after she'd stepped out of the shower, even after she'd taken her time getting dressed, even after she'd opened her door and stood staring down the stairs at the quite obviously closed door to his room, she knew.

Still, she'd hoped that he wasn't having true regrets. Maybe he was having only mild doubts, second thoughts. But looking at him standing there in her kitchen, poised as if ready to turn and run, she knew for sure.

For him, last night had been nothing but a big, fat, giant mistake. She was a fool for hoping he'd feel otherwise. She was a fool for hoping that somehow, someway, he'd fall in love with her. A very small, *very* foolish part of her had actually dreamed that Blue McCoy would make love to her—to no-frills, white-cotton Lucy Tait—and the earth would shake and the skies would open and he would realize that she was his life, his future, his reason for living.

Oh, yeah, she was a fool.

But at least she was a sensible fool. Her fantasies crushed and useless, she swept them away, out of sight, at least for now. She'd have plenty of time to feel badly later.

"Do you want breakfast?" she asked, her voice remarkably even as she busied herself with washing up her own breakfast dishes.

"I'll just fix myself some toast."

"That's good," she said. "You can bring it with you."

She could feel his surprise, even though her back was to him.

"We going someplace?"

Lucy wrung out the dish sponge and set it on the edge of the sink before she turned to face him. "I called Jenny Lee and asked if she would mind if we stopped by. She said yes, we should come around nine-thirty, and that that would also be a convenient time for us to take a look at Gerry's home office and—"

"Wait a minute, you lost me somewhere back around bringing my toast along to Jenny Lee's. I don't understand. Why are we going to her place?"

Lucy turned and stared at him. He truly didn't understand. For the first time since he'd come downstairs, he was looking at her, really looking at her, instead of through her or over her or under her or around her.

"I thought you were taken off the investigation," Blue said. "You said you quit. You're not even on the police force anymore."

Lucy nodded. "That's right."

"You don't need to do this," he said.

She nodded again. "Yeah, I know. But I *want* to do this. We're the only ones who want to find out who really killed Gerry. Travis Southeby is going to mess around until he finds enough circumstantial evidence to haul you in. If we don't try to discover who might've had a motive for wanting Gerry dead, the real killer is going to run free while you go directly to jail." She shrugged. "I currently seem to be between jobs and I have some free time on my hands, so..."

Blue was silent. He'd looked away from her again, and was studying the wide antique boards of the kitchen floor.

"You don't intend to just roll over and die, do you?" Lucy asked.

He glanced up. "No, but—"

"Neither do I," she said, well aware that her words had a deeper, hidden meaning.

"Why do you want to help me?" His question was point-blank, and it came with no warning. He was watching her again, his eyes almost piercing in intensity.

Because I love you. But she couldn't tell him that. Not so long as a small portion of her pride was still intact. "Because I know you didn't kill Gerry," she said, instead. "Because right now you've got no one else. And because I'm your friend."

He was silent again, still watching her, and she knew exactly what he was thinking. He was thinking about last night, about how their lovemaking had permanently altered their so-called friendship. What they were to each other wasn't as simple as being friends anymore. But it was clear that Blue didn't want them to continue on as lovers, so where, exactly, did that leave them?

He so obviously wanted to pack his bag and walk away from her. But where would he go? What would he do?

Blue needed her right now, whether he knew it or not. Lucy believed that. She *had* to believe that. It was all she had left.

"I *am* your friend," she told him quietly. "Last night we were lovers, but today I'm your friend again, McCoy. I expect nothing from you. I didn't last night, and I certainly don't this morning—nothing, that is, but friendship. So you can stop tiptoeing around me as if I'm going to act all hurt and upset because last night wasn't the start of happily ever after. I know nothing has changed, except that now I know exactly where to touch you to really turn you on."

He laughed, his voice tinged with a mixture of disbelief and respect. "Hell, you're not afraid to get right to the heart of the matter, are you?"

Lucy raised her eyebrows, crossing her arms in front of her. "Was I supposed to pretend I didn't notice you having some kind of morning-after anxiety attack?"

"Well, I don't know. Yeah. Most women would...."

"I was just supposed to let you walk away because suddenly *you're* uncomfortable with the fact that last night we got naked and had sex—*great* sex, I might add." Lucy glared at him. "You honestly expected me to just throw away your friendship? Forget it, McCoy. I can deal with your thinking that I might overreact. It's probably been your poor, pathetic experience that 'most women' do. But thinking I would just ditch your friendship... *that* hurts."

"I'm sorry," he said, and he actually looked as if he was. "It's just... I've never slept with a... a friend before. This is a new one for me. I'm not sure what to say to you... or what to do."

"You could say, 'Good morning, Lucy. Gee, you really rocked my world last night,'" she told him. She took the loaf of bread from the bread box on the counter and tossed it to him with a touch more force than necessary. "And then you could make your damned toast so we could get to work finding out who killed Gerry."

Blue sat in Lucy's truck and watched her drive. Going to Jenny Lee's hadn't given them any more answers.

No, Gerry didn't seem to have any enemies. Yes, his behavior had been odd over the past several days, but Jenny had believed it was due to Blue's impending arrival. Business had been picking up for his construction company over the past year. Gerry had had a number of projects in development and several in progress. Money was coming in and going out on a regular basis. His staff were all steadily employed; in fact, he'd had to hire carpenters and construction workers from an employment agency for a recent job.

A search of Gerry's office had provided no additional information. Nothing was unusual about any of his current projects. His files were all in order, his desk free from any mention or warning of any threats. His date book had no appointments circled in red saying "lunch with killers."

Gerry had had a normal amount of business meetings listed in his date book. Lucy had gone painstakingly through all the different names, matching them to his current projects. Some of them were clients he was wooing. And some of them were social appointments. He'd had lunch with Jenny Lee frequently, and he'd also apparently recently joined the Hatboro Creek Men's Club, R. W. Fisher's invitation-only elite organization that took on community projects. According to Gerry's notes, they were currently raising money to repair the roof of the county hospital.

No, this trip to the house that Gerry had shared with Jenny Lee hadn't provided any answers. However, it had raised some new questions for Blue.

Such as, why exactly was Lucy Tait going to all this trouble for him? Why had she slept with him last night? What did she really want? If there was one thing Blue had learned in life, it was that most people had motives for every little thing they did. What was Lucy's motive here?

She'd said she was helping him out of friendship, that she'd slept with him because she'd wanted to, no strings attached. But Blue found that hard to believe. Of course, he was suspicious by nature. Since he was small he'd had only himself to rely on. Trusting other people meant risking pain, so he'd learned to trust no one.

But then he'd become a SEAL, and he'd literally had to put his life in his teammates' hands. He'd learned to trust the men in his squad and unit, and that trust had grown deep and strong, bonded by friendship and loyalty.

SEALs had no ulterior motives, at least not beyond unit integrity. Sure, they had career drives and personal goals, but in the heat of battle, in the midst of an operation, getting the job done and getting everyone out alive and in one piece became the single motivating force.

Lucy Tait wasn't a SEAL, but she said she was his friend.

He had to smile when he remembered her direct confrontation in the kitchen this morning. He had to hand it to her; she was tough. He himself would jump into a fistfight without a moment's hesitation, but if the battle was an emotional one, he'd do all that he could to beat a retreat. Lucy, instead, had attacked.

Blue was glad that she had. Even though they'd gotten nowhere with their investigation by talking to Jenny Lee, he was glad Lucy hadn't let him walk away, glad he was sitting here next to her in her truck.

He liked having Lucy for a friend. It was odd—she was a woman, yet she *was* his friend. Even odder was the fact that they'd had incredibly intense sex last night, and this morning Lucy, somehow, was *still* his friend.

Blue couldn't remember ever having had a sexual experience as powerful. She *had* rocked his world last night. So why the hell had he backed away this morning? Why had he allowed the night to end? Why hadn't he stayed in her bed? They could have been there still, up in her bedroom, making love all day long. He could have been holding her, kissing her, gazing into her beautiful eyes, commanding her complete and total attention as he told her stories of the operations he'd been on, the high-risk missions he'd completed.

Why had he backed away?

Because he always backed away. He hadn't even considered the possibility of sticking around, of turning their one-night stand into a longer affair. He hadn't known that Lucy could still be his friend after becoming his lover. He simply hadn't known.

But could they honestly be friends during the day and lovers at night? Could that really work?

Something about it didn't sit right with him. Now that he'd had time to think about it, he felt as if he were taking advantage of her. It seemed as if he were using her. And he wouldn't—couldn't—do that to a friend.

It would probably be best if they kept sex out of their friendship. It wouldn't be easy, not with the memories of last night crashing into him every time he looked in Lucy's direction. No, it wouldn't be easy, but it would be the right thing to do.

Maybe Lucy was telling the truth and she was helping him find Gerry's killer purely out of friendship. If that was so, the least he could do was treat her with an equal respect.

Blue watched Lucy as she drove. She handled her big truck with the same air of calm confidence that she handled damn near everything. She wasn't wearing her uniform—she couldn't now that she'd resigned from the police force. Instead, she had on her worn-out blue jeans and cowboy boots and a plain T-shirt—white, cotton, no frills. Damn, but she looked good.

She glanced over, as if she felt him watching her. "What do you say we go over and talk to Matt Parker before lunch?"

Matt Parker. The "witness" who had "seen" Blue arguing with Gerry in the woods off Gate's Hill Road moments before Gerry's death. He had also been one of the joyriding dirt bikers who had obscured the tire tracks Blue had found. Blue nodded and smiled tightly. He definitely wanted to have a little talk with Parker. "Yeah."

Lucy looked at him again, concern darkening her eyes. "Just a talk, McCoy," she said. "Do you understand what I'm saying?"

He met her gaze evenly. "He's not going to tell us anything new unless we use a new approach. Like scaring the devil out of him."

"And if he turns around and calls Chief Bradley with an assault complaint, there's nothing I could do to keep you out of jail," Lucy countered. "And you know as well as I do that Travis Southeby is itching for a reason to lock you up."

Lucy could see real frustration in Blue's eyes.

"Why bother talking to Parker at all?" he asked.

"Because somebody is paying him to say what he's saying," she said, "and I'm betting no matter how much money he's making, he's feeling lousy about having to lie. I'm betting he won't be able to look you in the eye, because deep down he's probably a decent man, and he knows his story is a solid part of the case they're building against you."

"And you think he's going to take one look at me and confess?" Blue's voice dripped with skepticism.

"No," Lucy said calmly. "I think we're going to go over there, and he's going to stick to his story, and we're going to leave. And then he's not going to be able to sleep tonight, because he's going to be thinking about his words sending an innocent man to prison."

Blue laughed. "Get real, Pollyanna," he said. "He's gonna spend the evening counting his blood money and drinking himself into a stupor. The fate of my sorry ass won't even drift across his soggy mind."

"He may not even let us in the door," Lucy admitted. "But we have to try." She pulled her truck to a stop outside the Parkers' little bungalow. "After lunch, I want to go up to Gate's Hill Road and start canvassing the neighborhood. Somebody had to see or hear something unusual that night."

"And if nobody did?"

She met his gaze evenly. "Then we're going to check motor-vehicle registration records, find a list of all the owners of trucks with oversized tires. We'll go check 'em all out, find out whose tires still have new treads. And if *that* doesn't give us a lead, we'll get a copy of the guest list for that country-club party and go and talk to every single person on it. I still want to find out if Gerry was only pretending to be drunk at the party. Someone somewhere knows something."

Blue's face softened as he smiled at her. "You're not going to give up on this, are you, Yankee?"

Lucy shook her head. "No." He should know that she wasn't going to give up on this case—or on him. If she could endure that visit with Jenny Lee Beaumont, she could handle just about anything. Shoot, watching Blue put his arms around Jenny in a comforting embrace had been deadly. And sitting there like that in Jenny Lee's picture-perfect living room had been awkward—Blue together with both his high-school sweetheart and his lover from last night. Of course, Jenny probably hadn't known that Lucy and Blue were lovers. But Lucy had, and it was weird.

Lucy had expended a great deal of energy trying *not* to watch for signs of Blue's old chemistry with Jenny. Still, she couldn't help but wonder if Blue had closed his eyes and pictured himself making love to Jenny Lee last night. Lucy had had temporary possession of Blue's body, but Jenny probably still owned Blue's heart.

Lucy would have given just about anything to have even a short-term lease on Blue's heart. But that wasn't going to happen. He'd made *that* more than clear this morning.

The silence in the truck dragged on much longer than it should have as Lucy lost herself in the hot depths of Blue's eyes. He still wanted her. She could see desire swirling in among the blue. She could see it in the set of his jaw, in the tension in his lips. What had transpired between them last night hadn't been enough. He wanted more.

But he turned away, clearly intent on denying himself even the warm pleasure of the memory of their lovemaking. Was it seeing Jenny Lee again? Lucy wondered. Could Blue's former girlfriend still have that much power over him? Lucy's stomach hurt. She'd told Blue just this morning that she was his friend. But she was his lover now, too. She knew that if he came to her room again tonight, she wouldn't be able to refuse him anything he wanted or needed. She loved him that much.

But what about what Lucy needed?

Blue looked out the windshield at Matt Parker's house and took a deep breath. "Let's get this over with."

Chapter 12

They were in luck. Little Tommy Parker answered the door and let them in the house.

Lucy knew from the look in Matt Parker's eyes that he wouldn't even have opened the screen door to talk to them. But now they were here, in his tiny living room.

She looked around. The furniture was shabby, but clean. In fact, the entire house looked well kept. The ancient orange shag carpeting had been recently vacuumed and the surfaces of the end tables were clear and free from dust and clutter.

She could hear the sounds of Sunday dinner being cooked down the short hallway that led to the kitchen. Utensils banged against pots, and dishes clattered as a table was set. The fragrant smell of onions frying drifted out into the living room.

Blue went farther into the room and turned off the TV that was on.

"Travis told me *he* was handling this case now." Parker's eyes shifted from Lucy to Blue and then back. He was clearly remembering the fight outside the gas station. His nose was still swollen, and he touched it gingerly. "McCoy is not welcome in my house."

"We just want to ask you some questions," Lucy said soothingly. "You don't have a reason to want to hide the truth from us, do you, Matt?"

His eyes flicked back to Blue. "Of course not." He shifted slightly in his seat in a well-worn reclining chair. "But I answered all these questions already. My statement is down at the police station. Why don't you just get a copy of that, instead of bugging me again?"

"Well, we do have a copy of your statement," Lucy said, carefully keeping her voice reasonable and calm. "However, it raised an additional question or two, because Blue wasn't anywhere near Gate's Hill Road at the time you allegedly saw him there with Gerry."

Parker stood up. "Are you saying I'm a liar?"

"No, sir." Lucy gazed steadily at him. "You're too smart to get yourself into a situation where you'd have to perjure yourself in a court of law. You know the punishment for that can be a hefty fine along with jail time." She shook her head. "No, you're just mistaken about exactly what you saw. You must've seen someone else—not Blue. I'd like you to spend some time tonight thinking about it, because it would sure be a shame if your testimony sent an innocent man to prison, wouldn't it?"

She turned, heading back toward the door, and from the corner of her eyes she saw a shadow in the hallway, near the kitchen. It was Matt's wife, Darlene, but she disappeared before Lucy could even say hello.

"Let me know if you think of anything new," Lucy told Parker. She opened the front door and Blue followed her outside.

She could feel Parker—or maybe it was Darlene—watching them as they walked down the path to the street and her truck.

"You did okay," Blue told her as they got into her truck. "You said just enough to make the guilt stick—provided Parker has a conscience."

"Thanks." Lucy put the truck in gear and headed back toward the main road. "You did okay, too."

"I just stood there."

"Exactly." She glanced at him, unable to hide a smile. "You *didn't* slam him against the wall and threaten to tear his throat out. I know that's what you wanted to do."

His lips twitched upward into an answering smile. "I'm hurt and offended you could think such a thing, Yankee."

"Am I wrong?"

His smile became a grin. It transformed his face, making him look younger—and nearly paralyzingly handsome. "No, ma'am."

Lucy had to laugh. But when their eyes met, something sparked, something molten, something hot and liquid and filled with the trembling echoes of last night. As he'd done before, Blue was the first to look away.

Lucy turned her attention back to the road, trying not to care. Yet she couldn't help but feel disappointed. And she knew with a dreadful certainty exactly what she wanted, precisely what she needed.

She needed Blue McCoy by her side for the rest of her life.

Fat chance of *that* happening. But maybe if she played it right, she'd have Blue by her side again tonight. It was a pathetic substitute for what she really wanted, but it was all she could hope for.

Except Blue was still clearly uncomfortable with the hazy definition of their relationship. Were they friends, or were they lovers? He didn't seem to understand that they could be both. He didn't seem to realize that the best of lovers always were the best of friends, too.

If only she had enough time, she could set him straight. But time was not on her side.

Lucy glanced back at Blue, forcing a smile. "Come on, McCoy. Let's go knock on some doors up near Gate's Hill Road before lunch. Let's shake this town up. Maybe something of interest will fall out."

Dinner was over. The dishes had been cleaned up.

Lucy had gone out onto the porch to look up at the night

sky and get a breath of fresh air.

Blue knew he shouldn't follow her out there. He'd told himself at least a hundred times during dinner and probably a thousand times during the course of the day that sex could not be a regular part of his relationship with Lucy. He respected her too much to use her that way. Unfortunately, that didn't stop him from wanting her. And he did. He wanted her so badly it hurt. But he'd lived through pain before. He could do it again.

They'd talked about the investigation over dinner, going over and over the same facts again and again, trying to find whatever it was that they were missing, searching for some kind of lead.

They'd learned nothing from their endless knocking on doors and questioning the folks who lived near the spot where Gerry had died. They'd learned nothing from Jenny Lee, nothing from Matt Parker.

It was frustrating as hell.

Blue picked up the phone and tried calling the naval base in California again. But Alpha Squad was still off base and the officer from Internal Affairs was still taking all calls. Blue tried to squash the frustration that rose inside him. He needed some serious help, yet here he was, on his own.

Not entirely on his own—he had Lucy Tait on his side.

Wanting desperately to see her warm, familiar smile, Blue pushed open the door and stepped outside onto the porch. He was coming out here to say good-night to her. Only to say good-night.

She was sitting on the steps, looking at the stars. She glanced up when she heard the door and smiled. Blue felt simultaneously better and worse. Mercy, he wanted to make love to her again tonight.

But he couldn't let himself. It wouldn't be right.

He sat down dangerously close to her—on the steps instead of across the porch on the swing—even though he knew sparks were going to fly. But he was a demolitions expert. He was used to handling volatile substances. He could sit here, close enough to breathe in Lucy's clean, fresh scent, and he could still find the strength to stand up and walk away from her. He knew he could.

"Pleiades," she said, pointing up to the stars. "It's my favorite constellation. It's the—"

"That little tiny cluster of stars," Blue said. "I know the constellations."

Lucy looked at him. "Don't tell me SEALs are trained in astronomy."

"Intergalactic space navigation," he corrected her. "In case we need to run a rescue mission on some planet in the Andromeda galaxy."

She looked at him and laughed. He loved the sound of her laughter. He had to fight to keep from reaching out and pushing a strand of her hair back behind her ear.

"You know you say things like that so seriously I almost believe you," she told him.

"Alpha Squad *has* trained to fly the space shuttle," he said. "We haven't had the opportunity yet, but if the need arose, we'd be ready."

"You sound so casual about it," Lucy said, turning slightly on the stairs so that she was facing him. "As if hundreds, probably *thousands,* of hours of training are insignificant."

She'd changed from her jeans to a pair of cutoff shorts when they'd arrived home and Blue couldn't keep his eyes from traveling the long, smooth lengths of her legs. Just last night he'd run his hands and his mouth over every inch of those beautiful, sexy legs....

He forced himself to shrug, bringing his gaze back up to her face. "That particular training op was fun. Some of them aren't."

"Like what?"

He shrugged again. "Some of the guys really hate the submarine work. It's pretty claustrophobic stuff. Others turn green at the high-altitude parachute jumps. And most SEALs didn't have fun during the Arctic survival training."

"But those things didn't bother you."

"No." He smiled. "I could handle the physical training. My personal hell was trying to learn a different language. I busted my ass for that one."

Blue could see amusement shining in Lucy's eyes. "Are you serious?"

"I am now fluent in German," he continued. "And I can *parlez-vous* enough to get by in French and Arabic, but let me tell you it was a real uphill battle. I would've gladly taken a repeat session on Arctic survival, instead."

"Why did you have to learn a language, too?" Lucy asked. "I thought you said Joe Cat was the language specialist in your unit."

Blue shifted down several steps, leaning back on the porch with his elbows and stretching his legs out in front of him. He'd hoped his movement would get him away from the magnetic pull of Lucy's eyes, but now he was inches from the satiny skin of her thighs. He felt sweat trickle down the middle of his back.

"He is," he answered her. "But we all need to have at least one language besides English that we can speak fluently. It's important on an overseas mission *not* to look and sound like an American. That can be a real kiss of death. Part of SEAL Team Ten's counterterrorist training is learning how to insert into a country and blend in. Hide in plain sight." He sighed, shaking his head. "But I tell you, it was frustrating as hell watching Cat plow through language after language, sounding like a native after only a day or two of listening to the tapes. He was learning two different dialects of Russian while I was still stumbling over *'Guten Tag, wie geht es dir? Meine Nahme ist Fritz.'*"

"Your name is Fritz?" Lucy repeated, covering her mouth with her hand as she tried not to laugh.

"Fritz or Hans or Johann," Blue said, smiling back at her. "When I go on an overseas mission to someplace like Cairo or Kathmandu, I play a German because of my hair. I've even learned to speak English with a heavy Deutsch accent."

Lucy looked away from him and up at the stars again, trying to imagine the extent of the effort Blue had put in to become a SEAL. Clearly it wasn't all physical training. He had worked hard to get where he was. He'd truly wanted it badly enough.

The sound of insects scratching and buzzing and humming and rattling filled the night air. "You never fail to amaze me," Lucy finally said, so softly he had to lean forward to hear her.

"You're pretty amazing yourself, Yankee." Their gazes locked, and Blue felt himself drop into a wild free-fall of sexual energy that rivaled his most intense skydiving jumps. Except right now he wasn't wearing any kind of parachute. God only knows how he was going to land without hurting himself. Or Lucy.

"I'm not amazing. I'm a coward," she said, looking away from him. "You've gone so many different places and had so many adventures." She sighed. "You were right about Hatboro Creek. There are places that I'd rather be, but look at me. I ended up back here." She stood and gazed up at her big Victorian house, looming above them in the darkness. "Living here was my mother's dream, not mine."

"What's keeping you from selling and moving on?" Blue asked quietly.

Lucy held out her hand for him, and he hesitated only a moment before taking it and letting her pull him to his feet. But she let go of him almost immediately. He followed her in the soft moonlight around to the side of the house.

"I know exactly what I'm getting in Hatboro Creek," she said as they walked slowly into the backyard. "It's safe and secure—no risk. Like I told you, I'm a coward."

"Just because it's hard for you to throw away your mother's dreams," Blue said softly, "doesn't make you a coward."

Lucy turned and looked at him, the moonlight reflecting the surprise in her eyes. "Don't tell me. SEALs are trained in basic psychology."

"The psychology we learn isn't basic," he said with a smile. But then his smile faded and he gazed at her steadily, his eyes serious. "No, I'm talking from experience, Lucy. I stayed in Hatboro Creek as long as I did because it was *my* mother's dream."

Lucy's pace had slowed. She was watching him as they walked, waiting for him to tell her more. But now that he'd started this conversation, he wasn't sure that he could. He'd never talked to anyone about his mother, not even Joe Cat. But he wanted to make Lucy understand that she wasn't alone. It was the least he could do for a friend.

"My mother married Arthur McCoy because he was an honest and decent man. He wasn't necessarily a kind man, but she did the best she could in the time she had," Blue said. "See, she knew she had cancer—she knew she was dying. She married Arthur for me—so that I wouldn't be all alone in the world after she was gone."

Lucy was silent, just listening.

Blue took a deep breath and went on. "It was her dream that there would be someone in Hatboro Creek who would take care of me, someone who would love me and keep me safe. She wanted to know that I'd grow up here, in this little town, in a good home. She made me promise I'd stay until I finished school."

They'd walked all the way back to the end of the yard and up the trail through the woods to the back field where there was a small pond. The moon reflected almost perfectly on the glass-calm surface of the water. It was beautiful, but Lucy couldn't look away from Blue's face as he continued to talk.

"I made a promise, so I stayed." Blue's voice was softer now. "Even when it was clear that her dream wasn't going to come true—that Arthur McCoy had nothing to spare for me outside of a bed to sleep in and food to eat."

Lucy gazed at Blue in the moonlight. He was a man for whom talk did not come easily, and this was particularly difficult for him to talk about. As she looked in his eyes, she could see a distant reflection of the little boy he'd been, lost and alone. His basic needs had been taken care of, but he'd truly needed so much more. He still did.

Lucy knew at that moment that she loved Blue McCoy without any doubts, without any reservations. It had seemed so complicated last night and this morning, but it really wasn't. It was as simple as it could possibly be.

Her heart ached, and she had to wonder if anyone, *anyone,* had ever told this man that he or she loved him. She knew if she spoke the words that he would back away. She knew that he no longer wanted love, that he saw it as a burden, an unlucky twist of fate, a weight to be carried. And she knew that even if he were to change his mind, he wouldn't want her to be the one who loved him. He'd want someone perfect and feminine. Someone special and sweet . . . like Jenny Lee.

But he wasn't alone, and he wasn't unloved. Not as long as Lucy's heart was still beating.

"I always felt like there was something wrong with me," Blue told Lucy, "because here I was, living this dream of my mother's and hating every damn minute of it. It wasn't until I was older that I realized it was *her* dream, Yankee. Not mine. Sure, it would have been nice if it had all worked out, but it didn't, and that wasn't my fault."

Maybe that dream of Blue's mother had just taken a whole lot longer to work out than she'd anticipated. Because right now there *was* someone in Hatboro Creek—someone who would do her damnedest to take care of Blue and keep him safe. Someone who loved him. Someone named Lucy Tait.

But that, too, was something Lucy couldn't tell Blue. Her words would scare him away. Instead of telling him in words that she loved him, she would show him how she felt.

She reached out and took his hand, lacing her fingers through his.

But there was regret in his eyes as he looked down at her. "Lucy, I don't think—"

"Shh," she said, lifting herself slightly onto her toes to kiss him. His mouth was soft and warm and tasted like sweetened coffee. He groaned as she ran her tongue lightly across his lips and he pulled her into his arms, deepening the kiss.

Blue was spinning. One kiss, and he couldn't stop. One kiss, and he'd finally discovered the meaning of the word *impossible.* All his life he'd refused to acknowledge that anything could be undo-able. All his life *impossible* wasn't a word that was in his working vocabulary. Before this kiss, nothing was impossible. But now he knew he'd been mistaken. Staying away from Lucy, keeping the hot-burning sex, the uncontrollable *need,* out of their relationship was proving to be just that.

Her hands were up underneath the edge of his shirt, her fingers cool against his skin despite the heat of the night. Her touch left no doubt in his mind exactly what Lucy wanted. She wanted him. All of him. And she wanted him now.

And dear Lord, as much as he knew that he shouldn't, the truth was that he wanted her, too. He wanted her with a power that shook him to his very soul, a power that steamrollered over his resolve to keep sex out of their friendship, a power that neutralized his need to meet the impossible head-on and win.

Staying away from Lucy was going to be impossible, because as much as he wanted to do the right thing, he wanted even more to make love to her, to please her, to hear that incredible, sexy catch in her breath as he filled her. He wanted all that so much more.

He wanted to stop, but he didn't want to stop badly enough.

She was unfastening his shirt, and he helped her with the last button, then let it slide from his arms onto the grass. He unbuckled his shoulder holster as she pulled her T-shirt over her head. The moonlight glistened enticingly on her beautiful, smooth skin, on the curve of her breasts and the white lace of her bra. And then she was in his arms again and he was touching her.

Mercy! All day long he'd fought the urge to touch her. All day long he'd told himself Lucy couldn't possibly be as soft and as smooth and as delicious to touch and kiss and taste as he remembered. What they'd done last night had been damn good, but his imagination and raging libido had surely taken those memories and inflated them beyond reason.

He was wrong.

She was perfection.

And she was his.

"Let's go for a swim," she whispered, unbuckling his belt. Her eyes were shining a promise that took his breath away as she smiled at him. Blue knew without a doubt that she could have suggested that they go down into the darkest reaches of Hell and he would have gladly followed.

He kicked off his sandals and stripped off the rest of his clothes as Lucy did the same.

She was beautiful in the moonlight—so much so that his chest felt painfully tight at the sight of her. She started toward the water, but then stopped and turned to face him, as if she somehow knew that he wanted to take a moment to look at her. Her dark hair hung thick and shining around her shoulders—shoulders that were both strong and feminine at the same time. She was muscular and sleek, yet soft in all the right places. Her legs were long and well toned, leading up to slim hips and a flat stomach. The silvery light gleamed off her golden skin, casting enticing shadows, emphasizing the soft curve of her hips, the fullness of her breasts. Her nipples were taut with anticipation and need.

That need was echoed on her beautiful face. Her lips were moist and parted slightly and her usually dancing eyes were heavy-lidded and filled with a molten desire as she gazed back at him.

Lucy *hadn't* turned back to let him look at her, Blue realized suddenly, a jolt of new fire flooding through his veins. She'd turned back because *she* wanted to look at *him*.

Her gaze was almost as palpable as a caress as her eyes skimmed across his body. She boldly took her time when she reached the obvious evidence of his arousal. When she finally looked up again, she smiled into his eyes, a smile sweet and hot and filled with pleasure.

Then she turned, and a few short steps brought her to the edge of the pond. She did a surface dive out into the center, barely making a splash, then disappeared into the darkness of the water.

Blue followed more slowly, watching as she emerged on the other side of the small pond.

"Hell," he said as he stepped off the edge and found himself suddenly waist deep in icy water. "This water is *cold.*"

"There's some kind of underground cold spring feeding into this pond," Lucy said, drifting toward him. "It's great—normally around here a pond this size would become stagnant and turn into a swamp within a matter of months. But this thing has been around for years. I used to come out here and skinny-dip all the time back in high school."

"If only I'd known," Blue murmured, lowering himself so that the cool water went up to his chin. The cut on his arm stung for a moment, but only for a moment.

"I invited you out here for a swim once," Lucy said, treading water as she gazed at him. "I told you all about this pond. But you never showed."

He didn't remember.

"It was a really hot day, and you stopped to talk to me," Lucy said. "It was the only other time we actually spoke—besides that time you came to my rescue."

"You mean the time those damn fools broke your rib out on the baseball field."

"It was only cracked."

"Same difference."

"It was almost exactly a month after that happened," she said. "And it's not the same difference. It takes less time for a cracked rib to heal."

"I know. I've experienced both," Blue said. "Neither is any fun." He smiled at her. "Both times I thought about you, Yankee, while the doctor was taping me up."

Lucy splashed water in his direction. "You did not."

"God's truth," he said, dodging the water. "I honestly did. I thought what a tough kid you must've been to handle that kind of pain."

"You're just saying that to make up for not remembering the only other time we ever talked back in high school," Lucy teased to cover up her embarrassment. "Shoot, it was one of the highlights of my freshman year, and you don't have even the vaguest recollection."

Blue protested. "Remind me more about it," he said. "Maybe I'll remember."

"It was about a month after that fight. You and I nearly had a head-on collision in the hall outside the locker rooms," Lucy told him. "I was coming inside after a practice."

Blue felt his memory stirring. "And I just finished some long-distance run?"

"And it was about a million degrees out," Lucy said. "We were having some kind of weird heat wave."

"Yeah, that's right. It was October, right?" Blue said. He could see her, standing in the hallway of the school. She was wearing her baseball uniform, her knees all torn up from fielding ground balls, her hair falling out of a ponytail. Somehow he hadn't noticed her five-thousand-watt smile and her beautiful, sparkling eyes. He must have been blind, or a damned fool, or both. "But it was around ninety degrees, wasn't it? I do remember, Yankee. I was dying of heat."

"You were literally dripping with sweat."

"I was disgusting."

"You were sexy as hell."

She was sexy as hell right now, with the cool water barely covering the tops of her breasts. The first shock of the water had cooled Blue's overheated body down, but now he was getting used to the chilly temperature. And the thought of Lucy wrapping her long legs around his waist was creating quite a bit of new heat. Any minute now, this cold-water pond was going to start boiling.

"You were fifteen years old," he said. "You didn't even know what that word meant."

"Sexy?" Lucy's eyebrows went up. "Wanna make a bet, McCoy? One look at you and I was practically paralyzed."

He laughed again. "I thought you were just shy."

"Me? No way." She smiled at him. "No, I was just overdosing on a sudden release of hormones."

He could relate to that phenomenon, but it didn't make him paralyzed. She was still drifting in the water, about six feet away from Blue, but he meant to change that soon.

"I think I asked you how the baseball team was doing, right?" he inquired, moving in a big, lazy circle around her. He went briefly under the water and came back up, tossing his wet hair out of his face.

"You did." She turned in the water to keep facing him, paddling with her hands to stay afloat. "I told you we'd won our first six games, but that the team still had some personality problems to work through. I said that just that afternoon, the catcher and the center fielder got into a fistfight. You said that the unseasonable heat and humidity were making everyone more irritable."

Blue stopped swimming. "You really remember all that?"

Lucy smiled. "I wrote a word-for-word account in my journal," she confessed.

"That's when you told me about this pond of yours," Blue said. "You invited me over for a swim. I remember. It sounded really nice, and I told you maybe I'd drop by."

"But you didn't show. I was heartbroken."

Her voice was light and teasing, but Blue knew there had to be at least a touch of truth to her words.

"I was a fool, Lucy."

"I was way out of my league."

"You *were* a little young," Blue admitted. "I knew you maybe had a crush on me, but I didn't take it seriously. If I had—if I'd really looked at you..."

"You had Jenny Lee," Lucy said. "She was perfect. I was the poster model for bad-hair days."

"At least you weren't afraid to go swimming and get your hair wet," Blue said. "I swear, the entire time Jenny and I dated, she never went into the water."

"That's the problem with perfection," Lucy said wistfully. "Once you've got it, I imagine you spend a great deal of time worrying about losing it."

Blue knew that she was talking about more than just Jenny Lee Beaumont's hair. But as if she sensed him about to question her, she dove underneath the water. When she came back up, her hair was sleek against her head. She ran her hands back across it, pushing out most of the water.

Lucy met his eyes and smiled. "I used to see you down at the beach and over at the marina," she said. "I always wondered why Jenny wasn't with you. I didn't realize it was a hair thing." She shook her head and laughed. "God, if I had been your girlfriend, I would have followed you everywhere, including into the water."

If Lucy had been his girlfriend... Jenny Lee had given Blue an intense physical relationship, but she hadn't cared about him, not really. Lucy would have cared.

"It was more than a hair thing with Jenny Lee," Blue said. He started to swim in circles around her again. Each circle was tighter, bringing him closer to her. "If I had been smart, I would've had a cute Yankee freshman for my girlfriend."

"You had your chance," Lucy said. She started swimming in circles, too, at the same leisurely speed. At this pace, he'd never reach her. "I invited you out here for a swim. I had the perfect evening planned. You were the one who didn't show up."

"You quit too soon," Blue said. "What happened to that famous Yankee tenacity I always read about? You could've done something to get me to notice you."

Lucy snorted. "You wouldn't have noticed me even if I'd juggled chain saws. You wouldn't have been able to see me past Jenny Lee's big—"

Blue had to laugh at that. "Give me a break," he said. "I was eighteen years old, and Jenny just sort of hand-delivered herself to me. Did you know she asked me out first?"

Lucy silently shook her head.

He raked his wet hair back with one hand. "The first three times we went out, Jenny called me," Blue said. "Before I knew it, we were going steady." He laughed in disbelief. "I figured she really did love me, because all she ever wanted to do was come over to my house and hang out, just the two of us. We'd watch TV and you know...get real cozy on the couch. Truth was, there were more than two of us in that TV room. There was Jenny and there was me and there was Gerry—or at least the possibility that Gerry would appear. He came home from college a lot on the weekends. See, it turned out that Jenny was using me to get close to Gerry. Even back then, he was the one she wanted."

What was he doing, dissecting his relationship with Jenny Lee in front of Lucy? She didn't want to hear about this, so why was he telling her? He should be kissing her, not talking. All he seemed to do these days was talk.

But it was so easy to talk to Lucy. Blue never got the sense that she was listening with only half an ear. When she listened to him talk, she really paid attention. And she wasn't afraid of silence, like most people. Most people felt a need to fill in a pause in a conversation. Lucy seemed to understand that—at least for him—the pauses and silence added to what he was saying.

She was quiet now, just watching him. He wanted desperately to get back to where they'd been heading before he'd brought up the sobering subject of Jenny Lee.

Purposely, he made his voice light. "So tell me. This perfect evening you had planned for me that hot October night. What would've happened if I had shown?"

"You really want to know?"

"I certainly do," Blue said, smiling at her.

Lucy pushed herself backward in the water, treading with her arms and letting her legs float. Her toes broke the surface and she stared at them pensively.

"Well, you would've walked up here and found me already in the water, just like this," she said.

"Uh-huh."

"I would've smiled and waved and said, 'Come on in—the water is nice.'"

"And I would have."

"Nope." Lucy looked up at him and smiled, mischief lighting her eyes. "You would've said..." She mimicked his Southern drawl. "'Do you think your mama would mind if I went into the house and changed into my swimsuit?' And *I* would've said, 'You don't need a suit to swim in this pond, Blue McCoy. Don't worry—if you're shy, I'll close my eyes until you're in the water.'"

Blue laughed. "*Then* I would've gone in."

"Nope." Lucy bit her lower lip, barely able to keep from laughing. Her eyes were sparkling with amusement. "*Then* you would've stood there on the grass, deciding whether or not to be shy, and I would've said, 'I'm not wearing a suit, either. See?' and I would've done this."

Lucy had reached a shallow spot in the pond, and she now stood up, like a goddess rising from the deep, the moonlight glistening on her wet breasts, her nipples tightly peaked from the cold. The water didn't quite reach her belly button and she looked indescribably sexy as she smiled at him.

She laughed aloud at the look on his face. Her voice was musical in the night air.

"Sure, I was a little skinnier when I was fifteen," she told him, "but I can't imagine that you would've spent more than oh, five or ten more minutes up on shore, deciding whether or not to come into the water."

"Try five seconds," Blue said, starting toward her.

"After successfully enticing you into the pond," Lucy said, backing away from him, her eyes dancing with laughter, "I would've suddenly disappeared beneath the water. You would have stood there, wondering where I went—until suddenly I appeared."

Blue reached for her, but she deftly moved away, vanishing, just as she'd described, underneath the water. Only a small ripple or two marred the surface of the pond before it once again became still. He watched for any sign of bubbles, waited for any movement. But all he could see was the moon's silvery reflection. All he could hear was the sound of the crickets and his own breathing.

And then the water swirled around him, and Lucy was there beneath the water, swimming around his legs, touching him. She erupted, up and out of the water, sliding against him as she roped her arms around his neck and kissed him.

The sensation of her sleek, naked body suddenly pressed against his was unbearably perfect. He heard himself cry out at the pure, gut-wrenching pleasure of her kisses, and he swept his hands across her wet skin, unable to get enough of her, wanting more.

She pulled back, catching her breath and laughing.

"No way would you have done that back when we were in high school," he said. His voice sounded hoarse in the still night air.

Lucy's eyes were brimming with laughter as she pushed her wet hair from her face. "Of course not," she said. "I was fifteen years old. Just because I knew what sexy meant didn't mean I had a clue what to do with you if I got you alone." She shook her head, closing her eyes in pleasure as he swept his hands again over her slick body. "No, my perfect evening with you would have been taking a swim—*with* bathing suits on. Then we would have headed back to the house and watched the baseball game on TV while we ate popcorn. I would have been in teenaged heaven."

She kissed him along the side of his jaw, pressing herself closer to him. "But I'm not fifteen anymore. And my definition of heaven has changed a little bit."

Blue's definition of heaven was right here in his arms.

He kissed Lucy hard and deep, and she locked her arms around his neck and her legs around his waist. She was ready for him—he could feel her smooth, slick heat as their bodies strained to become one.

But he pulled back at the same moment she did.

"Condom," she breathed, her eyes wide as she gazed at him.

"Yeah."

"Will it work in the water?"

"Oh, yeah."

He scrambled up to the grass, to where he'd thrown his shirt. He rummaged quickly through his pocket, and was back beside her in a matter of moments. And then she was in his arms once more and he kissed her yet again. She pulled him closer to her, opening herself to him, moving her hips and sending him thrusting deeply into her hot tightness.

The sensation was incredible. Lucy's wet body was his to touch, to mold around him. As her strong legs locked around his waist, he held her derriere, pressing her tightly against him as together they set a feverish, passionate, primitive rhythm.

She pushed her wet hair out of her face, then swept Blue's hair back, too. She ran her fingers through the wetness and pulled his mouth up to hers for a hard, fierce kiss.

Blue couldn't believe he'd spent all day trying to convince himself that this shouldn't happen again. He couldn't believe he'd actually thought he'd be able to turn Lucy down. He couldn't believe he'd climbed out of her bed this morning, thinking he should run or try to hide from her.

Without a doubt, he was going to be in her bed again tonight. And this time he was going to do his damnedest to never leave.

Never leave.

Never.

The words surrounded him, pressing down on his chest with more suffocating force than the water around him. Blue could barely breathe—he was drowning in emotion. Damn, but where had that crazy thought come from? And it *was* crazy. He was career navy. He was a SEAL. And SEALs left. That's what they did. They left. Always. There was always someplace new to go, something else to do.

He wasn't in love with this woman. He couldn't possibly be. He'd felt no lightning bolt. He'd had no vision, seen no special sign. Fireworks hadn't exploded overhead the first time he'd gazed into her eyes. The earth hadn't moved under his feet.

But, mercy, it sure as hell was moving now.

His strange thought about never leaving had to be some kind of reaction to this intense physical pleasure. He had found his perfect sexual match in Lucy Tait; that was for damn sure. He'd always liked sex—hell, that was an understatement—but it had never been even remotely like this before.

Never.

Blue felt Lucy's lithe body tighten against his, and he knew she was close to her release. He was right there with her, and all his thoughts fled.

"Oh, Blue."

She pulled back to gaze into his eyes, letting him see the power he held over her. He saw something else, too. Something warm and loving. Something more than the raw physical lust that bound them together.

He knew in that instant that he wanted to take her with him to a place she'd probably never been before. He wanted to make this single moment she was sharing with him one that she'd never forget.

"Breathe," he told her hoarsely. "Take a deep breath."

The faintest flash of confusion appeared in her eyes, and then she understood. She breathed, filling her lungs and holding the air in. And then Blue pulled her back with him, underneath the surface of the water.

It was dark and so utterly silent. Blue loved it down there, in that other world beneath the water. He couldn't get enough of the strangely quiet blueness, of the sense of peace that being underwater gave him. He'd clocked a lot of hours with his scuba gear, and never passed up an opportunity to dive. Still, he knew that many people felt claustrophobic and closed in underwater. He loosened his hold on Lucy, ready to let her go if she panicked and suddenly sought the surface. She wasn't afraid, though. She kissed him with an urgency he matched, air bubbling up around their faces.

With his hearing muffled and his vision reduced, Blue's remaining senses heightened. The taste of Lucy's mouth turned sweeter. And his tactile sense sharpened, the sensation of their rhythmic movement making him delirious from the sheer, pure, focused pleasure.

Blue pulled Lucy up with him, up to the surface of the water, up to the air, and together they gasped for breath as still their rhythm didn't slow, didn't stop.

"More," she gasped.

It was all he had to hear. He waited only for her to draw in another long, deep breath, and then he pulled her back down under the water again, and again the magical silence surrounded them.

Lucy's hair floated around them, moving slowly, lazily, a direct counterpoint to the wild movement of their bodies. Blue found her breast with his mouth, drawing her taut nipple in, sucking, pulling. He felt her grip him even tighter, felt the turbulence as the waves of her release began. Then, there in the silence beneath the water, Blue lost control. He was totally decimated. Every cell in his body exploded in a dizzying rush of exquisite pleasure so overwhelmingly pure, so incredibly sweet.

He drew in a breath in an attempt to steady himself—and got a cold lungful of water.

Blue pulled Lucy up to the surface with him, sputtering and coughing. But his footing was unsure and he slipped, dunking himself again. The water closed over his head, and he felt a flash of panic as his lungs burned and his chest heaved. He was desperate to expel the water he'd inhaled, desperate for air.

But Lucy was there, pulling him up and out. With her help, he crawled out of the water and collapsed, facedown, on the grass, coughing and retching as his body fought to clear his lungs.

Finally, *finally* he could breathe, but still it took several minutes longer before he could speak. He could feel Lucy, sitting patiently beside him, soothingly stroking his hair.

He lifted his head and glanced up at her, chagrined.

"Are you all right?" she asked.

Blue nodded. His throat burned and his eyes watered, but he was okay. "I'm embarrassed as hell." He could do little more than whisper in a raspy voice.

Her eyes were dancing with amusement and she was trying as hard as she could not to smile. "It's not every day I have to save a Navy SEAL from drowning."

"It's not every day I try to breathe H_2O. You'd have thought I would've learned *that* day one of basic training." Blue pushed himself up and slid back down into the pond. He cupped his hands and brought some of the cold, clean water up to his mouth, swishing it around before he spit it back out.

Lucy's smile slipped out as she watched him. "You were distracted."

Blue couldn't argue with that. She was still distracting as hell, sitting so casually on the grass, the moon bathing her naked body with its silvery light. But the real truth was that he'd lost control. Totally. Without question. For the first time in his life he had been out of control.

The emotional impact of that hit him square in the gut, and he had to look away from her. He'd been out of control. Hell, he was *still* out of control.

He heard her stand up and turned to see her gathering up her clothes. "Let's head inside," she said, "before I become one giant mosquito bite." She nudged his shoulder holster with one toe. "Come on, McCoy. Grab your stuff."

Come on, McCoy. She spoke to him casually, lightly—the way she'd speak to a friend, not a lover. And she didn't wait for him to come out of the water. She started walking back toward the house without him. Doubt churned inside Blue, and he wondered if maybe she hadn't had the same incredible depth of sensations—he didn't dare call them feelings—that *he'd* had when they made love. But he could have sworn he'd seen something besides friendship and desire in her eyes.

But maybe he'd been wrong.

Of course, he was the one who hadn't held her in his arms after they'd made love. He should have kissed her, stayed close to her as the calming afterglow of their lovemaking surrounded them. Instead he'd tried to breathe water, and their intimacy had ended far too abruptly.

He pulled himself out of the water, then gathered up his things and sprinted after Lucy.

She was walking through her backyard buck naked, and he had to smile at her matter-of-factness. It was clear that she'd gone skinny-dipping in her pond on more than one occasion. She was quite comfortable walking back to her house without her clothes on. And she had every right to be. The neighbors' houses were some distance away, and the trees and bushes around the edges gave the big yard additional privacy.

On a whim, he dropped his bundle of clothes as he caught up with her. He pulled her into his arms and spun her around in an inexperienced attempt at a dance move. He'd never done more than a slow rock-and-grind the times he'd danced with women in the various bars and roadhouses that Alpha Squad had visited. But despite his clumsiness, Lucy dropped her own clothes on the lawn, spinning around him with a fluid grace.

"So you do dance naked in your backyard," he said. "I knew it."

She laughed. God, he loved the sound of her laughter.

"Only in the company of *very* good friends."

Friends. There was that word again. And again it was accompanied by that nagging sense of doubt, and an unidentifiable but decidedly unpleasant feeling in the pit of his stomach.

He spun her back toward him and into his arms, holding her close as they moved slowly back and forth in time with the silent melody of the night. Unrestricted by clothing, Lucy's body swayed against his, her soft breasts touching his chest, her stomach brushing his arousal. And he was aroused. Again. Or maybe not again, maybe *still* aroused. Maybe he was going to be aroused for the rest of his life, regardless of how many times he made love to this woman.

Lucy was looking up at him, her eyes wide, her smile fading at the sudden intensity of the moment. She felt it, too—she *had* to feel it, too. Whatever this was, this almost palpable connection between them, this sensation of breathless, out-of-control wonder as he gazed into her eyes, she felt it, too.

Blue lowered his mouth and kissed her, a slow, soft kiss that made his eyes tear from its sweetness. When he spoke his voice was husky. "You gonna invite me in?"

"I thought I already did." Her voice shook slightly.

"You didn't invite me up to your room."

"My door is still unlocked."

"I didn't want to—"

Lucy finished for him. "Assume. I know. Never assume." She threaded her fingers through the hair at his nape, smiling up into his eyes. "Although I'm going to risk assuming that you'd like to go upstairs in the very near future..."

"*That* assumption is correct." Blue smiled. "Of course it's based on fact—"

"A hard fact," Lucy agreed, her grin making her cheeks dimple. "A *very* hard fact."

Blue kissed her again. This kiss was still as sweet, but it was laced with a searing fire. She pressed herself against him and he had to release her. If he didn't, he knew they'd never make it inside the house. He grabbed their clothes from the ground and tugged her toward the back porch.

It was crazy, insane. They'd just made love. They'd just had a sexual experience so intense that Blue had lost all sense of up and down.

But already he wanted her again. Right there in the backyard. Right on the lawn. Or on the porch. Right there on the porch. He pulled her to him, kissing her feverishly as she opened the screen door and pulled him inside. Or maybe on the kitchen table. That was as good a place as any. He threw down their clothes, freeing his hands to touch her, to fill his palms with her softness as he kissed her again. But she escaped, pulling him with her up the stairs and down the hall to her bedroom.

The intensity of his desire would have been frightening if not for the fact that she clearly felt it, too.

She clung to him, kissing him fiercely as he somehow managed to cover himself, to protect them both.

And then she pulled him back with her onto the colorful sheets of her bed, crying out with pleasure as he filled her.

Oh, *yeah.*

This thing that he felt, whatever it was, Blue knew she *had* to feel it, too.

Chapter 13

"Who's the man in the picture?"

Lucy was lying with her head on Blue's shoulder, tracing the hills and valleys of the well-developed muscles of his chest. His words didn't make sense—not until she lifted her head and looked into his eyes. Even then she wasn't sure what he was talking about.

"What picture?"

"The one on your dresser," he said, gesturing with his head toward the other side of the room. "There's a framed photo of you with a man."

"Edgar Winston." She realized which picture Blue was talking about and pushed herself up so that she could look at him more comfortably. She rested her head on one hand, supported by her elbow. "He was a friend of mine."

Blue looked away from her, across the dimly lit room toward the chest of drawers where the photo sat. He couldn't possibly have seen the picture's details from here. Lucy knew he must have noticed it at some other time. But the thought of him in here without her, looking at her things, didn't upset or offend her. In fact, her response was quite the opposite. It made her feel good, warm. Blue was curious about her. He wanted to know more.

"A friend," he said quietly. He turned back to her, gazing into her eyes. His were serious and very blue. "The way I'm your friend?"

Was it possible that Blue was jealous? Lucy's heart started beating a little harder. If he was jealous, then maybe he felt more for her than simple friendship.

"Are you talking about sex?" she asked. "Do you mean, like, did I sleep with him?"

He smiled, the laughter lines around his eyes crinkling. "You know, that's what I do love about you, Lucy. You just grab right hold of the point of a conversation and shake it by the neck. No tiptoeing around."

That's what I do love about you... In the context of Blue's sentence, it was only a figure of speech. Lucy ached for it to be true. If only he loved her. The way he'd made love to her tonight, both out at the pond and here in her bed, she could almost believe that he felt something for her. Something powerful and strong. Something a lot like love.

But that was just her own wishful thinking.

"Isn't that what you're trying to find out?" she asked Blue. "Whether or not sex was part of my relationship with Edgar?"

"Yeah," he said, laughing silently. "You're right. That's exactly what I'm trying to find out." He leaned forward, propping himself up on his elbows in order to kiss her. "I'm sorry, though. It's not my business. I shouldn't have asked. You don't have to tell me."

"Don't you want me to tell you?"

He knew she was teasing him and he grinned good-naturedly. "What I *want,*" he said, "is for you to tell me everything there is to know about this Edgar guy, starting with the fact that there's no chance at all he's going to show up here angry as hell, wielding a double-barrel shotgun and threatening to blow me to kingdom come."

"There's no chance of that," Lucy said quietly. "He's dead."

Blue closed his eyes, silently cursing himself out. Of all the insensitive things he could have said.... "Aw, Lucy, I'm sorry."

"You didn't know. How could you have known?"

"I'm still sorry," he said again.

She reached out, touching the side of his face. Her fingers were cool against his skin and she touched him so gently. "He was my business partner," Lucy said. "And, yes, our relationship was totally platonic. No sex. Even if he was still alive, he wouldn't have shown up waving a shotgun. He would've approved of you. He had a thing for well-built blondes himself."

Her words took a moment to sink in. "You mean, he was...?"

"Gay," Lucy said. "I met Edgar in college. Two days after we first met, it was as if we'd been best friends forever. We went into business together after we graduated. Computer software design. We had an office in Charleston and we made money like crazy."

"I didn't know you had your own business," Blue said, taking her hand and lacing their fingers together. Her hands were slender but strong, with long fingers and short nails.

She made a face at him. "What did you think I did between college and six months ago when I joined the Hatboro Creek police force?"

He shook his head. "I don't know. I guess..." He shrugged. "I didn't think about it. I just always pictured you here in town all that time. But you were living in the city."

"Actually, I moved back to Hatboro Creek about a year ago," Lucy told him. "Right after Edgar died...."

He rarely saw her when she wasn't smiling, Blue realized. Lucy was usually so upbeat, with a smile or a grin at least lurking, ready to break free. But now her eyes were filled with a quiet sadness that made him ache for her.

"I'm sorry," Blue murmured. "How did he...?"

"AIDS," she said flatly. "It was awful. He got so sick. I just watched him...disappear." Her voice broke and she had to look away from him. Blue didn't want to hear this.

But he did. He touched the side of her face, gently pushing her hair behind her ear. Lucy glanced up into eyes so warm and blue and sympathetic she felt her own eyes fill with tears.

"It's hard to watch someone you love die," he said softly. "It's hard to know what to say or do." He paused. "I have a friend—Frisco. Alan Francisco. He didn't die, but he's wheelchair-bound. I never know what to say to him anymore. I don't know how to treat him."

"You treat him exactly the same way you did before," Lucy said. With her free hand, she wiped the tears from her eyes.

"Even when he shuts me out?"

"Especially when he shuts you out," Lucy said. "When Edgar got depressed, I stayed with him. I moved into his condo. I wouldn't let him give in. Did you know that it's a scientific theory that laughter and humor increase the odds of survival among patients with terminal illnesses?"

Blue shook his head. "No, I didn't know that."

"I stayed with Edgar till the end," Lucy said quietly. "I was holding his hand when he died."

"You don't run away from anything, Yankee, do you?" Blue continued. He smiled slightly. "You should've been a SEAL."

She had to smile at that. "Yeah, right."

"What happened to your software business?" Blue asked.

"When Edgar got sick, it was at the point where it could run itself," she explained. "We hired some key people to do the work for us and booked ourselves passage on a cruise around the world, but it was already too late. By the time Edgar found out he had AIDS, it was too far along. I think he knew he was sick for quite a while. He just put off getting tested. So we never got to Egypt and Kathmandu. Instead, I held his hand as he fought off all sorts of viral infections and three different kinds of pneumonia. The pneumonia finally won."

She took a deep breath. Blue was still listening, so she went on. "After he was . . . gone, I went to the office for the first time in months. I wasn't there for more than thirty seconds before I knew that I couldn't go back. I didn't want to be there without Edgar. The woman I'd hired as acting president asked me not to sell, at least not right away. She was afraid one of the larger companies would buy us out and all the employees would be excessed. I didn't want that, but I knew I couldn't stick around. So I just kept things as they were."

"That's when you came back here, huh?"

Lucy nodded. "My mother left me this house when she died. Hatboro Creek seemed like the logical place to go. And then the job opened up on the police force...."

"Law enforcement is pretty different from computer software design," Blue said.

"That was the idea. I wanted to do something entirely different. And it *was*. You should've seen me learn to shoot. At the risk of bragging, I got a high percentage of bull's-eyes the first time I was on the firing range. I was good at it. I figured the rest of being a cop would come even easier. Boy, was I wrong."

Blue watched Lucy, realizing that this was the first time she'd ever really told him about herself. He'd done a great deal of talking over the past several days and she'd mostly listened. It honestly hadn't occurred to him that she had had a life beyond Hatboro Creek. But it suddenly made incredible sense.

He knew she was a rookie—that she'd been on the police force for only six months. He *hadn't* known that before that she'd lived and worked in the city. She'd owned her own successful computer business. She'd probably gone to meetings with clients, worn business suits, high heels....

Well, no probably not. Lucy probably had one of those laid-back, jeans-and-T-shirts kind of computer business. That was more her style. But either way, she'd definitely had a life beyond Hatboro Creek.

He was glad for her, and saddened for what she'd been through with her friend.

"Being a cop isn't that easy." Lucy forced herself to smile, trying to disguise the unhappiness in her eyes.

Blue pulled Lucy to him, hugging her tightly. He bet she'd smiled at her friend Edgar all those endless months as he'd died. He could picture her smiling for Edgar's sake, even though she was crying inside. She was a remarkable person.

As he held her close, as she buried her face in his neck, Blue suddenly felt his own heart beating. It was slow and steady and quite possibly stronger and louder than he'd ever felt it beating before. He felt a sense of calm, a state of peace, more powerful and complete than any he'd ever felt in his entire life.

And that was odd as hell, since he was currently the main suspect in the murder of his stepbrother. He should feel turmoil, anger, frustration and grief.

But all those chaotic feelings were pushed aside, dwarfed by a powerful sense of completeness.

He was in love with Lucy Tait.

The thought popped into his mind out of nowhere, and his first reaction was to dismiss it entirely out of hand. That was ridiculous. He couldn't be. Love didn't happen this way. Love hit fast and hard and devastatingly intensely, like a wildcat bringing down its prey.

These feelings he had for Lucy—whatever they were—had crept up on him while he wasn't paying attention. He had become slowly and steadily surrounded by this gentle warmth, this calm happiness.

He liked her. He really, *really* liked her. Maybe that was what this was.

But he really liked Joe Cat, too, and the thought of being apart from Cat didn't shake him the way the thought of leaving Lucy did.

It was more than the sex, though Lord knows he'd miss *that* less than five minutes after he left her. It was her smile, her laugh, her bluntness, her cheerful honesty that he'd really miss.

Lucy lifted her head and still tried to smile. "I'm finding out the hard way that I'm better at designing software," she told him. "The truth is, I was a lousy cop."

"No, you weren't."

She shook her head, covering his mouth with her hand. "You know I wasn't cut out for the job, so do me a favor and don't try to pretend that I was," Lucy said. "I prefer the truth, McCoy—no matter how difficult it may be. Don't ever lie just to be nice."

He pulled her hand away, lightly kissing her fingers first. "I wouldn't," Blue said. "Honesty is real important to me, too, Lucy. All my life I've seen people use other people." He was quiet for a moment, then he added, "Do you know that you're the first woman I've . . . been involved with . . . who hasn't had some ulterior motive for being with me?"

Lucy looked away, hoping Blue wouldn't be able to see the secrets she was hiding. Because she did have an ulterior motive. She was in love with him—and she wanted him to love her, too. That was one major ulterior motive. "You're exaggerating," she said. "You've got to be."

"I'm not."

"You're telling me that you know for a *fact* that every single one of *all* the women you've ever been—"

"There haven't been that many," he interrupted quietly.

"That's hard to believe."

"It's true."

"And not one of them was with you simply because they liked you?"

"None of them ever tried to get to know me." He paused. "Except for you."

His soft words made her cheeks heat with a flush. If only she didn't want more from him—more than an easygoing friendship spiced with hot sex. But she did want more. She wanted so much more.

"Even back in high school," Blue told her. "Even Jenny Lee. . . ." Something shifted in his eyes. It was almost imperceptible. Almost. "In some ways, she was the worst. It took me a long time to get over her using me the way she did. After that I started to expect it. Some women liked being with a man in a uniform. Others were after an officer—it didn't matter who you were as long as you had some kind of rank. I once met a girl—she seemed really nice. Turned out she and her brother were writing a book about SEAL Team Ten."

Lucy sat up, her eyes narrowed slightly. "You, of course," she said, "having higher moral standards than those women, have never used another person in any way in your entire life. Every time you went home with a woman, you were searching for a meaningful relationship—something long-lasting, something special, right?"

Blue bowed his head in mock surrender. "Your point is taken. It's just that Jenny Lee..." He interrupted himself. "Let's not talk about Jenny anymore."

Good idea.

Lucy looked up at him. "So tell me honestly," she said. "Do you know how to break a man's neck the way Gerry's was broken?"

Blue nodded. "Yeah," he said. "I do."

She digested that information, still studying his face, her dark-brown eyes serious. "Have you..." She stopped herself. "Maybe I shouldn't ask you this."

"Have I ever done it?" Blue asked the question for her. "I've been in plenty of combat or counterterrorist situations where the enemy has to be permanently neutralized, often silently. So, yeah, I have done it. It's effective and efficient."

Lucy's eyes narrowed again. "You're talking about *killing* another person."

Blue shook his head. "A terrorist who kidnaps and tortures and murders a cruise ship full of civilians isn't a person to me."

"But that's how you feel in the heat of battle, so to speak," Lucy said. "After it's over don't you wonder who they were? Don't you feel badly then?"

"No," he said bluntly. "No guilt. No remorse. What good would feeling bad do me? The way I look at it is, I didn't kill them—they killed themselves by putting themselves in a situation where they'd have to go up against me."

"But every life is sacred," Lucy argued.

"You tell that to the terrorists," Blue said mildly. "If you can convince them of that fact, I'll be more than ready to agree. Until then, my job is to protect and defend—by deadly force, if necessary. I'm not an ambassador or a diplomat, Lucy. I'm a soldier. I'd far prefer it if the ambassadors and diplomats could get the job done. I'd be the first on my feet for a standing ovation if the entire world could live in perfect harmony. Hell, I'd gladly spend the rest of my life rescuing victims of natural disasters. But that's not the way it's gonna be anytime in the near future."

"I know that," Lucy said with a sigh.

"We're doing more research into weapons that aren't deadly," Blue said. "If there was some kind of stun gun or tranquilizer gun that guaranteed neutralization for a definite, extended period of time, we'd consider using it. In certain situations, when the terrorists are asleep, for instance, we do inject tranquilizers, using syringes. But tangos who aren't sleeping don't often sit still and wait for you to stick 'em with a needle. And with a gun, it's harder to be accurate.

"And that makes it tough when you're in a life-and-death situation. Everything you do is focused on staying alive, on keeping your squad alive. If you only tranquilize Terrorist X instead of killing him, you're going to expend a certain amount of energy and brain power wondering if maybe you didn't do it right, and maybe he's going to pop back up and mow down half your squad with his HK-93. But dead is dead. You do it right, and you know it. Terrorist X doesn't pop back up and kill anyone after his neck has been broken."

Lucy was still watching him. "I see your point of view," she said. She didn't necessarily agree with him, but it was clear that he'd given this a great deal of thought. He was a soldier. He had taken others' lives—not because he wanted to, but because he *had* to. She'd read about some Special Forces operators—Navy SEALs and Green Berets and others—who'd actually enjoyed the act of killing. Blue clearly wasn't one of them.

But he also wasn't going to apologize for what he did. Protect and defend. Lucy knew he would give his life; he would *die* in order to get his job done.

How many people did she know who could say the same?

She glanced up at him. He was watching her. She could see in his eyes that he was waiting for her to make some kind of negative comment. He was bracing himself for her condemnation or disapproval.

"You know, I really like you, Blue McCoy," Lucy said with a smile.

Blue had to smile, too. Her comment was pure Lucy. She really liked him. It made him feel warm inside. Warm, but wistful, too. Was it possible he would have rather heard her tell him that she *loved* him?

Mercy, the complications that that would bring were mind-boggling. But he wanted it, he realized. He wanted her to love him.

"We should try to sleep," Lucy said, lying back in the bed. "We've got a big day tomorrow."

"Are we planning to crack the case?"

Lucy sighed as he put his arms around her, pulling her so that her back fit snugly against his chest. "No," she said. "Tomorrow we're going to drive into Charleston and hire a private investigator—someone with more than six months' experience. He or she will crack the case."

"Excuse me, Officer Tait...?"

Lucy glanced up from filling her truck's gas tank to see a tired-looking woman on the other side of the self-serve pump, filling the tank in her own car.

It was Darlene Parker, Matt's wife. Her old station wagon was loaded full to the top, and Tommy, her young son, sat in the front seat. Matt was nowhere in sight.

"I was going to send this to you," Darlene said, handing Lucy an envelope, glancing furtively around to make sure no one was watching them, "but as long as you're right here, I figured I may as well risk hand-delivering it. Don't let anyone see."

"Are you leaving town?" Lucy asked, folding it in two and putting it in the back pocket of her jeans.

Darlene nodded. She seemed relieved that the envelope was out of sight. She lowered her voice even further, her thin face pinched and nervous. "I wrote to tell you what really happened the night Gerry McCoy died."

Lucy felt a surge of hope. "You know who killed Gerry McCoy?"

But Darlene shook her head as she finished filling the tank and replaced the gas cap. "No. But I know that Matthew was paid quite a bit of money to make up that story about seeing Blue up in the woods, arguing with his stepbrother. I know for a fact that Matt didn't see anything of the sort. He was with me that entire night. It's all in the letter. When you read it, you'll see."

Darlene hurried to the gas-station office to pay. As Lucy watched through the window, Darlene quickly threw several bills onto the counter. She headed back to her car, but Lucy intercepted her.

"If you leave town," Lucy said quietly, "you won't be able to make a statement about this to the police."

Darlene was already shaking her head. "No," she said. "I'm not going to do that. I've already done more than I should. They killed Gerry McCoy. They won't think twice about killing again."

"Who are 'they'?"

"R. W. Fisher," Darlene whispered. "And the police. You're the only police officer I was absolutely certain wasn't involved."

The police? And R. W. Fisher? Killed Gerry McCoy? Lucy's head was spinning.

Darlene pushed past her and opened the door to her car. "I'm leaving with Tommy while I still can," she said. "Matt is gonna wind up with his own neck broken, but that's his own damn fault."

She closed the door with a slam, then locked it. Lucy leaned in the open window. Tommy gazed sullenly at her from where he was sitting, surrounded by bags and unpacked things his mother had thrown, last minute, into the car.

"How do you know about this?" she asked. "Darlene, I need to know where you got this information."

Darlene started the car with a roar. "I've already told you too much."

"At least give me your forwarding address, so that I can reach you in case—"

"You're kidding, right?"

Darlene put the car into gear and pressed the gas pedal. Lucy had to jump away to keep the rear tire from rolling over her boots.

Darlene's reedy voice floated back through the open window. "If I were you, I'd get out of town before you end up like Gerry McCoy, too."

Lucy pulled the envelope Darlene had given her out of her pocket. She dug in her other pocket for a pen and jotted down the station wagon's license-plate number. Just in case. She paid for her gas and got back into her truck before opening the envelope.

It was a single-page, handwritten letter. Darlene's cursive writing was scratchy and hard to read.

A glance told Lucy that the letter wasn't signed. Without Darlene around in person to back up the contents, it would do little to discredit Matt Parker's story. Still, she read it slowly, working through the nearly illegible words.

Just as Darlene had said, she'd written that Matt had been home all evening on the night that Gerry McCoy had died. She said that after Matt had issued a statement that he'd seen Gerry and Blue near Gate's Hill Road that night, he suddenly had lots of money. When Darlene asked him about it, since he was currently unemployed, he told her to mind her own business.

But later Matt had told her that he'd gotten the money from R. W. Fisher, and that in a few months, after the uproar died down, he was going to have a guaranteed job working for the Tobacco King.

R. W. Fisher.

It seemed ludicrous. The wealthiest, most successful man in town involved in murder?

And the police were supposedly involved, too. Darlene didn't say why she thought that was true or who had given her that information. She just stated that the police couldn't be trusted.

Lucy looked up from the letter, staring sightlessly at the morning sky. Blue had seen Fisher deep in discussion with Gerry at the country club on the night Gerry had been killed.

She'd wanted to go and talk to R. W. Fisher in connection to the autopsy report's odd findings about Gerry's blood-alcohol levels at the time of his death. She'd wanted to ask Fisher if he'd thought that Gerry was drunk prior to the dance-floor altercation with Blue and Jenny.

She'd told Chief Bradley about wanting to talk to Fisher....

And he'd responded not just by taking her off the case, but by suspending her from the police force and telling her to get out of town.

What if Darlene was right and the police—including Sheldon Bradley—were involved in some sort of conspiracy?

And what if, by wanting to talk to Fisher, she'd been getting too close to the real truth?

Whatever had come in with the morning mail was causing quite a stir in Chief Bradley's office. Despite that, Annabella stopped Lucy as she was heading past her desk.

"I thought you got axed," the older woman said with her usual sensitivity, lighting a cigarette with a snap of a match.

"I'm just getting...something from my locker," Lucy said. "Packing up some of my stuff." Curiosity got the better of her, and she motioned toward the commotion. "What's going on?"

"Blue McCoy's military records just arrived," the raspy-voiced dispatcher told her, exhaling a cloud of smoke. "Did you know that he's got some kind of expert status in martial arts–style hand-to-hand combat?"

"Well, yeah, umm...actually, I did," Lucy said.

Lucy couldn't quite believe she'd dared to come inside the police station. The normally bland beige walls seemed to be dripping with conspiracy. The familiar faces of her co-workers seemed suddenly sinister.

She was probably overreacting. She was going on the unsubstantiated statement of Darlene Parker—a woman who, for all Lucy knew, could have paranoid delusions. If R. W. Fisher and the *entire* police department had killed Gerry McCoy, there had to be some kind of reason, some sort of motive. Darlene hadn't provided her with one of those, and Lucy was having a hard time coming up with one of her own.

But she couldn't totally discount what Darlene had told her. In fact, Lucy took Darlene's warnings seriously enough to want to be armed. Of course, she'd turned in her police-issue weapon when she'd had it out with Chief Bradley two days ago. But she had a personal license for a smaller gun—which happened to be inconveniently stored in her locker in the basement of the police station.

This entire day wasn't going at all the way she'd planned. She'd awakened alone again and had a moment of frustration until she caught the fragrant smell of coffee and frying pancakes floating up from the kitchen. When she went downstairs she found Blue cooking breakfast. He'd greeted her with a smile and a maple syrup–flavored kiss. That was nice—she couldn't complain about that.

But after breakfast, Lucy had left the house alone, intending to drive into town to the library to photocopy the Yellow Pages listings of private investigators from the Charleston phone book. Today she had intended to seek professional assistance in this murder investigation.

Instead, here she was, spooked by Darlene Parker's crazy suspicions, creeping down the police-station stairs, hoping she'd get to her locker, get her gun and get the hell out of there before anyone besides Annabella noticed her.

Not a chance.

Chief Bradley stopped her in the hall on her way back to the door.

Lucy kept her face carefully expressionless, hoping the fact that she suspected him to be part of some wild, murderous townwide conspiracy didn't show in her eyes.

But he didn't ask her what she was doing there. He glared at her and said, "You knew Blue McCoy had extensive martial-arts training?"

Lucy looked down toward Annabella's desk, where the dispatcher was smoking yet another cigarette, watching with unabashed curiosity.

"All Navy SEALs do," she said evenly. "I'm surprised you didn't know that."

"No, I did not know that," Bradley fumed. "Just now Annabella told me you knew about McCoy's martial-arts training. And I happened to be talking to Doc Harrington's pretty little wife yesterday, and *she* mentioned the fact that you're some kind of walking fountain of information about the military's Special Forces divisions."

"Sarah was exaggerating. I don't know *that* much—"

"What I want to know is why the hell didn't any of that information bubble over onto my desk?"

"I didn't think—"

Bradley shoved several pieces of paper into Lucy's hands. It appeared to be pages photocopied from Blue's personnel file. Much of the text was blacked out, censored no doubt for security reasons. But there was a full listing of the areas in which Blue held expert-level—or higher—status. Martial arts and hand-to-hand combat were high on the list.

Lucy flipped the page, fascinated despite the fact that this was Blue's private file, despite the fact that she was surrounded by people who were allegedly involved in Gerry McCoy's death.

She skimmed the brief psychological evaluation that was written at the bottom of the second page. "Carter McCoy is a perfect candidate for the SEAL program," she said. "He is a tenacious, usually steady, thoughtful individual who is not afraid to take action. Negatively, his temper can be volatile at times. He also is very much of a loner, unwilling or unable to share his thoughts and feelings with anyone other than his very closest friends, if even them. Carter McCoy is—"

"You look at that file," Chief Bradley interrupted her, "and you tell me if you think McCoy has the skill and training necessary for him to be able to snap a man's neck."

Lucy gazed up at him. She didn't want to answer that. She *couldn't* answer that, not without damning Blue. But if she refused to answer, Bradley would assume she was hiding the truth.

"Blue McCoy is a lieutenant in the Navy SEALs," she told the chief. "He's the executive officer of SEAL Team Ten's Alpha Squad." She slapped the papers against her hand. "According to this, he's won countless medals for bravery—"

"I didn't ask you for a background sketch of the man," Bradley said. "I asked if Blue McCoy has the skill and training to kill in that manner—"

"He'd never do such a thing," Lucy protested.

"It's a yes or no question, Tait. Does he or does he not have the skill and training to break a man's neck?"

Bradley was watching her. Annabella was watching her. Farther down the hall, Travis Southeby and Tom Harper were watching her. They were all waiting for her answer.

"*All* SEALs do—"

But Chief Bradley wasn't listening any longer. "That sounded like a yes to me. Run next door to the judge's chambers," he said to Travis. "Let's get a warrant and bring that son of a bitch in. We got motive and now we've got means."

"Motive?" Lucy asked, following Bradley down the hall, back toward his office. "What motive did Blue McCoy have for killing his brother?"

Bradley stopped and looked at her as if she were first cousin to the village idiot. "Jenny Lee Beaumont," he said. "She's motive enough for damn near any man."

"That's ridiculous—"

"You got a better motive?" Bradley said, turning back to glare at her. "Or maybe you've got an entirely different suspect in mind?"

They killed Gerry McCoy, Darlene Parker had said ominously. *They won't think twice about killing again.*

Lucy shook her head, backing slowly away. "No," she said. "No, I don't." She gazed into the chief's eyes, trying to see if he was capable of murder. As much as she disliked the man, she found it hard to believe. But she'd been wrong about a lot of things before.

"Got the warrant, Chief," Travis called.

"Take Tom and go pick up McCoy," Bradley said to Travis. He turned to Lucy. "He still staying out at your place?" He smiled knowingly. "In the *guest* bedroom?"

Lucy's stomach was in a knot. They were going to arrest Blue. They were going to bring him in, charge him with murdering his stepbrother. Or maybe they *weren't* going to bring him in. Maybe they were simply going to kill him, instead, claiming he resisted arrest.

"Let me go along," she said to Bradley, her mind going a mile a minute as she searched for a way out. "I can talk him into coming in quietly."

"Yeah, or you can tip him off—warn him so that he gets away. You don't work for me anymore, remember?" Bradley said. He nodded to Travis, who headed for the door, Tom Harper one step behind. "No, I want you to sit down right here in my office and stay until I receive word that McCoy is behind bars."

"You can't keep me here," Lucy said tightly, her fear for Blue stronger and sharper than her concern for her personal safety.

"Yes, I can," Bradley said. "We can do it one of two ways. You can sit down nice and quiet, or I can have you arrested. Which will it be?"

Lucy walked out into the hall, toward the front door. "Arrest me."

"Have it your way," the chief said. He called down the hall, "Annabella, get Frank Redfield up here to arrest Lucy Tait."

Lucy could see Annabella flipping frantically through her code book, trying to find an appropriate ten code for the situation. The dispatcher finally gave up and just picked up the phone.

But Frank was already upstairs. He stepped out into the hallway in front of Lucy, blocking her exit out of the building."

"Come on, Lucy," he said. "Why do you want to make trouble for yourself?"

"If you're arresting me," she said, "what are the charges?"

"Attempted obstruction of justice," Chief Bradley volunteered.

"That's ridiculous," Lucy said, turning to face him, "and you know it. You *try* arresting me for that. Just try it."

She stepped around Frank, who looked down the hall at the chief, waiting for instruction. But the chief didn't say a word. He was silent as Lucy pushed open the door and went down the stairs into the hot morning sunshine.

She'd called Bradley's bluff.

Lucy ran for her truck, and started the engine with a roar even before she shut the door. She pulled out of the parking lot with a squeal of tires and headed up toward Fox Run Road, praying that she wasn't too late.

Chapter 14

Blue went out onto the porch as the police car pulled into the drive.

Lucy was still downtown, and he recognized Travis Southeby behind the wheel. That wasn't good. But at least Tom Harper was with him. Tom had no doubt read all of his civil-rights handbook, while Travis had clearly skipped a few chapters.

They'd come to arrest him. He knew that even before they got out of the car. And the two police officers got out of the car with almost comedic differences in style.

Tom stood up and straightened his pants, nodding a greeting to Blue, closing the car door behind him.

Travis drew his weapon, and, flinging his car door open and using it as a shield, he aimed his gun at Blue.

"Blue McCoy, you are under arrest," he shrilly announced.

Tom glanced at Travis, then looked apologetically at Blue. "We've got to bring you in," he said. "We're making the charges official."

"I didn't kill Gerry," Blue said evenly. "If I had, I would've been long gone."

"Keep your hands where I can see 'em," Travis said sharply.

Blue glanced back at Travis and his gun. "You're too far away to get an accurate aim with that thing," he said. "Put it away before you accidentally hurt someone." He turned back to Tom. "You're making a big mistake here. You're wasting your time on me while Gerry's real killer is running around free."

Tom actually looked sorry as he snapped a pair of handcuffs on Blue. He quickly searched him as he recited Blue's Miranda rights.

Travis approached, obviously keeping his hand close to his reholstered gun. "We've got enough evidence to put you away, McCoy," he said. "We've got a motive of jealousy—"

"That's total bull."

"Is it really? I didn't think so. Chief didn't, either," Travis said. "We've got a witness who places you with the victim at the scene of the crime—"

"You've got a liar who's probably getting paid a small fortune to make up stories," Blue countered.

"We've also got a hundred other witnesses who saw you threaten the victim earlier that evening. Are *they* all getting paid off, too?" Travis was enjoying this way too much.

Tom opened the door to the patrol car, and Blue started to climb in. It wasn't easy with his hands bound together behind his back.

"And," Travis said, playing his winning card with a flourish, "we've got military records that peg you as a martial-arts expert *and* we've got our own local military scholar—of sorts—who will be called to testify that as a Navy SEAL martial-arts expert you have the knowledge and skill necessary to be able to break a man's neck the way Gerry's was broken."

Blue straightened up. Was he talking about...?

Travis smiled at the look on Blue's face. "That's right," he said. "Lucy Tait. And she'll be doubly valuable to the prosecution considering you've been shacking up with her for the past few days. Imagine how that'll look to the jury—

your own lover testifying against you." He made tsking sounds.

"Lucy would never do that," Blue said. He could feel anger starting inside him, burning hot and tightly contained.

"She will if she's subpoenaed," Travis said. "And she'll be subpoenaed. All she'll have to do is repeat what she said this morning down at the station."

Blue got into the car. "Play your head games with someone else, Southeby," he said shortly. "I know for a fact that Lucy wasn't at the police station this morning."

"Well, I know for a fact that she was," Travis said, slamming the door behind Blue and climbing in behind the driver's wheel. He put his arm along the back of the front seat, twisting to look at Blue. "She came in to give you up. She provided us with that last bit of information we needed to come on out here and bring you in."

Blue just laughed and told Travis in quite specific language exactly what he could do with himself.

Travis turned to look at Tom, who'd climbed into the car and was fastening his seat belt. "McCoy thinks I'm telling tall tales," he said. "He thinks I'm making this all up. Isn't that exactly what happened this morning, Tom? Lucy Tait walked in, told the chief that McCoy had the martial-arts training needed to cleanly snap a man's neck, and five minutes later I was holding the warrant for McCoy's arrest in my hand."

Tom glanced at Blue, clearly sympathetic. "I don't know exactly how it happened," he said. "I didn't hear all of it, but Lucy *was* at the station this morning, and I did hear the chief ask her if you had the skill to break a man's neck. Right after that, we had the warrant."

Part of Blue up and died. Just like that. Sudden, instant, tragic death.

He stared out the window of the police car as Travis pulled out of Lucy's driveway. Summer had hit full stride, and the trees and meadows were bursting with life and color. Wildflowers were everywhere. A breeze ruffled the green leaves, making the trees seem like some giant, moving, living thing. There was all that life out there, yet Blue felt dead inside. Dead and brown and dried up and broken.

So tell me honestly, Lucy had said to him last night, after they'd made love for the second—or was it the third?—time. *Do you know how to break a man's neck the way Gerry's neck was broken?* Their legs were still intertwined, and he had been running his fingers down her back, from her shoulder all the way to her thighs. Her skin was so soft and smooth he couldn't stop touching her.

They'd just talked about honesty, about how Lucy was the first woman Blue had known who hadn't had some sort of ulterior motive for being with him.

But she had. She'd had one hell of an ulterior motive, hadn't she? She'd used sex and the intimacy it created between them to get the information she'd needed to send him to jail.

He'd almost let himself love her. Damn, he was such a fool.

Blue was silent as Travis Southeby and Tom Harper led him into the station, silent as they took his fingerprints and mug shots, silent as they told him his bail would be set that afternoon, silent as they put him in the holding cell and locked the door.

It wasn't until Travis came back, telling him that Lucy Tait was outside, that she wanted to see him, that Blue spoke.

"I don't want to see her," he said, amazed that someone who felt so dead inside could still speak.

Lucy stared at Travis Southeby. "But..."

"He said he doesn't want to see you," Travis repeated. He smiled. "Can't say I blame him, seeing how you were the one who provided the final piece of evidence in the case against him. He wasn't too happy when I told him about that."

"You told him *what?*"

"Nothing but the truth," Travis said smugly. "You came in here to tell the chief that Blue McCoy had the ability to break a man's neck. Not everyone knew that he had that particular skill, you know. Your little tidbit of information proved vital in our case against him."

"You *son* of a bitch!"

Could Blue really believe that she would betray him that way? She wouldn't have thought so, but apparently he had.

"Watch your mouth, missy," Travis said primly.

Lucy took a deep breath. Slamming her fist into Travis's smug face wasn't going to do her—or Blue—any good. She forced herself to calm down. "I'm sorry." She took another deep breath. She'd gotten to her house too late. Blue was gone and Travis's patrol car was nowhere in sight. She'd turned right around and come back to the station. "Please, you've got to let me see him anyway."

"Can't do that."

The front doors opened, and Lucy turned to see Jenny Lee Beaumont walk into the police-station lobby. She was wearing a rose-colored suit with a frilly white blouse. The frills made her generous bosom look even larger. Her hair was up in an elegant bun and she had high heels on her tiny feet, pushing her height up to a full five foot three.

Travis moved toward her. "Ms. Beaumont," he said. "What can I do for you, ma'am?"

Jenny took off her sunglasses. Her eyes still looked smudged and bruised from grieving. "I received a call from Blue McCoy," she said in her breathy Southern accent. "I'm here to see him."

Travis nodded. "Right this way, ma'am."

As Lucy watched, Jenny turned back to Annabella, who was sitting at the dispatcher's desk. "My lawyer should be arriving soon. Will you please bring her back to us when she comes?"

Lucy watched as Jenny Lee Beaumont was ushered down the hall, toward the holding cells. Blue had called Jenny Lee. *Jenny's* lawyer was coming to help him. He trusted Jenny, not Lucy....

But Jenny didn't know that some—if not all—of the police officers on the Hatboro Creek force were involved in the cover-up of Gerry's death. And Jenny didn't know that R. W. Fisher had allegedly paid Matt Parker large sums of money to make up his story about seeing Blue in the woods with Gerry on the night of his death.

And Jenny didn't love Blue.

Lucy did.

And somehow Lucy was going to find Gerry's killer. Somehow she was going to prove Blue's innocence. Somehow she was going to prove to him that she *didn't* betray him.

Or she was going to die trying.

"Bail is set . . . for five-hundred-thousand dollars."

A murmur went through the courtroom. Half a million dollars. Lucy's stomach clenched. Where was Blue going to get half a million dollars?

"Can the defendant make bail?"

As Lucy watched, Blue turned and glanced at his lawyer, who turned and looked back at Jenny Lee. Jenny shook her head. "Not at this time, Your Honor," the lawyer said. She stood up. "Your Honor, my client is a lieutenant in the U.S. Navy. A navy attorney will be arriving sometime next week. May I suggest my client remain in custody in Hatboro Creek until that time?"

The judge shook his head. "Those facilities aren't adequate," he said. "The defendant will be transferred immediately to the correctional institution at Northgate."

Several armed guards approached Blue. He stood up and let them lead him away. He had to know Lucy was there, in the back of the room, but he didn't look up. He didn't even glance in her direction.

Blue hated Northgate prison. He hated the feeling of being locked up. He hated being stripped of his clothes and forced to wear ill-fitting blue jeans, and a white T-shirt, and sneakers on his feet. He particularly hated the sneakers.

He stood in the courtyard alone, watching from the corners of his eyes as a large group of men gathered, then approached him. They were clearly the prison's movers and shakers—among the inmates, they were the ones in charge. They surrounded him, their body language threatening.

He ignored them. It wasn't until one of the men got right in his face that Blue even looked up.

"You Popeye the sailor man?" the inmate asked, grinning at his own clever humor.

"No," Blue said. "I'm Blue McCoy, the Navy SEAL."

At least one person in the crowd knew what that meant, and as Blue stood there, a murmur spread from man to man. He couldn't hear the words, but he knew what was being said. A Navy SEAL. A snake eater. One of the toughest sons of bitches in the military.

Like magic, the crowd disappeared. No one wanted to pick a fight with a man they couldn't possibly beat.

Blue was almost disappointed. He could have used a good brawl to get this pain out of his system, this heartache of knowing that Lucy had used and then betrayed him.

She was so damn good—he hadn't suspected a thing. Her sunny smile had been genuine. Her kisses had been so sincere. How had she done it? How had she looked at him with all that emotion in her eyes without feeling a thing?

Blue wanted to be out of this prison. He wanted to be far away from South Carolina and Lucy Tait. Damn, he never wanted to see her again.

He wanted to take a sailboat out onto the ocean, out of sight of land, and just be one with the water and sky. He wanted to erase Lucy's face from his memory.

It wasn't going to happen.

He wanted to stop thinking about her, but she followed him everywhere, filling his mind, overwhelming him with her presence.

Why had she done it? How could she have done it? It didn't make sense. Did she really think he'd killed Gerry? Or worse, could she possibly be part of some conspiracy against him?

It didn't make sense.

It didn't make any sense at all.

He closed his eyes, and she was there, in his mind, arms crossed, mouth tight, glaring at him with barely concealed impatience.

"Why?" he asked, speaking the word aloud, causing some of the inmates to look curiously at him and then to move farther away.

Blue needed to know why. Of course, Lucy couldn't answer.

Lucy sat outside the gates of R. W. Fisher's plantation-style mansion, slumped in the front seat of Sarah's car. She'd borrowed her friend's shiny black Honda because she knew her own battered truck would stand out on this well-manicured street like a sore thumb. She had also borrowed a microcassette recorder from Sarah's husband's office, and she'd dug up a pair of binoculars from her own attic.

The night was endlessly long. It was only 3 a.m. and she felt as if she'd been sitting out here for half an eternity instead of eight hours. She'd followed R. W. Fisher home from his office at a little after seven. He'd gone inside and hadn't come out since.

The binoculars weren't much use. The house was dark, and through the binoculars it was simply larger and dark.

The microcassette recorder wasn't much use, either. Lucy managed to amuse herself for about five minutes by recording her voice as she sang the latest country hits, and then playing back the tape. But since most of the popular songs were about heartache and love gone wrong, she quickly stopped.

She forced herself to stay awake by chewing some caffeinated gum that she'd picked up at a truck stop. She didn't dare drink any of the coffee she'd brought, for fear she'd have to leave her stakeout to find a bathroom.

The night was sticky and hot, but she didn't turn the car on and sit in air-conditioned comfort; she was afraid a neighbor would notice the running car engine and call the police.

The very same police who were somehow involved in a murderous plot with R. W. Fisher.

So Lucy just sat. And sweated. And wished that Blue hadn't been so quick to doubt her. She wondered if Northgate was as awful as she had heard. She wondered where

Blue was, if he was sleeping or still awake. She prayed that he was safe.

At 5:57 a.m., Fisher's gate swung open. Lucy sat up straight, then scrunched down even farther in her seat to hide. Fisher appeared, driving a big, off-road vehicle with oversized tires. Lucy would have bet both her house and the computer software company she owned in Charleston that the tread on those big tires was nearly brand-new. And she would have gone double or nothing on those tires being the same ones that had left those tracks Blue found in the woods near where Gerry's body was discovered.

As she watched, Fisher turned to the right out of his driveway and moved swiftly down the street.

She started Sarah's car, waiting until he was some distance away before pulling out after him.

He didn't go far. He made a right into the parking lot of the middle school and stopped.

Lucy drove past without even braking, but quickly pulled off the road several hundred yards farther down. She grabbed the microcassette recorder—just in case—and scrambled out of the car, backtracking on foot through the woods.

Fisher stood near his truck, one foot on the bumper as he tightened the laces of his sneakers. He was wearing running shorts and a T-shirt, and for someone pushing seventy, he was in outrageously good shape.

He did several more stretches, adjusted his headphones and Walkman, then started running along the edge of the middle-school playing field. Lucy followed, running a parallel course through some impossibly dense woods.

He was in *hideously* good shape, she realized when she was out of breath after only a short distance. Of course, Fisher wasn't running in long jeans and cowboy boots, leaping over roots and rocks and getting smacked in the face with tree branches and vines. She saw that she was losing him and she pushed herself harder, faster.

He reached the corner edge of the field and took a trail that led into the woods. He slowed his pace slightly, but not much.

Lucy was glad for the headphones Fisher was wearing, glad he couldn't hear her. She was making more noise than a herd of wild elephants. She remembered the way Blue had been able to run silently through the woods. And tirelessly, too. As a particularly thick branch smacked her square in the forehead, she wished that he were there with her. But he wasn't. If she wanted to keep up with Fisher, she was going to have to do it on her own.

You gotta want it badly enough. The words of Blue's SEAL training instructor flashed in her mind. She did. She wanted it. Badly. She wanted a happy ending to this nightmare. She wanted to find the proof that would free Blue from jail. She wanted him to walk out of the county prison and into her arms. And as long as she was making up happy endings, she wanted him to kiss her and tell her that he loved her. She wanted to marry him and live happily ever after.

God, she was stupid. It wasn't going to happen that way. Even if she didn't get herself killed, even if she succeeded in getting Blue out of jail, he was going to ride off into the sunset with perfect, pink, frilly Jenny Lee Beaumont.

Lucy cursed as she tripped over a root and fell, tearing a hole in the knee of her jeans. She ignored the pain, ignored the scrape and the blood, and picked herself up and ran.

R. W. Fisher was way ahead of her along the trail.

Of course, if Fisher really was just out for a morning run, Lucy was going to feel pretty idiotic. She was praying that he was meeting someone, praying that something would happen to—

Lucy stopped suddenly, dropping down into the underbrush.

Fisher had stopped running. He stood now in the middle of the trail, catching his breath, headphones off, leaning against a huge boulder. He hadn't heard or seen her, thank God.

Slowly, carefully, trying her hardest not to make a sound, Lucy crept forward.

Please, she was praying in rhythm with her pounding heart. Please, please, please, please, let him be meeting someone, please, please, please....

Then she heard it. The sound of a dirt bike coming along the trail. She used the cover of its engine to creep even closer and to take out the microcassette recorder.

But then Lucy realized it was not one dirt bike she'd heard but two. The riders braked to a stop and cut the engines. They were both wearing helmets, and as she watched, they pulled them off.

Travis Southeby. And... Frank Redfield? Oh, my God, if kind, gentlemanly Frank was involved in this, maybe Tom Harper was, also. And Chief Bradley—why not him, too?

"What are we going to do about McCoy?" Fisher asked.

His voice carried clearly to Lucy. She quickly switched on the recorder and pushed the microphone level up to high.

Fisher shook his head in disbelief. "Jesus, didn't I just ask that same question a week ago? Didn't we just have this conversation?"

"This time it's a different McCoy," Travis said. "But I don't think we have a problem, Mr. Fisher. Blue McCoy is in Northgate prison, and he's gonna stay there. There's no way in hell he can make that bail."

"Seems he's got some special navy lawyer flying in," Fisher said. "When I heard about that, I came very close to calling New York and—"

"Snake doesn't want to get involved," Travis said. "He did his bit—"

"By breaking Gerry's neck?" scoffed Fisher. "He should've made it look like some kind of accident. But a broken neck...? That was asinine."

"Blue was easy to frame," Travis said. "He'll take the fall."

"But what about this navy lawyer?"

"It's not a problem," Frank interjected. "McCoy is up at Northgate, right? There's going to be a fight in the cafeteria at noon. Blue McCoy is not going to survive. I can guarantee it."

Lucy stopped breathing. Blue McCoy was not going to survive? Not as long as she was alive and kicking.

Fisher nodded, his well-lined face looking suddenly tired and old. "All right."

"What *I'm* interested in knowing is how you plan to fill the gap that Gerry's death left," Travis said. "How the *hell* are we going to get that money into the system and back to New York by the syndicate's deadline?"

"Matt Parker," Fisher said. "He's been willing to help up until now. I'm sure he'll be happy to continue our relationship. I'll arrange a loan with the bank. Nothing that draws attention in our direction, of course. But it'll enable Matt to purchase a suitable business—maybe even McCoy's construction company. Construction was the perfect way to launder the money."

"Too bad Gerry chickened out," Travis said.

New York syndicate. Launder money. My God, that was what this was all about. Someone named "Snake," probably from that same New York syndicate, had broken Gerry's neck because Gerry hadn't wanted to play along.

"We'll be rich yet, gentlemen," Frank said, putting his helmet back on. "Next year at this time, we'll be rolling in money."

Lucy lay hidden in the underbrush long after the dirt bikes had pulled away, long after Fisher had run back down the trail. She wasn't sure exactly where she'd be next year at this time, but she knew one thing for certain. R. W. Fisher and Frank Redfield and Travis Southeby and anyone else involved in Gerry's murder were going to be in jail.

Even if she had to put them there herself.

Chapter 15

Lucy ran back toward Sarah's car, faster even than she'd run while following R. W. Fisher.

According to her watch, it was nearly six forty-five. She had to get up to Northgate by ten-thirty for morning visiting hours to warn Blue that he was in danger. It was about an hour's drive, but that was okay. She could make it.

Of course, once she got there, there was no guarantee that Blue would see her.

She was drenched with sweat and covered with burrs and dirt as she climbed into the car. She started the engine with a roar and headed quickly for home.

She had to call someone. Say what she'd overheard—what she'd gotten on tape.

She couldn't call the local police. They were involved. She knew that for sure. How about the state troopers? Hell, there was no guarantee *they* weren't in on the deal. And the local federal agents? Shoot, she was so paranoid now she was afraid to call anyone.

Lucy pulled into her driveway with a spray of gravel. She ran up her porch steps and quickly unlocked her kitchen door, then closed it behind her.

Think. She had to think.

She picked up the phone, then hung it back up. Then, with a sudden burst of inspiration, she picked the phone back up and pushed the redial button. She closed her eyes and prayed that Blue had been the last person to use the phone and that the last call he'd made had been to Seal Team Ten's headquarters in California.

It was ringing. Wherever she'd dialed, it was ringing. She could only hope it wasn't ringing in the local pizzeria.

"Night shift," said a deep voice on the other end of the phone.

My God, of course, it was three hours earlier in California. Out there, it was five o'clock in the morning.

"Who's this?" she asked.

There was a pause. "Who's this?" came the wary reply.

Lucy took a deep breath and a big chance. "My name is Lucy Tait, and I'm a friend of Blue McCoy's," she said. "He's in big trouble, and I need to speak to Joe Cat right away."

Another pause, then, "Where are you calling from, ma'am?" the voice asked.

"Hatboro Creek, South Carolina," she said.

"Can you be more specific about this 'trouble' you say Lieutenant McCoy is in?"

"Who is this, please? I can't say more until I know who I'm talking to."

There was another brief silence, then, "My name is Daryl Becker," the voice said. "Blue calls me 'Harvard.'"

Harvard. She'd heard that name before. "You went through BUDS with Blue and Joe Cat," she said.

"How do you know that?" he asked suspiciously.

"Blue told me."

"We talking about the same Blue McCoy?" Harvard asked. "The Blue McCoy who hasn't said more than three full sentences in his entire life?"

"He talks to me," Lucy said. "Please, you've got to help. I need to speak with Joe Cat."

"It's 0500 here on the West Coast," Harvard said. "We just got back last night after several weeks away. Joe is with his lady tonight."

"Veronica," Lucy said.

Harvard laughed. "If you know about her, Blue *has* been yapping his mouth off. You must be special, Lucy Tait."

"No, just a friend."

"I'm his friend, too," Harvard said. "So tell me what's going on."

Lucy did, telling him everything from the money-laundering scheme to Gerry's murder, the charges against Blue and the impending murder attempt at Northgate prison. Afterward, Harvard was silent.

"Damn," he said. "When that redneck white boy gets in trouble, he gets in *big* trouble, doesn't he?"

"I need help," Lucy said. "I can't do this on my own, but I don't know who to call. I need to know who I can trust."

"Okay, Lucy Tait," Harvard said. "This one is too big for me, too. Lay your telephone number on me. I'll risk certain death by calling Cat and waking him from his blissful slumber. He'll know what to do. I'll have him call you right back."

"Thank you," Lucy said, giving him her number.

She hung up the phone and opened the refrigerator, pouring herself a glass of orange juice as she tried not to watch the clock. God, she was a mess. She was soaked with sweat and dirt, her hair straggly and stringy, her knee still bleeding through the hole in her torn jeans.

Three minutes and forty seconds after she hung up from Harvard, the telephone rang.

Lucy scooped it up. "Yes?"

"Lucy? This is Joe Catalanotto from Alpha Squad."

Lucy closed her eyes. "Thank God."

"Look, Lucy, Harvard filled me in on what's happening out there. I've already called the admiral and arranged for emergency leave. I'm on my way, but it's going to take too long to get there, you hear what I'm saying?" Joe Cat's voice was pure urban New York. It was deep and rich and filled with the confidence of a Navy SEAL commander.

"Ronnie is gonna get in touch with Kevin Laughton, a FInCOM—Federal Intelligence Commission—agent I trust...works out of D.C. He'll send someone out to Hatboro Creek—someone you can trust with that tape of yours."

Ronnie? Veronica. Of course. His wife.

"What I want you to do," Joe continued, "is go out to wherever Blue is being held and tell him about this noon assassination attempt. Do whatever you need to do, Lucy, to get him out of that prison."

Lucy took a deep breath. "You want me to tunnel him out of there?"

Joe laughed. He had a deep, husky laugh. "If you have to, yeah. Do whatever it takes. Just don't get Blue or yourself killed."

Before Joe hung up, he gave her his home phone number, the SEAL Team Ten headquarters number, and Kevin Laughton's, the FInCOM agent's, number. Just in case.

Lucy hung up the phone.

Do whatever it takes. Whatever it takes. Whatever.

She picked up the phone and dialed Sarah's number. She knew she was going to wake her friend up.

"'Lo?" Sarah answered sleepily.

"It's me," Lucy said. "How much money do you have in your savings account?"

Lucy worked quickly. She dug out the files for both her house and her business from her home office. She found the title for her truck. She gathered her savings-deposit passbooks and uncovered her checkbook from her dresser.

She searched the Charleston Yellow Pages, making phone call after phone call until she found exactly the right type of entrepreneur she needed. She gave him directions to Hatboro Creek and made him promise to arrive no later than 9:00 a.m., when the local bank opened.

She made a copy of the microcassette, using her telephone answering machine to play the miniature tape and holding the microcassette recorder above the speaker. The quality of the tape was going to stink, but she didn't care.

As long as the words were faintly audible and the voices were identifiable. She stashed one of the tapes in the kitchen utensil drawer for safekeeping.

At 8:57 a.m. she climbed into Sarah's car and headed downtown.

Sarah was standing on the sidewalk in front of the bank. Lucy parked and got out of the car.

"I can't believe I let you talk me into this," Sarah said worriedly. "It's the thirty-thousand dollars Richard was intending to spend to modernize his office."

"You'll get it back," Lucy said, hoping she was telling her friend the truth. "I can't tell you how much I appreciate this. Your money pushes me over the top."

"I had no idea you had that much," Sarah said.

"It's mostly tied up in the business," Lucy said. "Look, before I forget, I hid a tape in my kitchen, in the utensil drawer. If anything happens to me—"

"Oh, God, don't say that."

"It's important," Lucy said. "On my bulletin board is a phone number of a federal agent named Kevin Laughton. Make sure he gets the tape."

"The tape from the utensil drawer." Sarah nodded. "Why the utensil drawer?"

"I was going to hide it in the toaster, but then I thought, what if someone comes in and wants some toast...."

Lucy looked up as a heavy man in a business suit and an incredibly obvious toupee approached them. It had to be Benjamin Robinson, the man she'd found in the Yellow Pages. It *had* to be.

"Ms. Tait?" the man said, looking questioningly from Sarah to Lucy.

Lucy held out her hand. "Mr. Robinson," she said. "I'm Lucy Tait. Shall we go into the bank and get down to business?"

A skinny man stopped near Blue in the prison courtyard during the morning exercise period. He lit a cigarette with hands that shook and stared up at the sky.

"You gonna be snuffed," he said.

It took a moment before Blue realized the man was talking to *him*. He looked away from the man, down at the ground at his uncomfortable sneakers, as the meaning of what he'd said sank in. Snuffed. Killed. "When?"

"Lunch," the man replied.

That soon. Blue felt the familiar surge of adrenaline as his body prepared for a fight. "How many?"

"Too many. Even if you fight back, they gonna get you. If you don't show up at lunch, they do you at dinner."

"How many?" Blue asked again. There was no such thing as too many. He just had to know in advance so he could plan, strategize against an attack.

"There's thirty of 'em, bubba. All hard timers."

Thirty. God. Not impossible, but not good odds, either.

"They gonna get you," the man said.

Thirty. This was gonna be a tough one. This guy was quite possibly right. "Why tell me about it, then?"

"I'm telling you because if it was me gonna die, I'd want to know." The man flicked ash from his cigarette, still not looking at Blue. "Write a will," he said. "Make peace with whichever God it is you believe in. Or get on line for the telephone—call your girl and tell her you love her." He started to walk away. "Tie up loose ends."

Get on line for the telephone. Lord, if only he could. But Blue didn't have telephone privileges yet. Not for another week. And according to the skinny inmate, Blue wasn't going to live that long.

Blue went inside the main building to the library.

"I'd like a pen and a piece of paper, please," Blue said to the burly inmate who was acting as librarian.

Silently the man laid both on the counter. Blue could see reflections of his imminent death in the silence of the man's eyes.

"Thanks," Blue told him, but the inmate said nothing, as if Blue were already dead. The pen was attached to the counter by a chain so no one could steal it and turn it into some kind of weapon. He stood there, lifted the pen and held it poised over the paper.

Damn. This was going to be harder to write than he'd thought.

He started it off easily enough: "Dear Lucy." But after that it got much harder.

He didn't have time for it to be hard. He didn't have time for it to come out perfectly. He knew what he wanted to say, so he just had to say it. He wrote, trying hard to print legibly.

> I've had a lot of time to think over the past twenty-four hours, and every time I try to fit you into this puzzle of who killed Gerry, the picture comes out looking all wrong. Whenever I think of you going to the police station, intending to deliver information that would strengthen their case against me, I just can't believe it.
>
> I've been thinking about Travis Southeby, about the way he stood up against me at the Grill, about the way he took such pleasure in telling me you had turned me in. At first I accused him of playing head games with me, and now I can't help but believe that he was indeed messing with my mind. I believed Tom Harper when he said you'd been to the police station, but what if he was lying, too? Or what if you'd been there, but for some other reason entirely?
>
> I guess it all boils down to the fact that I don't want to believe them. I won't believe them. But I'm afraid it's too late. I'm afraid they already won.
>
> It kills me I didn't see you when I had the chance. I'm not sure I'll have that chance again, because someone in here wants me dead—probably so that I won't be able to prove my innocence and open up the question of who really killed Gerry.
>
> Maybe I'm a fool, and maybe you're involved with these murderers. But I don't want to believe that. I'm not going to believe that. If I'm going to die, I'd rather die loving you.

Blue took a deep breath, then plunged on.

I've never said these words to anyone ever in my life, let alone written them down, but somehow over the past few days, I fell in love with you, Yankee.

I thought you should know.

He started to sign the letter "Carter," but crossed it out and wrote in "Blue."

He folded the letter in thirds and pushed the pen back toward the librarian, who again said nothing. He asked for an envelope and a stamp, and the librarian pointed silently down the hall toward the tiny room that served as the mail drop-off and pick-up point.

While Blue was there, several guards came in. They rattled off a series of numbers. It took him a moment to realize they were ID numbers—*his* ID numbers. They were looking for him.

"You're wanted in the warden's office," they said as he dropped his letter into the mail slot.

Was it possible the warden had somehow found out about the death threat? Was he going to put Blue into solitary until the danger passed? It was a long walk to the warden's office near the front gate of the prison, and Blue had plenty of time to speculate.

But when the guard opened the office door and Blue walked inside, the warden's words surprised him.

"Your bail has been made," the man said. "Sign the paperwork, change your clothes and you're free to go."

His bail had been made. Half a million dollars. Who the hell had come up with half a million dollars just like that? And just in time, too.

The clock on the warden's wall read 11:10. In twenty minutes, the inmates would be lining up to go in for lunch. In twenty minutes thirty men would be looking for him, ready to snuff out his life. But he wouldn't be there. He wasn't going to be forced to fight with thirty-to-one odds. Relief flooded through him, hot and thick. He wasn't going to die today. At least not before lunch.

"Who posted bail?" he asked.

"Does it really matter?"

Blue shook his head. "No."

He quickly changed his clothes, strapping his belt back on. They hadn't found the knife hidden inside the buckle. That was good. Maybe his luck was starting to change.

The guards led him down the hallway to a locked gate. He went through it, then down another corridor toward another locked gate. He could see someone standing on the other side of the thick security wire. As he got closer, he realized exactly who was standing there, waiting for him.

Lucy. God, it was Lucy. His luck was definitely changing.

Her face was wary, as if she wasn't sure of her reception. She held his gaze, though, searching his eyes as the guard unlocked this final barrier.

And then he was free. He was outside the prison, in the visitors' waiting area.

"*You* paid my bail?" he asked. It wasn't what he really wanted to say to her, but it was better than just standing there, staring.

She nodded.

"Where the hell did you get half a million dollars?"

Lucy nervously moistened her lips and shrugged, giving him only a ghost of her regular smile. "Remember that computer software business I own?" she said. "Business has been extremely good lately."

"But you couldn't have had that much cash...."

She shook her head. "No, it's almost all tied up in the working capital. I used the business as collateral, along with some other things and some borrowed money, and..." She shrugged again. "I didn't have anything to do with your arrest, Blue," she said, her voice fast and low. "I mean, I was there at the station, getting my gun from my locker, and Bradley asked me a question, and I answered it as best as I could and all of a sudden Travis Southeby had a warrant for your arrest. I didn't...I wasn't..." There were tears in her eyes, but still she held his gaze, silently begging him to believe her.

"It's required by law that I escort you to the front gate," the guard told Blue.

He ignored the guard and took a step toward Lucy. "I know," he said.

She wiped at her tears with the heels of her hands, refusing to cry. "You do?"

"Yeah," he said. He wanted to pull her into his arms, but he was oddly nervous. He was in love with this woman. Somehow knowing that changed everything. He was afraid to touch her, afraid of giving himself away. Sure, he'd just written his deepest feelings in a letter, but there was no way he could say any of that aloud. "It took me a while, but I finally figured it out. Lucy, I'm sorry—"

"Come on, folks," the guard said impatiently. "Save the teary reunion for outside the gate."

Lucy turned to face the guard, her chin held high, her eyes blazing. "I just paid half a million dollars so this man could walk out of here with me—and we're going to walk out of here on our own good time, when *we* want to, and not one minute before. Thank you very much."

Blue felt himself smile for the first time in what seemed like centuries. "I think I'm ready to leave," he told her.

The guard escorted them to the door, and then they were out in the humid air and finally outside the gate.

Freedom.

"Was it awful?" Lucy asked quietly.

"It's over," Blue said.

Their eyes met, but only briefly, only for an instant, before Lucy looked down, and Blue knew with a deadly certainty that if he reached for her, she would pull away.

When he'd first seen her standing and waiting for him on the other side of that gate, when he'd realized that *she* was the one who'd paid his bail, he thought for a moment that it had to be proof that she loved him. What woman would risk everything she owned for a man she didn't love?

But then he remembered her friend Edgar. Lucy had only been friends with Edgar, yet she had sacrificed much to be with him in his last few months.

Her loyalty to her friends was clearly unswerving. But Blue didn't want to be only her friend any longer. He wanted more, God help him. He wanted more, but the fact that he'd lost his faith in her just might have destroyed whatever fragile love she was starting to feel for him.

Blue had to reach for her; he had to try. But before he could, Lucy started walking, heading toward the parking lot and her truck.

"Matt Parker's wife told me R. W. Fisher was paying Matt lots of money to say he saw you in the woods with Gerry," Lucy told him.

R. W. Fisher?

"She also said that some of the men in the police force were involved," she continued.

Blue knew that. He'd had a gut feeling about that right from day one.

"So I followed Fisher, and sure enough, he met with Travis Southeby and Frank Redfield," Lucy told him. "I have their conversation on tape. They're involved with some kind of money-laundering scheme set up by an organized-crime syndicate from New York. The way I figure it, the mob gives them money and they inflate the income of their businesses, take a cut high enough to pay the higher taxes and then some, and give the rest back. Gerry was involved up to some point. My guess is he went along with it for a while, using his construction business to get a lot of the mob's dirty money back into circulation. But he probably started feeling guilty and wanted out. When he made noise, they killed him. The mob sent some guy named Snake down to do the deed."

Blue was astonished. "Shoot, you've been busy."

"There's more," she said. The dust from the parking lot coated her boots, and she stopped to face Blue, wiping the dulled leather on the back of her pant legs. "Alpha Squad is back from their training exercises. I spoke to Joe Cat. He's on his way. In the meantime Veronica contacted somebody named Kevin Laughton over at FInCOM. It's just a matter of time until the FInCOM agents get out here."

Blue had to laugh. "You did all that *and* raised the money to pay my bail?"

Lucy nodded. She started walking again. Her truck was down at the end of a row of parked cars. "All we need to do now is find someplace safe to hide until the FInCOM agents arrive.''

Blue stopped suddenly and grabbed Lucy's arm. ''Someone is hiding behind your truck,'' he said in a low voice.

Lucy went for her gun, but she wasn't fast enough.

Travis Southeby stood up, aiming his gun directly at Blue. ''Don't move an inch,'' he warned Lucy, ''or I'll put a hole in him.''

''Let him shoot me,'' Blue told her, his eyes never leaving Travis. ''Then plug the son of a bitch between the eyes. I know you can do it. You told me you were a good shot.''

''I'll kill him,'' Travis said. His voice was high, his hands shaking slightly, his florid face tense. ''Slowly put your hands in the air.''

Lucy did. ''I can't risk it,'' she whispered to Blue.

Travis held his gun on Blue as he came toward them and quickly took Lucy's gun from under her jacket, from her shoulder holster.

''Damn,'' Travis said. ''I couldn't believe it when the warden's assistant called and told me that Blue McCoy had made bail. Half a million dollars.'' He looked at Lucy, using the back of one hand to wipe his perspiring forehead. ''What the hell were you doing working on the police force with that kind of money in your bank account?''

''What the hell are *you* doing on the police force with your kind of morals?'' Lucy responded tightly.

Travis just handed Lucy a set of keys. ''My car is right here, next to yours,'' he said. ''Get in.''

Blue took the keys from Lucy's hand. ''I'll drive,'' he said. ''She doesn't need to come along.''

''I'm afraid she does,'' Travis said. He was being very careful to stay at least an arm's length away from Blue. He knew if he got close enough, Blue would try for him, regardless of the weapon Travis held. He aimed his gun at Blue's head. ''Get in the car, or so help me God, I'll drop both of you right here and right now.''

Lucy's heart was pounding. She knew that Blue didn't want to get into that car. She knew he wanted to stay right there, out in the open of the parking lot. She knew he was just waiting for the right opportunity to go for Travis. She knew if Blue had been the one carrying a gun, he would have jumped Travis when he got close enough. But Lucy couldn't ignore the fact that Travis's own gun was aimed steadily at Blue.

Blue had his thumbs hooked in his belt, one hand resting on his buckle. His eyes flicked to Lucy for half a second. "Do what he says," he told her softly. "Get in the car." He reached out, the car keys held flatly in the palm of his hand. "Please."

Whatever Blue was planning to do, he wasn't going to do it until Lucy was at least somewhat removed from the scene. Whatever he was planning to do, the fact remained that Travis had a gun and Blue didn't. If someone was going to get hurt or killed, it was likely to be Blue.

Lucy took the keys from him, letting her fingers linger in the warmth of his hand, well aware that this moment could be the last time she touched him.

And suddenly all of her doubts about exactly what their relationship was, all of her doubts about Jenny Lee, all of her fears that given the choice between the two of them Blue would choose Jenny, all of that ceased to matter. Nothing mattered but the way Lucy felt.

Blue looked at her again, just briefly, sending a silent message with his eyes. But the message that she wanted to give him in return, the words she wanted him to hear, were not ones she could trust to be conveyed through a single look.

"I love you," she breathed.

Blue looked back at her, his eyes betraying his surprise.

She turned and climbed into Travis's car.

Blue forced his eyes away from Lucy, back toward Travis and his gun. She loved him. Lucy *loved* him. She was his friend, but she also loved him.

Blue knew that if he could just make it past the next few minutes, he was going to have a real honest-to-God shot at living happily every after. Lucy loved him and he sure as hell loved her.

This was what Joe Cat and Veronica had found. This was why Cat had been nearly insane with worry when terrorists had hijacked the cruise ship Veronica had been on. Blue stared into the little black barrel of Travis's gun, silently willing the man to keep that gun aimed right at him. If he turned and aimed that thing at Lucy, Blue wouldn't be able to fight back. He wouldn't be able to risk it.

And he'd just about worked his knife free from his belt buckle....

"You get in now," Travis said to Blue, gesturing to the car with his head. "We're gonna go for a ride."

Blue didn't move. At least not his feet. "I don't think so," He said. "You're gonna have to shoot me. And then, when your gun is empty, I'm gonna walk over there and snap your neck the same way Gerry was killed. Don't worry—it doesn't hurt. I imagine the last thing you'll hear is your bone cracking. It's probably powerfully loud. But only for an instant."

Sweat was rolling off Travis now and his hands shook even harder. "I said, get in the car."

Inside the car, Lucy could see Blue, his hands still resting clearly in Travis's view, thumbs looped around his belt and...

Blue's belt. Blue was working to get his knife free. As Lucy watched in the rearview mirror, she saw Blue put his hands down at his sides, and she knew he'd somehow palmed the knife.

God, a knife against a gun. She had to do something to put the odds more in Blue's favor, and she had to do it now.

Blue moved toward the car, waiting for the perfect moment to strike. He had Travis shaken up. He just needed some kind of distraction and...

Lucy started Travis's car with a roar. Startled, Travis looked away from Blue.

It was only for a split second, but Blue didn't hesitate. He threw with unerring accuracy, and Travis fell with a scream, his gun bouncing on the dirt parking lot as he grabbed his wounded leg. Blue grabbed the gun, holding the barrel under Travis's chin as he took Lucy's gun from the man's pocket.

The knife was buried up to its hilt in Travis's thigh.

"You're still going to die," Travis hissed at Blue.

"I wouldn't pull that knife out if I were you," Blue told him. "At least not until you get to the hospital. I aimed for a major artery. If you pull that out yourself, you'll bleed to death in about two minutes."

Travis's pale face got even paler.

"Get in," Lucy said urgently to Blue. "Fisher's truck just pulled into the parking lot."

As if to punctuate her words, a shot rang out, and the rear windshield of Lucy's truck shattered.

"At least they have lousy aim," Blue said, throwing open the back door of Travis's car and climbing in behind Lucy.

Lucy pulled out of the parking lot with a squeal of tires as Blue climbed over the seat back into the front. She glanced at him. "I'm surprised you didn't kill Travis," she said.

"Are you kidding?" Blue said. "And miss seeing him stand trial for Gerry's murder?" He turned around, squinting to get a better view of the truck that was chasing them.

It was a monster truck, with big, oversized tires. It looked as if Fisher himself was driving. But someone else was next to him, riding shotgun. Literally.

"What if he bleeds to death?" Lucy asked about Travis.

"He won't," Blue said. "I was messing with his head when I told him I hit him in an artery. That was total bull. I was trying to immobilize him."

Another shot rang out, but as far as Blue could tell, it didn't hit Travis's car. Lucy pushed the car even faster, but the truck kept up. Easily.

Blue turned around, quickly scanning the interior of the car they were in. It was an upscale foreign car with a big engine, loaded with all the extra features. Travis even had a car phone built into the hump between the two front seats.

They were heading north on Philips Road. Lucy was taking the curves faster than she should and the tires squealed and moaned. Blue tried to visualize exactly where they were. Philips Road intersected with Route 17 not far from Northgate prison. And somewhere west off Route 17, between Philips Road and the turnoff to Hatboro Creek, was the local television station where Jenny Lee worked. Bingo. Blue picked up the car phone. He had a plan.

He glanced back at the truck just as the rear windshield shattered. The shooter had put a scope on his rifle. They were in trouble now.

"Faster," he said to Lucy. "And keep your head down."

"I can't do both," she said tightly.

"You have to," he said.

"Shouldn't you be shooting back at them?" Lucy asked.

Blue shook his head. "Handguns don't have the same range as a hunting rifle. It'd be a waste of bullets."

"Blue, I can't take this road any faster!" There was more than a touch of panic in her voice.

He put down the phone and drew Travis's gun, instead, then braced his arms on the back of the seat. "Hit the brakes," he said to Lucy. "Now."

She looked at him in shock. "What . . . ?"

He raised his voice. "Do it!"

She did. The car slowed, shuddering slightly, and the truck roared into range.

"Drive!" Blue shouted, emptying the magazine of the gun in rapid succession. He saw the truck's front windshield shatter, saw the telltale spray of red on the back windshield, and he knew someone had been hit.

If it was the driver, he hadn't been killed. As Blue watched, the truck pulled over to the side of the road and came to a stop. Lucy was watching, too, in the rearview mirror. "Keep going," Blue said to her. "As fast as you can."

"They stopped," she protested.

"That doesn't mean they can't start after us again," he said.

Several minutes passed in tense silence as Lucy drove as fast as she dared and Blue watched out the back for any sign of the truck. They were going up a small hill, and bits and pieces of the road behind could be seen in the valley below. He caught a glimpse of the monster truck, back on the road, still following them.

Lucy swore like a sailor when he told her. She glanced at the speedometer, pushing the car even faster, but otherwise didn't take her eyes off the road. "We're coming up on Route 17. Which way?"

"West."

Blue picked up the car phone again, dialing a number he obviously had memorized.

"Who are you calling?" Lucy asked.

"Jenny Lee."

Lucy felt herself grow very, very still. Jenny Lee. Blue was using the car phone to call Jenny Lee. She shouldn't have been surprised, but somehow, foolishly, she was. She was surprised and hurt. God, it was shocking how much it hurt. She'd anticipated this scenario. She'd been prepared for it. Or so she'd thought.

Somehow Lucy managed to keep on driving. Somehow she made the turnoff west onto Route 17. She had told Blue that she loved him, and he didn't even have the decency to wait until they were out of danger before he called Jenny. Maybe that was what hurt the most.

"Jenny Lee Beaumont, please," Blue told the receptionist, then waited while his call was connected.

Lucy was really able to open up out on the state road. She pushed Travis's car faster, listening to the rush of the tires on the road, trying not to listen to Blue talk to Jenny Lee. But it was hard not to overhear him.

"Remember when you came to the jail and I told you to be ready for me?" Blue said to Jenny. "Well, I'm on my way." There was a pause, then he said. "Ten minutes." Another pause. "Right." Then he hung up.

He turned to Lucy. "You know where the turnoff is to the television station?"

She nodded. She knew.

He looked at her closely. "You all right?"

Lucy nodded. "I'm fine." She glanced at him. He really didn't have a clue. He was gazing at her, concern in his eyes, puzzlement on his face. "Considering people who want to kill us are chasing us in a truck that can probably go a lot faster than this car," she added.

Blue turned around, looking out the broken rear window. "I winged one of them," he said.

"I thought you were supposed to be a sharpshooter," she said.

He turned to her again, and she could feel him studying her face. She held her jaw firmly, her mouth tightly, her eyes carefully on the road.

"I am," he finally said. "Travis's gun really sucks. I didn't have time to figure out which way it pulled. I didn't have time to compensate."

Blue turned around to watch out the rear window. Several more miles sped by with only the sound of the wind whistling across the broken window, breaking the silence.

"This is almost over," Blue finally said.

Lucy nodded. They were almost at the station. What he intended to do there, she didn't have a clue. She was afraid to ask. Maybe Blue planned to take Jenny Lee and escape in the television station's helicopter. After all, he was a Navy SEAL. He could fly a helicopter, no problem. Or maybe he intended to hole up in Jenny's office, using Lucy's gun to keep Fisher and whoever was with him in the truck—probably Frank Redfield—at bay until the authorities made the scene.

But maybe Blue wasn't talking about the danger they were in. Maybe he was talking about his relationship with Lucy. And it was true. It was almost over. If Blue was planning to be with Jenny from now on, there was no way his friendship with Lucy could continue on the way it had.

Blue swore, suddenly and loudly, and Lucy glanced up. The monster truck had reappeared in the rearview mirror. It was growing larger by the second, gaining on them.

Lucy could see the turnoff that led to the television station up ahead.

They weren't going to make it. Lucy could see the hazy sunlight glinting off the barrel of the hunting rifle as she glanced again in the rearview mirror.

"Get down!" Blue shouted, and she ducked. A shot rang out and Blue cursed.

Oh, my God. Blue was hit. The windshield had been sprayed with his blood. Somehow Blue wiped a clear swatch with his hand.

It was his arm. He'd been shot in the arm and he was bleeding.

"Blue," Lucy said. "Oh, God, Blue...."

Another shot rang out and the windshield broke, spider-webbing. Again Blue was there, kicking it out so that she could see.

"Your arm," she gasped, the force of the wind in her face taking her breath away.

"I'm fine," he said, his voice still soft and calm as he quickly ripped the tail off his shirt and tied it around his arm to stop the bleeding. "It's nothing. Just messy, that's all. Come on, Yankee. Here comes the turnoff. Don't slow—just take it."

Lucy pulled the wheel hard to the right and they skidded around the corner. It took a moment for their tires to get traction, but then they were off again, doing eighty down a road with a fifteen-mile-an-hour limit.

At the first speed bump they nearly launched into the air.

The truck was right behind them, and it bounced up and almost on top of them.

But then they were in the parking lot, heading toward the main building.

Lucy could see a small crowd standing out in front. It looked like a television crew, complete with at least two cameras and a whole bunch of technicians. What the heck...?

"Don't hit the brakes until we're almost past them," Blue told her. "Then just get down and stay down, do you understand?"

Yes. Lucy understood. Suddenly she understood.

She saw Jenny Lee Beaumont, dressed in pink as usual, standing in front of the crowd, a microphone in her hand, reporting live from the front of the television station.

Lucy understood. If R. W. Fisher and Frank Redfield were going to kill Blue and Lucy, they were going to have to do it on live television.

It was perfect. It was so perfect she had to laugh. Blue had no doubt set this plan up with Jenny Lee. He had no doubt figured that the time would come when the people who killed Gerry would try for him, too. But no one in his right mind would commit murder in front of an audience of two-hundred-thousand-plus viewers.

She hit the brakes hard and felt the car go into a skid and then finally stop. She didn't get down quickly enough, and Blue pulled her down, covering her with his body.

Lucy could hear shouting. She could hear the squeal of tires as the monster truck did a quick U-turn out of the parking lot. She heard the drumming of helicopters overhead as the FInCOM agents made the scene and took off after the monster truck. Then she heard the quiet sound of Blue's breathing and the pounding of her heart.

Blue shifted slightly so that most of his weight was off her. Lucy turned her head and found herself looking directly into his eyes.

"You all right?" he asked quietly.

She nodded. "Are you?"

He nodded, too. "My arm was just nicked," he said. "It's nothing to worry about."

Their legs were still intertwined. That felt too intimate, too wrong. Or maybe it felt too right.

She looked up to see Jenny Lee peering in the window at them.

"Whoopsie," Jenny said. "We'll get this interview a little bit later. Sorry. Didn't mean to interrupt, Carter."

Lucy sat up, hitting her head on the steering wheel. Blue helped her up and into the driver's seat.

"I'm okay," she said, rubbing her head. "I'm all right. You can go. I'm fine."

"Go," Blue repeated. "Go where?"

Lucy forced herself to smile. "Go to Jenny," she said. "It's all right." But then she caught herself. What was she saying? "No, it's not all right," she realized. "In fact, it stinks. In fact, you're a jerk, and I don't even know what I saw in you in the first place—"

"Lucy, what the hell . . . ?"

"Go ahead," she said, glaring at him. "Go spend the rest of your life with Jenny Lee. I hope you like lace doilies and little pink flowers, because your house is going to be covered with them."

Blue was confused as hell. "Why would I want to spend the rest of my life with Jenny?"

"Because you childishly imagine you're in love with her."

Blue had to laugh. "Lucy, did you hit your head harder than I thought?"

"No."

She wasn't kidding. There were actually tears in her eyes. She was mad at him. She was *serious.* Blue stopped laughing. Where the hell had she gotten this idea? He ran his fingers through his hair, and when he spoke it was slowly and calmly. "I'm not in love with Jenny Lee."

"My point exactly," she said hotly. "You only imagine you are."

"No, I don't. I—"

"Yes, you do," Lucy insisted. "And you know what's going to happen if you marry her? After six months, she's going to bore you to tears."

"Lucy, I'm not—"

"That is if you don't suffocate underneath all those little pink flowers first."

"Why," Blue said as clearly and distinctly as he possibly could, "would I want to marry Jenny Beaumont when I'm in love with you?"

Lucy was silenced. The silence continued for several very long moments.

"Excuse me?" she finally said.

"You heard me the first time, Yankee," Blue said quietly, dangerously. "Don't make me say it twice."

"But I want you to say it twice," she said. And then she smiled.

Her eyes glistened with tears, but her smile was pure sunshine, pure joy. When she smiled at him that way, Blue could refuse her nothing.

"I love you," he said, touching the side of her face, losing himself in her eyes. Hell, that was easier to say than he'd thought possible. So he tried saying something that was even more difficult. "I think you should marry me, Lucy."

Lucy felt her smile fade. Marry. Blue. My God. She'd never dreamed... Well, actually she *had* dreamed. But she'd imagined they were just that. Dreams.

Blue made an attempt at humor. "You need me to say that one again, too?"

Lucy shook her head. "No." Her throat was dry and she swallowed. "No, I heard you."

She could see uncertainty in his eyes.

"What do you think?" he asked.

He honestly didn't know what her answer would be. Lucy cleared her throat. "You mean, move to California?" she asked, stalling for time. Did he know what he was asking? Was he just caught up in the emotion of the moment? How could she know for sure?

Blue nodded. "That's where Alpha Squad is stationed these days." He searched her eyes. "I've got an apartment outside Coronado. It's kinda small—we could get something bigger...."

Lucy didn't speak. She couldn't speak. He seemed to have given this some thought. He seemed lucid and certain.

Blue mistook her silence for hesitation. "I know being married to a SEAL isn't always fun," he said quietly. "I'd be gone a lot—too often. But I swear to you, while I'm away, I'll be true. Other wives might wonder or worry, but you'd never have to, Lucy. And when I'm home, I'll do my best to make up for all the time I'm away—"

Lucy interrupted. "Are you sure?" She couldn't stand it any longer. She had to ask.

"It's always hard when you've gotta leave on a mission, but Joe Cat and Veronica are making it work and—"

"No, I mean, are you sure you want to marry *me?*"

Blue laughed in surprise. "I guess you really didn't hear me the first time—or the second time, either. I love you."

He cupped her chin in his hand, leaned forward and kissed her. His mouth was warm and sweet, his lips as soft as she remembered.

"It wasn't love at first sight," he told her in his black velvet Southern voice, kissing her again. "It took longer than that. I can't tell you when I knew for certain. All I know is little by little, bit by bit, I realized I want you next to me, Lucy. I realized that I love you. I want you wearing my ring, taking my name, having my babies. I want you to be my friend and my lover for the rest of our lives. So please, marry me."

Lucy's heart was in her throat, so she opened her mouth and gave it to Blue. "Yes," she said.

Blue smiled and kissed her.

Blue sat down next to Lucy on the porch swing. "I spoke to Joe Cat," he told her. "I caught him before his plane left Kansas City. As long as I'm out of trouble, he's just going to turn around and head back home to Veronica."

Lucy leaned back against him, looking out at the deepening twilight. He smelled sweet and clean from his shower. He'd shaved, too, and she rubbed her own cheek against the smoothness of his face.

"One of the FInCOM agents stopped by while you were getting cleaned up," she told him. "Travis signed a full confession. Apparently he *was* there—along with Fisher and Frank Redfield—on the night Gerry died."

Blue nodded, just waiting for her to tell him more.

"According to Travis," Lucy continued, "Gerry was involved with some kind of money-laundering scheme. R. W. Fisher apparently knew some mob boss from New York who convinced him Hatboro Creek was the perfect sleepy little town to launder drug money. Fisher got Gerry into the deal, along with the Southeby brothers and Frank Redfield. Everything was moving along smoothly until Gerry started going to Jenny Lee's church. When Gerry got God, his conscience started bothering him, and he told Fisher and the others he wanted out of the deal.

"They threatened him and he was running scared, trying to figure out what to do. When you showed up, Fisher was afraid Gerry would go to you for help, so he told Gerry if he as much as *spoke* to you, they'd bring this hired gun from New York—a man named 'Snake'—to kill *you.* Instead, Snake killed Gerry."

Blue swore quietly.

"Travis said that Gerry *wasn't* drunk that night. He was sober. The drunkenness *was* just an act. Gerry was trying to make you leave town."

"He was trying to protect me," Blue said.

Lucy nodded. "Yeah. All those awful things he said to you weren't true. He cared about you—he didn't want you to be hurt."

"I could've helped him," Blue said.

"I know."

They sat in silence for a moment, just listening to the sound of the crickets whirring and chirping in the early evening.

"I told Joe Cat about you," Blue said.

She turned and looked at him. "Really? What did you say?"

"That I fell in love with a friend of mine. He seemed to understand." Blue leaned forward and kissed her. It was a slow, deep, lazy kiss that promised forever—a sweet, dizzying happiness for all time.

"I can't wait to meet him," Lucy said, settling back against Blue again, shifting so that her head was in his lap, so she was gazing up at him. He pushed the swing and they rocked gently. "Tell me more about him. Tell me about all the guys in Alpha Squad, and about California. . . ."

Blue smiled down at her as he began to talk.

Smiling into Lucy's eyes was easy. Telling her that he loved her was easy, too. Asking her to marry him had been a breeze. Kissing her and making love to her were as easy and as natural as breathing. But sitting here on the porch swing, swaying gently as the evening descended upon them, Blue knew that talking to Lucy—his friend, his lover, soon to be his wife—was easiest of all.

Epilogue

Lucy stood in the back room of the naval-base chapel as Sarah adjusted her veil.

"I feel stupid," Lucy grumbled. "What is this thing hanging in front of my face? Is it supposed to hide me? Do I look *that* hideous? Why do I have to wear this anyway?"

"Because it's traditional," Sarah said calmly. Nora, her baby, now three months old, smiled happily at Lucy from the backpack Sarah wore. "You look beautiful, and you know it."

"It's not very traditional for the bride to be given away by her best friend and her godchild," Lucy commented.

Sarah gazed at her for a moment, then took out the pins that held the veil in place and tossed both pins and veil aside. "Fair enough," she said.

"I wish I were wearing my jeans," Lucy said wistfully.

Sarah shook her head. "Nope," she said. "Nice try, but I draw the line at the veil. No way am I letting you march down that aisle in blue jeans."

"I just feel so...not me," Lucy said. The dress was cut low, off her shoulders, with tiny cap sleeves, a tailored bodice and a long, full skirt, complete with a train.

"You look incredible," Sarah said. Nora gurgled and chewed on her mother's hair in agreement.

The music started, and Sarah took Lucy's arm. "Come on." Sarah smiled. "Wait till you see what's waiting for you at the other end of this church."

Self-consciously, Lucy let Sarah lead her out into the church. And then she stopped feeling self-conscious at all. Because standing there in the front of the church was Blue. Next to him stood the six other members of Alpha Squad. All seven men were wearing white dress uniforms and the effect was nearly blinding.

Lucy's gaze ran across their now-familiar faces. Joe Cat's smile was genuine and warm, but he couldn't keep himself from glancing across the chapel to smile at his wife, Ronnie. Lucy's first impression of Ronnie had been that she was an ice queen—until Lucy had walked into the Outback Bar to find the usually proper, English-accented woman cutting loose, dirty-dancing with her handsome husband.

And then there was Harvard. Daryl Becker. Along with his Ivy League education, Harvard possessed a first-class sense of humor. His shaved head gleamed almost as much as the diamond he wore in his left ear.

Cowboy, Wesley and Bob all grinned at Lucy. Cowboy winked. He was the youngest member of the squad and he did his best to live up to his reputation as a hothead.

Lucky O'Donlon was smiling, too—and oh, my God, standing next to him was none other than Frisco. Alan Francisco. There weren't seven men up there—there were *eight*. The big, towheaded former SEAL was standing with the rest of Alpha Squad. Blue had taken Lucy to meet him at the rehab center several months ago, and Frisco had been in a wheelchair. It had been years since he was injured, and all the doctors had sworn he would never walk again. But today he was *standing*. He had a cane, but he was standing. Lucy looked around, but she didn't see any sign of a wheelchair. Had he actually *walked* to the front of the church?

And Lucky—Frisco's best friend and swim buddy—looked happier than she'd ever seen him. The two men were almost the exact same height and build. Lucky's hair was brown, while Frisco's was blond, but other than that, even their faces were similar enough that they might have been brothers.

Except Frisco couldn't hide the lines of pain around his eyes. He may have been standing, but it was hurting him to do so.

"Thank you so much for coming, Alan," Lucy said to him, emotion breaking her voice.

Frisco nodded. "I wouldn't have missed it for anything," he said.

And then, suddenly they reached the front of the church. Sarah kissed her on the cheek, and then Lucy was face-to-face with Blue.

Blue McCoy.

He looked incredible in his white dress uniform. Lucy hadn't seen him dressed up since Gerry's funeral, and before that at the party at the country club. Today, like that night, she was wearing a dress that made her feel peculiar, as if she were masquerading as someone else.

But Blue looked different, too. His shining blond hair was perfectly combed, every wave and curl in place. The rows and rows of medals he wore on his chest were overwhelming. His uniform was so clean, so starched and stiff and gleaming white. He gazed, unsmiling, into her eyes.

Who was this stranger, this sailor she was marrying? For one heart-stopping moment, Lucy wasn't sure she knew.

Then she looked down and caught sight of Blue's feet. He wasn't wearing dress shoes like the rest of Alpha Squad. He was wearing his old, familiar leather sandals.

He was wearing his sandals, and she was wearing her cotton underwear. It was fancier than usual, but it was cotton. She'd insisted. They both had their hair combed differently, and both of them were dressed differently, but deep down inside they knew exactly what they were getting—exactly *who* they were going to spend the rest of their lives with.

Lucy smiled.

Blue smiled, too. And then he kissed the bride.

* * * * *